THE REPORTER
AT
THE REPORTER

by
John Barry Quin

www.johnbarryquinn.com   Word Count:87,450

CHAPTER 1

WELCOME HOME

Jude knows he should be asleep; ensuring he'll be in the best shape possible to start his new job, begin his new life. But sleep is as elusive as the moonbeams threading through the thin curtains of Jude's little bedroom, above the entrance to the public bar of *The Proud Stag*.

'It's hopeless,' he realizes, pulling himself up and along the soft mattress into a sitting position. Jude's head is a jumble of excitement and fear about the following day and realising sleep is as about as likely as winning the Pulitzer Prize on the first day of his new career as a journalist, his only option is to get up. 'Maybe a run will clear my head and then let me sleep?' He gingerly walks the three steps across the faded cold lino to the window and pulls back the curtain.

The view across the New Forest is impressive and huge, silent and open. To Jude its intimidating and unsettling, in its own way so bright and noisy. 'In the city,' he thinks, 'you're wrapped in a duvet of dull light and quiet hum that helps you relax and sleep. But here, miles from any other dwelling, the Forest's heathland is so silent. Then, maybe a mile away, an owl will screech or a pony bray and it sounds like the bloody thing is next to you, in your bedroom.' As he watches, the cloud parts and the moon emerges. Jude's bedroom transforms from battleship grey to bright silver and, outside, the impossibly large, full moon seems closer and brighter than he's ever seen. Eyeing the dark, flat silhouettes behind the gorse bushes that stretch as far as he can see, he decides it's definitely bright enough outside for a run. 'It's like that old Cat Steven's song, *Moonshadow*,' he thinks, and his eyes are drawn to a moon-illuminated movement on the horizon. Jude peers and spots the shape of a motorcycle and rider, lights turned off, silently heading down the hill on the single-track road towards *The Proud Stag*. 'Strange,' he thinks, but dismisses the idea – it is his first night staying in the remote pub – but carries on furtively watching. The rider glides the bike to a halt in the pub's small carpark and pulls the heavy machine silently onto its stand.

'Country folk, a weird lot,' Jude thinks and checks his watch, '2AM on a Monday morning?' The helmeted and black leather-clad biker bends over and picks something up from the pub's flowerbed. He or she, Jude can't tell for sure, draws back their arm and hurls whatever they'd picked up. An explosion of glass shatters the night, followed by a second of total silence, which is, in turn, shattered by the barking of a dog and joined by the cries of a baby. Unhurriedly the biker walks back to his machine, rolls it off its stand and kicks it into life, revving its powerful engine. Now, with headlight switched on, the rider speeds back up the hill. Jude has the presence of mind to grab a pen and scribbles the bike's numberplate onto the back of his hand.

The sleeping pub ignites into life. Jude stumbles downstairs to see the naked figure of his cousin, Gerry, the pub's young landlord, moon-silhouetted in the doorway, screaming obscenities in the direction of the biker's flight. His strong left hand holds the collar of his barking puppy Alsatian, Rin Tin Tin, the dog desperate to chase after the motorbike.

Jude heads towards where he thought the light switch is – he'd entered *The Proud Stag* for the first time some four hours earlier – and screams. The welsh accent of Milly, Gerry's wife, cuts through the chaos. 'Jude, stand bloody still, can't you, there's glass on the floor. Gerry, calm down. And stop Rin Tin Tin barking; give him some crisps from behind the bar and lock him there, safe from the broken glass. Right, hang on.' There's a click and the lights come on throughout the public bar. Milly was the only one of the trio dressed, a dressing gown quickly thrown on. She chucks Gerry's woollen dressing gown at him. 'No one wants to see your old meat and two veg. When the dog's calm, can you grab a dustpan and brush? Right, Jude, I'll get you some slippers, a bandage for that cut on your foot and some trousers. Mind, you look alright in Y-fronts.' She smiles; it was a matter of personal pride to Milly never to appear rattled or upset, a trait, she believes, from her Welsh Calvinist upbringing and her mother's heartfelt belief that 'God helps those who help themselves.'

Mollie marches back upstairs towards the crying of their baby, George, who sounds desperately upset to be missing out on all the fun. Rin Tin Tin's barking subsides into the occasional yelp and, now wearing jeans and T-shirt, Milly reappears, laden with the items she promised and a simpering infant on her hip.

She passes her cousin-in-law a pile of bandages, clothes and slippers. 'Sort yourself out Jude, just don't stand on any more of that glass, right?' Milly walks to the back of the bar to pat and calm down Rin Tin Tin. On the floor she spies, then picks up, a mauve pebble the size of a large egg. 'I'll put that back in the rockery tomorrow. The bastard.'

Gerry is obviously use to doing as Milly orders and finishes sweeping the glass shards into a dustpan. 'Bastards? I'll give 'em bastards. How dare they come here, to our pub, to our home, in the middle of the night, with our baby asleep. That bloody pebble could've killed George.'

Jude has managed to stem the bleeding from his right foot and wraps the bandage over a piece of lint he presses onto the cut. He makes a white figure of eight by circling the crepe around his foot and ankle and ties the bandage. Jude leans back to admire his handiwork and flexes his ankle. The bandage immediately goes loose and falls down his shin.

'I'll do that,' Milly says, looking at Jude, 'are all the Devlin men useless or is just you and your cousin?' She unties the bandage, unwraps Jude's feeble efforts and, within a few moments, his foot is professionally bound. Milly looks at her husband across the room. 'Gerry, have you upset someone? What was that all about. Shouldn't we call the police?'

'It's as much a mystery to me, love. Maybe we'll call them in the morning? Not much point now, is there. They won't want to come all the way out her in the early hours of a Monday morning for a broken window.'

Milly gives Gerry the look that a wife gives a husband when she knows she's not being told the full story. 'Right, if you don't mind finishing clearing up, I'll try and get George back down and get some sleep myself; I've got a breakfast conference call with a client at seven bloody thirty. Don't be too long you two.' Milly disappears upstairs with George again on her hip, his eyes alternating between open and asleep.

The clearing-up finished, Gerry hovers in the pub's lounge, and Jude senses that his cousin wants to talk. Jude grabs his car keys from the hook and suggests the pair 'inspect the damage from outside.' He feels inside his old Peugeot's glovebox, eventually finds his instamatic camera and tells Gerry to stand next to the pub's broken window. 'One for the record, you might need it for the insurance.' The little camera's powerful flash ignites the building's exterior and sears Gerry's retinas.

After a desultory and depressing look around, the pair head back inside to the pub. 'Why don't you pour us each a pint of your Ringwood Fortyniner and tell me what's this is all about?' Jude suggests. Similar in build and outlook, although Jude is slightly the taller, the pair were born the same year, 1955, and have always enjoyed and easy, understated relationship. Neither of the 32-year-olds can remember a time they hadn't been friends, although they'd seen little of each other over the last decade.

'It's nothing, not really, but let's have a pint to welcome you home. We didn't get a proper chance earlier, did we.' Gerry drains off a half glass to clear the pipes before expertly pouring two pints and the pair sit at a table by the broken window, looking out into the moonlight, appreciating the light, forest-scented breeze on the warm August night.

'Gerry, don't give me the old bollocks it was nothing. I couldn't sleep, was thinking of going for a run to clear my head and looked out the window to see if it the moonlight was bright enough. That's when I saw a motorcyclist drive down, his engine and lights turned off, pick up the pebble, throw it and smash your window, then drive off. He came here for a reason. Have you been up to no good with a regular's missus or what?'

'Are you joking? The baby, the puppy, this place and my little gardening business... I'm too exhausted to raise a smile, let alone anything else.' The old friends laugh lightly.

'Look,' Jude holds out his arm, showing the writing on the back of his hand, 'I've got the motorcycle's registration. I reckon the police will be able to track him down pretty quickly.'

'There's no need. I know who it is. Well, not exactly who, but why. I had two big guys, strangers, in here last Wednesday lunchtime. They said I needed bouncers on the doors and they could help me with that. I laughed; as you can see, we're a quiet country pub that does a bit of food at the weekend, not a city centre disco, for God's sake. They said it was insurance. I said I had insurance. "Not like ours," one said and I asked them to leave, polite but firm. They said we'd be hearing from them. Well, I reckon, we just have.'

'Bloody hell, that's a story. We should tell the police.'

'No, it's not a story, not for a newspaper. Look, there's been rumours about a protection racket at local pubs for the last few months; that's why I got Rin Tin Tin.'

Over two more pints the pair reminisce, laugh and retie the old bonds that had slipped and unknotted over the 10 years that Jude has spent in exile, away from Southampton, his home.

Exhausted and a little drunk, Jude starts up the stairs, then turns to his cousin. 'I really appreciate you letting me stay here until I find somewhere permanent, in the city. We'll catch up over the weeks, it'll be like old times.'

'I couldn't let you stay in some dingy B&B with only corn-flakes and cold milk for breakfast. Well, I could, but Milly wouldn't hear of it. And it was about time you met George.' Gerry smiles. 'Jude, there's one thing I've got to ask. What about Sue? Aren't you going to see or contact her? Don't you owe her that? You'd have been married, what, 10 years?'

'I'm thinking about it,' Jude climbs the rest of the staircase towards his room. 'Night Gerry,' he stage-whispers, hoping to claim the four hours of potential sleep left before his alarm will sound.

CHAPTER 2

LET'S GET YOU STARTED

Hung over, 15 minutes late and buttered crumbs sticking on his tie from the toast Milly had insisted he ate, Jude realises this isn't a great way to start his new job, let alone his new life. What did his old sales manager used to say? 'You don't get a second chance to make a first impression.' With a boss like that, was there any wonder he had left the exciting world of electrical wholesaling…?

Through the frosted glass of the office door, he watches the outline of moving bodies before catching his own reflection – it is worse than even he'd imagined – and reads again the large calligraphically on the glass: *The Reporter, Newsroom,* followed, in smaller font, *Journalists and Photographers Only!* Jude straightens his tie, runs his hand through his blonde hair and takes a deep breath. 'Well, that's me, from today. So, why am I nervous? This is the job I've worked so hard to get,' he tells himself. 'A new job and new life. Just smile, push the bloody door open and say "Hello, I'm Jude." Do it!' For once, he follows his own good advice, but rather too successfully: the door flies open, smashes against the adjoining wall and spits out its frosted glass window with the force of an infant who decides that they now hate carrots. The glass shatters impressively on the wooden floor. 'That's two windows in two days. Is that 14 years' bad luck or does that only apply to mirrors?' Jude wonders, before realising that three faces and five eyes are staring at the suited, booted and, now, pink-faced trainee reporter. 'Hello, I'm–

'A man who obviously likes to make an entrance. Tea? I've been waiting for you to turn up before making it. How do you take it?' The welcome came from a short, smiling, impish looking woman in her late 20s with sparkling eyes and dark red hair. 'White and no sugar, no doubt. Step over the glass and we'll get Old Jones to clear it up, he's always desperate to please. I'm Sarah and you must be the dramatic Jude.'

Jude nods a thank you for the offer of tea and starts a clumsy apology, embarrassment hindering his normal easy charm and relaxed smile. The staccato stutters are halted by a tall angular young man, who walks with difficulty towards the new reporter and grins. 'Sorry, can't shake hands,' he looks down at his long gangly arms, each half immersed and moving inside a large black bag. 'I'm developing pics from Saturday's game. Well, first I'm trying to wrestle the wretched film out of its canister, but it's a bit stuck. Robert, Robert Freeman-Adams. As you've already deduced, no doubt, the photographer on this great journal. Good to meet you, Jude.'

Before Jude can reply a deep northern accent emanates from the remaining figure in the office. 'Now, don't take no notice of either of those.' Jude thinks the voice is rather deep for the diminutive middle-aged, grey-haired man sat behind a large desk which is all but concealed under mounds of untidy newspapers, opened envelopes and books. In the middle of the desk is a battered grey typewriter, and tidy columns of typed pink paper. 'They're only lead you astray.' He minutely adjusts the black patch over his right eye. 'I'm the editor, your boss. Remember that and we'll get along fine. Call me Jimmy, it's not my name, that's James Graves, but as long as I can remember everybody has thought calling me Jimmy Graves was hilarious, although I hate bloody football.' The editor shakes his head.

Without apparently being summoned 'Old Jones,' dressed, as always, in a long brown overall that, like its owner, has seen better days, slouches into the office and surveys the scene. 'Ooh, that'll be expensive, with the signwriting on and everything.' He turns and looks sternly at Jude, appraising him from head to toe. 'You must be the new journalist. Hope they're going to pay you well; they'll take the cost of the window out of your wage packet. Well, your first story can be on office vandalism, written in the first person.' The blood-induced pink colour that had started to fade from Jude's cheeks flushes back with a vengeance, causing Old Jones' face to split into a wide grin. 'Only joking, lad, only joking. I've got a mate who does that calligraphy stuff. He'll do it as a favour, no worries. And remember, if there's anything you want to know about this place, ask me, not this bloody lot.' Old Jones offers his hand and Jude shakes it, feeling slightly bewildered. The caretaker starts clearing up the broken glass. 'Is that coffee I can smell, Sarah? I'm feeling a little parched…'

'Right, Jude the destroyer, sit yourself down over there.' Jimmy nods towards a dark wooden desk of indeterminable age, inhabited by an old Imperial typewriter sporting a *Death to the Ruling Class* bumper-sticker on one side. Next to the typewriter is 'the spike,' a dangerous, sharp thin stiletto of metal projecting into the air. 'The sticker was Kevin's, your predecessor. He left here for The Times and didn't think it would fit well with the ethos of his new employer. Right, make sure you take a carbon copy of everything you type and keep it on your spike for future reference. Don't go and fall on the spike. Bloody Robert did last year, he'd only been here a month, and couldn't take any photos for weeks.'

'Jimmy, you know I was only off work for two days. The spike went right through my finger,' Robert protested.

'Anyway, you can forget all that next week, when the fancy new computers turn up, God help us. The managing editor probably told you that at your interview, we're going to be the first newspaper in the whole company to have Apple computers. No more paper, at least that's the idea. We're the guinea pigs for the whole group because we're the smallest office, so any problems can be sorted out before the bigger papers get the technology. That's what they reckon. Next Monday and Tuesday we're all going to be trained how to use them. I tried to book the week off as holiday but they wouldn't bloody let me.' Jimmy again shakes his head.

Sarah places a large mug, with 'Editor' written in tall slim blue letters on its side, on Jimmy's desk. 'You'll be fine, Jimmy. You're pick it up in no time.' Sarah dishes out the drinks, including a large green mug of coffee for Old Jones, who joins the group as if he was one of the journalists. Jude sits at his desk, his home for at least the two years it will take to qualify as a senior reporter, like Sarah. He feels the tension in his neck ease a little; despite his dramatic entrance, this small group of real journalists, who obviously like and support each other, have welcomed him. He, Jude Devlin, is a reporter.

They drink their teas and chat amicably, asking Jude where he'd gone to college and seem pleased when he tells them that he is looking forward to working in his home city. 'It's about time we had someone who actually knew a little about this place we cover,' Jimmy says, only half joking.

Jude had thought it was weird that the managing director, Alex Pointing, had interviewed him for the job without the editor being present. Well, interview wasn't quite what happened: Alex had spent 45 minutes telling Jude what a brilliant journalist he'd been before he 'revolutionised the newspaper industry' with the launch of an 'ever-growing stable of free newspapers.' Jude reckoned he'd landed the job as junior reporter because he'd managed to convey his agreement to everything Alex had said without ever interrupting him! It was obvious the managing director hadn't bothered to tell his editor anything at all about his new trainee.

Jimmy rises from his chair and limps a little as he walks the 10 paces to lean on Jude's desk. 'Right, lad, let's get you started.' Jude, aged 32 and over six feet tall in his socks, feels it odd to be called 'lad' but in this environment, he realises he's the baby. Despite successfully completing the National Council for the Training of Journalists one-year course in Darlington, he realises that his real journalism education is about to begin. Jimmy brings the trainee back to the moment. 'Here's a press release about a Donkey Derby next weekend at our local sanctuary. It's just on the edge of Southampton, so it's an excuse to get photos of dumb animals in the paper, which, apparently, our readers love. Get 150, no 200 words out of it to go with Robert's heart-warming photos of the rescued brutes.' Jimmy stands and looks over at Robert. 'Any decent snaps from the sanctuary we haven't used before?'

Robert shakes his head. 'Jimmy, you know I don't take snaps. They are compositions in light. And the answer is no, we've used all the stock photos I've taken from the sanctuary, some a couple of times over. I'm free this afternoon and the weather's supposed to be good, so I could pop out then and shoot some new stuff. I'll do enough to ensure we've got a good supply for the future as well. There's nothing else in the diary.'

The editor turns back to Jude. 'Right, lad, call the donkey sanctuary straight away and try to organise Robert's photo shoot for after lunch, the number's on the press release. Don't expect a photographer to organise their own pictures, a phone is too technical for most of them, even the upper-class ones like our Robert here. As soon as you're off the phone, nip up to The Dell: Southampton Football Club, The Saints, are revealing their new signing, a centre forward, apparently. Don't worry, it won't be anyone famous or any good. Robert will take you, show you the ropes; he loves the bloody Saints, knows everyone. Do you know anything about football?'

'I used to be a season ticket holder at the Dell; I'm a big Saints fan.'

'Well, you've just saved yourself some money. You'll get in free from now on – into the press box; you'll be writing a match report on every home game, Saturdays or on a Wednesday night, to fill The Reporter's back page. Just don't ask for overtime.'

Jude waits in the paper's car park for Robert to move a small mountain of empty crisp packets, sandwich wrappings and well-thumbed scuba-diving magazines from the passenger seat of his old Renault 5 and they drive to the football ground.

The editor is wrong; the Saints signing is good: Colin Clarke, a 23-year-old free-scoring striker from neighbours Bournemouth. It's a big move for Clarke, who is getting a crack at the big time: the First Division. The club refuse to say how much they've spent on the striker to obtain his signature and, after the press conference, the national newspaper journalists, 'the pack,' huddle together, excluding Jude, and discuss the player's value. Robert uses the opportunity to quietly introduce Jude to the Saints manager, Chris Nicholl. The reporter is embarrassed when Robert reveals to the team's boss that it was Jude's first day as a reporter, and the trainee quickly changes the subject, telling Chris that he'd been a season ticket-holder.

The manager smiles. 'It'll be good to have a fan covering the team. Write down my direct line number and call me if you've a query or want to know something and I'll try and help you out, just don't use it too often. What do you think of Clarkey, the new signing? We've done well to get him; Man United were interested.'

Jude is surprised; the fact that the biggest club in the country had been interested in the centre forward hadn't come out during the press conference. 'Can I use that? That Saints beat Manchester United to buy Colin Clarke?' Jude asks the manager. Chris nods, adding that he wouldn't have said it otherwise. Jude is delighted, realising he has an exclusive line that won't looked dated in three days' time, when the weekly *Reporter* is delivered to every house in the city. 'Thanks, Chris, I owe you,' and the pair shake hands.

Robert is happy with his photo; the old cliché of the new signing putting his new team's scarf round his neck still works, apparently. Jude has enough quotes for a double page spread, although Jimmy only wants '300 words, tops.'

Now for the donkeys. 'I'll drop you back at the office,' Robert kindly offers.

'No, I'll come with you, I've got to start making my own contacts, they were keen we did that, back at college.'

'Your call,' Robert says and the pair head out of Southampton to the other side of Totton, right on the edge of *The Reporter's* distribution area.

The donkey sanctuary owner, Meg Tomlins, fits the stereotype: aging hippy, long flowery dress, flowing hair tied in an Indian scarf. She welcomes Robert like a long-lost friend and is genuinely pleased to meet Jude. 'Tea? We only have camomile but it does smell divine.'

'Camomile. Well else would it be?' thinks Jude, and tucks into the proffered homemade walnut and oatmeal biscuits. Meg is upbeat and passionate about the donkeys, who owe their lives to her and a team of volunteers, and tells Jude of the sad histories of a few of the animals.

The Donkey Derby isn't going to be so much of a race. The 'jockeys' are large corn dollies, fastened to the animals' midriffs with rope so it's more a way of getting visitors to the sanctuary to raise money. 'Is funding a problem?' Jude asks politely – it obviously was, looking round the dilapidated sprawling site and 'the office,' a battered old caravan not large enough to swing a Manx cat.

The ever-smiling Meg looks, for the first time, very serious. 'If you only knew. The farmer who owns these fields is really generous; charges a peppercorn rent. And I don't take out one penny. But we'll soon need feed for the winter months, then there's vet's bills and when I look at the bank statements, well, there's less red on a post box.' With resignation Meg smiles. 'My husband is very supportive, but I don't know what I'm going to do.'

Jude has a quiet word with Robert and asks him to make sure he has a photo of the warm and ever-smiling Meg looking sad, even if it means catching her off guard.

Back in the office, Jude just has time to phone his other new contact, Saints' manager, Chris Nicholl, who laughs at his request. 'OK, why not? Tell the organiser I'll support her donkey charity. In fact, I'll do more, I'll bring the family with me and visit the Donkey Derby on Sunday and even give out the prizes, if she likes.'

Then Jude is brought back down to earth. Jimmy calls him over to the editor's desk. 'Jude, being a journalist is a great job, possibly the best, apart from being Master Blender at the Macallan Distillery on Speyside. But it's not a bloody holiday, to go off visiting donkeys. All you had to do was turn the press release round for an extended picture caption.'

'But Jimmy, I got a story. The sanctuary is skint. It's desperate for cash.'

'Yes, and the Pope is Catholic. Look, animal sanctuaries are always skint.'

'No, really skint. And we could save it. The Saints manager has just agreed to give out the prizes at the Donkey Derby, that's a start.'

'Fine, write it up and let's have a look, but, in your early days here, check with me before you decide to go out on a job next time. OK?'

Jude nods, returns to his desk and threads two sheets of pink paper, divided by a sheet of dark blue carbon, into the platen of the old Imperial. 'Bollocking or not,' the trainee thinks, 'I AM a reporter,' and, smiling, starts to type.

CHAPTER 3

FAIRY FUCKING STORIES

First thing next morning Jude turns straight to the sports sections of the nationals and the Saints' signing of Colin Clarke dominates the back pages, but no paper reports that Manchester United tried to buy the striker – he still has his exclusive angle! All the papers confidently report that Clarke has cost the Saints £500,000. 'The pack,' after a little discussion, had obviously decided on the figure yesterday and their fiction is today's reality. Jude realises, for the first time, the power of the press but he's not allowed long to dwell on the shortcomings of the industry he's just joined.

'It's fucking emotional blackmail, that's what it is!' Sarah explodes, as she slams the phone down on its cradle.

Jude has no idea what is going on and looks beseechingly at his new colleague. Sarah ignores him and stares at Jimmy. 'I don't believe her. She says if we don't pull the story, the donor won't give the money and there'll be no MRI for Southampton General Hospital. We should run it anyway.'

Jimmy fiddles with his eyepatch, thinking, and the trainee reporter uses the space to ask Sarah what is going on. 'The head of fund raising at The General is, well, was, a good contact of mine and told me the city is to get its first MRI scanner, our front page exclusive for this week. That was her on the phone, saying the company that's making the donation for the scanner wants to announce it themselves, with their annual financial results in two months' time. If we break the story now, she says, there'll be no donation and no MRI machine for our city. Fucking emotional blackmail.'

Jimmy sighs heavily. 'Sarah, you're right. That's exactly what it is. And we have to accept it, we don't have a choice. More importantly, we've got two hours before deadline for a decent splash to fill the gaping hole that is currently our front page. Any ideas, anyone?'

The office is a morgue.

'Right, I'm not worried.' The editor stands up to his full five foot five inches. 'I know that by the time I get back from picking up a copy of *The Echo* to see what they've got today; you'll have a great splash for this week's paper.'

'Thanks a fucking lot,' Sarah says towards the office door that has closed behind Jimmy's exit. 'Our editor's gone missing when we need him.'

'Does Jimmy always check the Echo on our deadline day?' Jude asks.

Robert responds. 'Yep. The Echo may be infinitely better resourced, have 10 times the editorial staff and be our paid-for sister evening paper, but Jimmy thinks we should compete and beat it.'

Sarah shakes her head in a frenzy, her straight red hair obscuring her face. She stops. 'Right, what do we have?'

Jude cowers behind his typewriter and the ever-polite Richard answers: 'Nihil,' adding, 'Forsan et haec olim meminisse iuvabit.'

'Bloody public-school education. What's that in English?' Sarah demands.

'Perhaps even these things will be good to remember one day. It's by Virgil.'

'Bloody hell, Richard. That's your contribution? What, we don't have a front page, but one day we'll all have a good laugh about it.'

'Hang on a minute,' Jude surfaces from behind his chunky

typewriter. 'That's made me think. On Sunday night my cousin's pub had a window smashed.'

Sarah picks up her phone and speaks into it without dialling a number. 'Printers, hold the front page, "Pub Has Window Smashed exclusive..."'

'No, listen a minute. It turns out he was told by two heavies that his little country pub needed bouncers on the door. They were really demanding protection money. When he didn't pay up, he got a warning: the window smashed in the middle of the night. I've even got a photo of my cousin standing next to the smashed window; it's undeveloped in the camera in the car.'

Sarah looks pensive before breaking into a big smile. 'Right, we have a splash. Give Richard the film and I'll call the Hampshire Police press office to get a quote. With a bit of luck, my mate Del – Sergeant Derek Simpson – will be on duty, he'll always help us out. Right, what are we waiting for?'

When Jimmy arrives back into the office, *The Echo* under his arm and 'Nothing much in it,' on his lips, Jude is busy typing away at the old Imperial and Sarah is shouting advice and reading out the police quote. 'This is not the first such case we are aware of and Hampshire Police takes any claim of money being demanded with menaces very seriously indeed. There has been obvious criminal damage and we will do whatever is required to bring the perpetrators to justice.'

An hour later the finished copy is placed on Jimmy's desk. Jude's story does not hold back, quoting landlord Gerry Devlin as saying, 'My little baby boy could have been killed.' Jude's photo shows the worried and startled publican caught in the camera's flash next to the broken window, the scene's drama magnified in the moonlight. Jimmy adds the headline 'PROTECTION RACKET HITS CITY'S PUBS' and a reverse white on red strapline across the top 'attack on quiet country inn.'

'That's great work,' Jimmy beams. 'A real team effort. I knew you could do it. And your first byline is on the splash, well done, Jude,' Jimmy beams. 'Right, off to *The Osborne* for you lot. I'll see you in there in an hour when I've finished laying this out. Tell Jackie that the first round's on me. Let's celebrate Jude's first splash; despite everything we've produced a good paper this week, as usual.'

When Jimmy joins the rest of the editorial team in the lounge bar of *The Osborne* he holds up the proof of *The Reporter's* front page for all to see. Jude reads his name on the splash – next to the word *Exclusive* – and can't believe how intoxicated it makes him feel. Jimmy smiles, recognising and recalling the emotion. 'Get used to it, lad. It won't be the last. Just make sure you keep a copy of the paper. It's like your first time with a woman, you'll never forget it, it's special.'

'It's brilliant!' Jude grins from ear to ear, showing all his perfect white teeth. But the smile dissolves into a frown. 'I'm delighted, of course. But my surname and Gerry's are the same – we're cousins, after all. Isn't that a problem?'

'No one, except other journalists, read bylines,' Jimmy explains. 'And if anyone else does notice, they'll just think it's a coincidence.'

After a few celebratory pints, Jude, heads for the Gaumont cinema, where he's to review a new film, *Highlander*. After the film, he sits in his car and writes his review in his notebook, whilst his thoughts are fresh. He dismisses the movie as 'some nonsense about an immortal swordsman starring an aging Sean Connery,' who, the trainee reporter suggests, 'must need the money to appear in such tosh.' It means Jude doesn't get home until much later than usual, and eats alone in the pub's kitchen because Gerry and Milly are working in the bar whilst monitoring little George's sleep via a walkie-talkie. Next morning, he leaves early for work before anyone else is up and about.

The Reporter is printed overnight and, on Thursday afternoon and early evening, a small army of poorly paid schoolkids, pensioners and the unemployed deliver 120,000 copies, posting them through every letterbox in the city and its suburbs. Distribution can be haphazard, with the newsroom often receiving phone calls reporting piles of the free paper dumped in hedgerows or bundles found in builders' skips.

Jude bathes in the glory of his first week's work and his name on the front page. He's still elated as he walks into *The Proud Stag's* kitchen that evening, until he's hit by a chill from the obvious permafrost between George and Milly . Only George is immune to the atmosphere, sitting in his highchair, playing a game of 'how many bread crusts can I fit into my mouth at once.' Regardless, Jude couldn't stop himself smiling with pride as he spots a copy of *The Reporter* on the kitchen table, complete with Gerry's startled face staring from its front page. Milly stops stirring the contents of a saucepan on the Aga. 'Jude, sit down, I'm about to serve up dinner. Anything else you need to tell me that my husband has kept secret?'

Jude sits down but looks blank. Milly stares at him. 'Don't know what I'm talking about, Jude?'

Gerry answers. 'Milly, Jude didn't know I hadn't told you. At least he's not guilty of that, just everything else,' his expression is somewhere between outrage and self-pity.

'Look, I'm sorry... what exactly have I done?' Jude asks, looking at Gerry.

Milly replies. 'Gerry didn't tell me about the threats, the demand for protection money.'

'What? Not even after the broken window?' Jude is genuinely startled by the revelation.

'No, I bloody didn't, OK? I didn't want to worry you, Milly. I'm your husband, I'll sort it out.'

'So much for being a team,' says Milly.' So much for taking on the world together. I'm a bloody barrister, for God's sake. I know the law; I'm paid to be a bloody expert. But no, you prefer to tell your trainee journalist cousin, who hadn't even started in the job. Bloody hell, Gerry!'

'Milly, you're an expert in marine contract law, not gangs demanding protection money. And I told Jude in confidence, not so he could plaster it all over the front page of his fucking free newspaper.'

'Watch your language in front of George. So, it would have been alright to tell him and not me if he hadn't printed it in the paper, would it?'

Milly raises her serving spoon accusingly, and a drop of casserole falls to the floor.

'Shit. Right, sit down Gerry, I'm serving up. I've spent long enough cooking it, it's not going to go to waste, let's try to enjoy it.' Gerry sits as he's told and the three of them all fail to enjoy what, under normal circumstances, would have been a very tasty lamb stew.

After the meal, as soon as Milly leaves the kitchen to carry a tired and crying George up to his cot, Gerry turns on Jude. 'You do realise what you've done, don't you?'

'I'm sorry, I just assumed that you'd told Milly.'

'No, not that, she'll get over me not telling her soon enough. I asked, no, told you it wasn't a story for the newspaper.'

'Gerry, I didn't think you meant it... the paper was short of a splash and I had the photo, had witnessed it all with my own eyes.'

'You think you're the top reporter? Well, Scoop, what do you think is going to happen next.?'

'I don't know, perhaps–'

'Perhaps nothing. Do you think this gang is going to be pleased to read about themselves on the front of the local freesheet? Or do you think they are going to be really, really pissed off and come after the man who's told the police? The man whose photo is on the front of the paper for all to see? Well?'

'It might scare them off, you know, there's the quote from the police.'

'Jude, are you naïve, thick or just don't give a shit about us, your family. If you think for one moment that this gang is scared off by a police station eight miles away that is only staffed on a Tuesday morning, well, you shouldn't be writing news stories, you should be writing fairy fucking stories.' Gerry storms out, slamming the kitchen door and reigniting George's cries.

CHAPTER 4

THE RAID

Jude leaves for work early, before breakfast, desperate to avoid seeing Milly or Gerry. All night he'd been going over the story, asking himself if he'd realised the potential implications when he wrote the story or had he just pretended to himself that everything would be OK? He knew he'd let his cousin down.

Jude's phone rings for the first time since he started working on the paper. 'The Reporter newsroom, Jude Devlin speaking.'

'Well of course you are, I phoned your direct line, Jude. You might want to relax a little, you sound like you're working for an insurance company.'

'Oh, do I, er, sorry. Look, who's calling?'

'It's Del. We haven't spoken but you must have heard of me? Sgt Derek Simpson of the Hampshire Constabulary press office, your new best friend.' The bright, ever so slightly camp tones and relaxed over-familiarity made Jude instantly warm to Del. The sergeant asks about Jude's background and is delighted to learn that they're both 'local boys.' They chat for 10 minutes, Del welcoming, helpful, charming and funny. 'Look, Jude, I only phoned up to say I loved your piece on the donkeys. So did Meg. She just called me to say her phone hasn't stopped ringing this morning. Said she's had offers of enough free hay for the next two years and counting. People have been calling to ask for directions to the Donkey Derby. BBC's South Today are sending out a film crew to do an interview–'

'You know Meg, Meg Tomlins?

'I should do; I sleep with her.'

Jude is confused. 'What do you mean? You've got different surnames.'

'Jude, don't be such a prude. Meg is my other half. Just 'cause we're in our 40s doesn't mean to say we have to be married to live together. We've just never got around to it, but we've been together for years; we've got two kids. Enough about my love life, you must tell me about yours soon, much more interesting.'

'If only, Del, if only.' Jude looks at the ceiling.

'Anyway, one good turn deserves another. Saturday night, be at the central nick for 8pm and bring the well-spoken Comrade Robert along. Tell him to pack his long lens. You won't regret it. Ask for me at the front desk. Byee.' And the phone line goes dead.

Jude replaces the handset into its cradle and wonders what had just happened. He looks at Sarah. 'The Donkey Sanctuary has been offered enough free hay for the next two winters and Sunday's Donkey Derby looks like it's going to be a big success.'

Sarah shook her hair in delight, flashes Jude a huge smile, jumps up and heads for the editor's desk. 'Jimmy, looks like we've got next week's splash sorted, "The Reporter Saves the Donkeys!"'

Jimmy looks up from a car magazine he was absently reading. 'That's good news. Jude, phone Meg, that's her name, right? Phone Meg to check how well the appeal is going and ask her not to speak to anyone else after Sunday: she'll have to speak to other reporters until then, otherwise they'll blank her in the future and she can't afford that. And you and Robert cover the derby on Sunday: lots of smiley photos and happy, supportive quotes and we'll get the centre spread out of it as well as the splash.'

Later that afternoon, when the office is quiet – Jimmy is still in *The Osborne* and Sarah is out, interviewing someone for a feature – Jude pours the tea for himself and Robert. 'Are you free on Saturday night?'

'Jude, I'm free every Saturday night and every other night,

come to that. If you've had a four-month-old baby and your wife only trusts her family, who all just happen to live in Surrey, to babysit, you'd be free every night. That's if being free is sitting on the sofa, watching the old goggle-box with your significant other and listening for the slightest of baby sounds from upstairs.'

Although Robert's public-school accent added weight to his words, Jude fails to feel sorry for him; Sarah has already explained that Robert is very happily married to a beautiful, funny and charming woman whose family's wealth allows him to 'play at being a photographer' and that the pair of them dote on their baby, Elizabeth-Jane. 'That's good; Sgt Derek Simpson wants us at City Police Station for 8pm, says to bring a long lens with you and that "we won't regret it."'

'That's going to piss off my significant other. I wonder what he's up to? And a tip, Jude: don't call him Derek, he hates it, always Del. He's no fool, although he likes to act like one.' Jude files the information and nods his thanks. Robert continues, 'I think Del wishes he had joined a newspaper himself, rather than the Hampshire Constabulary. But he's a good friend to *The Reporter*. He looks out for us and reckons our ethos is the same as his: communist. I saw Del on a job a couple of weeks ago and he starts calling me 'Comrade Robert' – reckons *The Reporter* could be secretly funded by the Soviets, "Your paper's more Trotsky than *The Socialist Worker*, which you have to buy. *The Reporter* tells stories against the corrupt bourgeois state and is delivered, free, to every home in the city. If that's not egalitarian, what is? Marx could have written for it." He can be a bit barking, but he's got a point.'

Jude laughs aloud. 'I think the reporter is more like the NHS; free to all at the point of delivery, but if you can afford something better, *The Echo* or *The Times*, you go for that instead, like paying for private health treatment.'

On Saturday, Robert and Jude meet at the Central Police Station car park and, after some speculation about what could be in store for them, ask the desk sergeant for Del. The press office sergeant was right, they're not disappointed: there's a major drugs raid planned and they're invited to 'tag along'. Del throws the pair a stab vest each. 'Stick these on and don't get in the way. And use your long lens, Comrade Robert, that will make it safer for everyone.'

Del ushers the two journalists into a packed briefing room where some 30 or so police officers are chattering excitedly. As they enter, the room turns in on itself and immediately goes silent. Even Del's effusive personality can't break down the barrier as he introduces the journalists to the hostile crowd. 'Here are the two representatives of the enemy. May I have great pleasure in offering you, all the way from *The Reporter's* offices in Millbrook, Jude Devlin with his poisoned pen, and Robert Freeman-Adams and his 12-inch lens.' The officers are clearly underwhelmed to meet the journalists who are to accompany them on the raid. Del appears not to notice his colleagues' negativity and remains upbeat. Turning to the journalists he says loudly, 'Lads, you're going to get a great story and photos. This is likely to be the city's largest ever drug's haul, if all goes according to plan.'

Del is interrupted by the shortest person in the room. 'I'll do the explaining, if that's OK with you, sergeant?' Chief Inspector Peter Scott steps onto the raised platform at the front of the briefing room. Del flounces his disapproval as the chief inspector clears his throat. 'Good, right. This is a major and unique operation, as you can tell by the size of the team assembled this evening. Tonight is a key plank in our plan to remove the city's major drugs gangs from the streets and we expect to catch these villains with a significant amount of both cash and cannabis. The cannabis has been smuggled through Southampton Docks by two crew members off *The Pride of Calcutta,* a Panamanian-registered, Indian-owned freighter out of Tangier. With help from "friends" at the docks, the crewmen have evaded customs and are, as we speak, delivering their cargo to gang members at the multi-storey car park in the city centre. Special Branch are monitoring the handover and will intercept and arrest the crew members later this evening. I'm happy to let Special Branch have their fun and all the paperwork that goes with arresting foreign nationals.' The group give a knowing laugh. 'Right, the sergeants will form you into smaller teams for different parts of the operation, then I'll continue.'

The assembled police officers fidget and chat amongst themselves quietly as the sergeants reassemble the team into groups of threes and fours. 'Bloody hell,' Jude thinks, realising his pulse is galloping. 'This is the real deal, an actual drugs raid and I'm going to be on it.' He looks slowly, intently around the room and notices that, although all the officers were dressed in black only three or four are wearing normal uniforms, the rest are in clothes that look more like tracksuits.

Jude is brought back to the moment by the chief inspector raising his voice. 'OK, let's go again. We have good intelligence that the drugs will be taken to an address off Derby Road, in the city centre, where it will immediately be distributed among the five different gangs we are anticipating being in attendance. We expect them to arrive from 10pm to collect their shares – more on that in a minute. Our job is to observe the cannabis – given the amount, it should be pretty easy to spot – and the arrival of those gang members. Once we are confident the cannabis and villains are inside, the order will be given to raid the building, arrest everyone present and safely collect all money and drugs on the property. We also have extensive intelligence that the house has security inside, both passive and active, although, from the outside, it looks like every other building in the terrace.'

The chief inspector scratches his neck. 'Look, we need to get in bloody quickly, before they know what's hit 'em or can start destroying the drugs. And we need to show an overwhelming degree of force, making the gang members realise that any resistance will be futile. Should there be any resistance, it must be subdued immediately using whatever level of force is needed. Understood?' There's a murmur of agreement, but the chief inspector is not satisfied. He looks keenly at each and every officer and waits for their individual nod of assent.

Chief Inspector Scott smiles and continues. 'Good. All of you here have carried out drug raids before, which is why you've been chosen. But tonight's operation is different and unique. The leaders of the city's gangs will, for the first time, be in the same room and I expect them to be on edge. On the surface they may have forgotten their local rivalries to co-operate and buy in bulk, but they will all be very nervous, hence the need to subdue all of them very quickly. The gangs have pooled their funds to purchase a huge quantity of Moroccan Black cannabis resin, known on the streets as hashish, directly from India, rather than buy smaller quantities from London or Liverpool dealers as is their normal modus operandi. Make no mistake; what we are going to do this evening will be a major attack on the city's drug supply and the criminals behind it. Right, before we get into specifics of who's doing what, and study the building's layout, are there any questions?'

Chief Inspector Scott waits a second and is about to continue when Jude raises his hand. Chief Inspector Scott shakes his head. 'I mean questions from the active participants, not the observers. For clarity, the observers will only enter the building once I have personally authorised it and that will only happen if and when I am confident it is safe to do so. The observers, who will be accompanied by Sergeant Simpson at all times. Now, if you two gentlemen of the press wish to go and get yourselves a coffee before I get into detailed operational matters with the team, I'll not stand in your way.'

Jude and Robert realise they are, politely, being kicked out and Jude nods a thank you towards the chief inspector, knowing he'd committed a faux pas by trying to ask a question. Del joins them in the corridor.

Robert re-checks his cameras and Jude asks, 'The chief inspector didn't really want us in there, did he?

Del smiles his disarming grin. 'Scotty's all right, just a bit on edge before the raid – there's lot that could go wrong and it's his officers who could get seriously hurt if it does. Gangs don't take kindly to being arrested with their pockets stuffed with drugs. But he realises good publicity and his photo on the front of The

Reporter won't do his reputation and career any harm.'

Jude is told, although asked not to report, that a microphone had been planted, thorough an adjoining chimney, in the house and officers listening in heard how the gang leaders, rather than being on edge like the police expected, are quite relaxed. It seemed they were only worried about the threat posed by each other and not the police. When they were all in the same room, they were heard joking about how much more money they were going to make now they'd cut out the middlemen.

Jude, Robert and Del are stationed in an unmarked police car 50 yards from the drug den and, through one of its side windows, Robert's long lens captures the drugs being carried into the house: four very large canvas bags, with handles on each side, and two massive backpacks, all stuffed fit to burst.

The gang leaders are already inside; they were all so scared of being stitched up by each other, they'd all arrived early. The chief inspector gives the order and Robert photographs an officer smashing open the front door with one well-directed swing of his door ram. The photographer keeps shooting as more officers, all in full armour, charge into the terraced house. Their speed surprises the gangs and the sight of the leading sergeant, his automatic weapon pointing at them, is enough to make them realise that the game is up. Two of them try to run out the back, but are tripped to the ground by officers waiting just outside. The whole raid is over in less than a minute, including the initial search and making safe of the rest of the building.

It wasn't much longer before Robert's camera is recording images of a dozen handcuffed men of varying ethnicities, all aged in their teens or 20s, being marched out of the building, surrounded by armed police officers. They are led to a series of police Transit vans which arrive right on queue. The street lamp outside the house means the arrested men's faces are clearly visible, although Robert wonders aloud if he'll need to blur them, for legal reasons, when he prints the photos in *The Reporter's* darkroom.

It's another half an hour before Del leads Jude and Robert

into the house and there, on a table in the front room, are 300 blocks of compressed hashish. Despite each block being wrapped first in plastic and then a brown paper outer skin, the room still reeks of the unmistakable smell of dope. There is cash, but only around£1,500 - a decent amount of money, but nowhere near enough to pay for the drugs. There's an assortment of knives, baseball bats and old school knuckledusters, all found in a box at the entrance of the passage – the gangs had obviously agreed to leave their 'tools' by the front door. The chief inspector refuses to be photographed holding the drugs but readily agrees to Robert's request to pick up the box of weapons for a photo. The pair then spend five minutes together, Robert clicking away, the Chief Inspector standing in front of the stash of drugs on the table. He looks serious but co-operates with Robert's requests, although he refuses to smile, and answers Jude's questions, giving excellent quotes.

Later, back at the station, Del chats away as he escorts the two journalists to their cars. 'Scotty's happy with the result and reckons everyone arrested will plead guilty to something or other. No one can pretend they weren't there. And it helped that everyone in the house, except the two Greek guys caught running out the back door, were stoned – apparently, they "needed" to try out the dope first, which is why the smell inside was so strong.' Del shakes his head from side to side and grins at the same time.

Robert is surprised. 'When I was taking the chief inspector's photograph, he didn't look very happy, he looked, well, puzzled, like something was troubling him.'

'There is, but it's not for publication, OK, Jude?' Del looked quizzically at the reporter. Jude nods his assent. 'Right, Scotty had intelligence that the Quirk family had organised tonight's events; that it was them who convinced the other gangs to forget their quarrels, pool their resources and to buy, in quantity, directly from abroad. He was convinced the Quirks were the brains behind it all, that they guaranteed the safety of the leader of each gang and their minder.'

Jude has never heard of the Quirks before, but realises there's no reason he should have. 'Sounds like they're pretty smart bunch, this Quirk family.'

'Well, they can't be that smart, because they didn't show, the only significant group from the city's criminal fraternity that weren't represented tonight. I suspect that, for once, Chief Inspector Scott got it wrong.'

Robert looks at his watch and Jude understands the photographer is impatient to get home to his wife. 'We better get going, thanks for tonight, Del. Can I phone you on Monday to get a value of the drugs?'

'Of course. I'll have to let the Echo and TV and radio know about the raid. But none of those will have your first-hand account or photos. Speak next week, guys.' Del smiles, waves and heads back inside the police building.

CHAPTER 5

THEY'RE NOT CHEMISTS

It's a gorgeous late summer's day, just perfect for Robert's photos of the Donkey Derby. Jude's also smiling, happy he has all the quotes he needs and more, turned into his shorthand squiggles and safely in his notebook. The reporter, watching the photographer lift his khaki-coloured camera bag into the boot of his car, laughs aloud. 'Robert, there's never a dull moment, is there? Police drug raid one night, Donkey Derby the next day. In truth, that's why I was so pleased to get the job on *The Reporter*. I knew that working on a freesheet, I'd get to cover every story going.'

'That's one interpretation, Jude. The other is our paper is ridiculously understaffed and we get worked like dogs for starvation wages.'

'It's funny you say that; I realise I've not had a day off in the two weeks I've been at the paper. I'm not moaning, I'm loving it, but I need to do some washing soon. I took this shirt out of the dirty laundry basket this morning.'

'It's not normally this busy, and it's worse in summer, with fetes and processions that need covering. One tip, don't even think about asking to be paid for overtime, it won't happen; you're in the wrong industry for that, Jude. But if you ever need a day off or to go to the dentist or something Jimmy's pretty good. Right, I'm going to pop back to the office and dev these films from the Donkey Derby and from the raid last night. Reckon we'll have some good stuff. I'll print them up tomorrow, see you then.'

Jude thinks about joining Robert to type up the drugs raid but decides he needs to first ask his editor what angle the paper wants on the story. As for the Donkey Derby, well it was a huge success but they won't need many words to go with Robert's photos for the centre spread, and the splash would write itself: 'The Reporter Saves the Donkeys.' So, Jude decides to head home. 'Right, see you bright and early,' he says to Robert, gets into his old Peugeot 304 convertible and enjoys taking the roof down for the drive back to *The Proud Stag*. 'Perhaps I can take little George out in his pushchair and earn some brownie points by giving Gerry and Milly some time together,' he thinks, as the oak branches speed by overhead.

Jimmy asks Robert to print out the photos from the Donkey Derby first and Jude to write 150 words to go with them. That will allow him to lay out the centre page spread 'nice and early, for a bloody change.'

At lunchtime, Jimmy scratches his thinning grey hair and reckons he'll celebrate his brilliant design work with a trip to *The Osborne* 'for just the one celebratory ale, anyone joining me?' Jude and Robert are both too busy following up on the police raid from the weekend and, with Sarah out of the office on an interview, Jimmy enjoys his pint alone and in peace.

Robert is unusually diffident as he places a series of black and white photos – *The Reporter*, like most papers, doesn't have colour, except for the blue of its masthead – in front of Jude. 'Look at the top one, Jude. I wouldn't say this in front of Jimmy, but there's something I'm concerned about. In the top photo, forget the drugs on the table, look in the kitchen doorway, do you notice anything unusual?'

'No, not really. I don't remember seeing those cardboard boxes stacked on top of each other in the kitchen. But there was a lot going on and–'

Robert nods. 'That photo is the only one with the door open, where we can see into the kitchen. I think someone had just walked through from the lounge as I clicked. The door is firmly shut in all the rest of the photos. Did you go into the kitchen at all, Jude?'

'No, now you come to mention it, I didn't. I went to go in once but a sergeant said the scenes of crime team were inside, taking prints, so the kitchen was out of bounds.'

Robert removes the first photo to reveal a grainy close-up underneath. 'I've blown up the top of the uppermost box about as much as our old enlarger will allow. What do you think is inside the cardboard box?'

Jude studies the photo for some time, not wanting to make a mistake and appear an idiot to his new workmate. Then, he was sure. 'Bloody hell!' he almost shouts, and feels goosebumps on his arm. 'That looks the same as the packets of drugs that are stacked on the table. Plastic and then badly covered with brown paper. What do you think?'

Robert nods. 'The same. I can't be totally sure, but it's very, very similar to the blocks of hashish carefully arranged and on display on the table in the lounge.'

'And if those boxes underneath are full of the same, well it's half as much again as the cannabis stacked on the table.' Jude lets out a whistle. 'Robert, how big would you say each block on the table was? I reckon, what, 8 inches by 3 wide and 2 high.'

'I wouldn't argue with that estimate, why?'

Jude starts to scribble numbers in his reporter's notepad. He's concentrating but pops his head up once. 'And the bags used to carry the cannabis into the house, what size where they? I reckon those big duffel bag type things were about 4 foot long, 18 inches in diameter? The backpacks were big, say three foot tall, two foot wide and 15 inches deep?'

'I imagine you're close, but I could scale it off the photos if you need a more accurate measurement. Can you work out the volume?' Jude nods in reply and Robert is impressed. 'That's very clever, I don't ever remember studying that at my school. Maths wasn't really my thing; I was quite good at Latin. Not a lot of help, though, is it?'

Jude re-checks his figures. 'Those bags were definitely full when they went into the house on Saturday night, right? But the drugs on display for us to photograph would have taken up about half the available space of the backpacks and the four duffel bags. Two thirds, tops.' He scribbles some more, nods and re-checks the numbers. 'But if those cardboard boxes in the kitchen, if they were full of bars of hashish, that would account for the difference.'

Robert look at the reporter and shakes his head. 'Well... there could be a perfectly reasonable explanation.'

'Let's find out.' Jude picks up the telephone, checks his contacts book for the number, and dials. 'Del, we've got some terrific photos for Saturday night, thanks for that. Robert said if you want any pics for the Hampshire Police newsletter, let him know.'

'Great, thanks. You two should have stayed, not long after you disappeared, we all went for a few beers. Ended up a lock-in and a couple of the local working girls came in and joined in the fun. I'm not sure how I got home!'

'Your Meg must be a very understanding woman. Did you get a street value for the cannabis?'

'And a very lucky one. Street value? Of course, young man. And it is a record for the Hampshire force to seize. The 300 blocks, that Comrade Robert so lovingly photographed, each weighed about a quarter of a kilo and have a street value of some £264,000.'

Jude is stunned. 'A quarter of a million. Fuck me! 'Scuse my French, Del. Really, wow.'

Robert hears the number and sits down, shocked at the value of what he's photographed.

Dell explains. 'Well, work it out for yourself, the smallest amount, a sixth of an ounce, goes for about £15, maybe a bit more. That's roughly a hundred quid an ounce on the street.'

Jude grabs a pen from his desk – he'd snapped the end of

his pencil when he heard the street value of the drugs. 'Del, you could buy a street of three-bed semis in Southampton for that amount,' he laughs. The reporter thinks quickly, the 'missing drugs' must also have a huge value, and his voices switches to serious. 'Del, one last question, well a statement really. In one of Comrade Robert's photos, we can see a box in the kitchen and inside the top box is, or looks like, wrapped blocks of cannabis.'

'Ah, you saw those couple of blocks, did you?'

'Well, we didn't see them at the time, but they're in one photo. Why aren't they on display.'

'Right, no need to publish this or use that particular photo; I'm sure you've got enough to choose from. And you won't find this in any police training manual or be told officially, but it's standard practice, all the forces do it, to keep a little back. It's used for training sniffer dogs what to go after and teaching new recruits what to look for. Otherwise, Hampshire Police would have to go and buy fresh dope off the street from dealers and that wouldn't look very good in the annual accounts, would it?'

Jude laughs. 'I suppose not. But a couple of blocks, at a quarter of a kilo each, wouldn't be heavy or large enough to fill the bags or weigh enough. You saw how those guys carrying the bags struggled to get them out of the car.'

'Remember, Jude, these guys are tough ugly drug dealers, not dispensing chemists, weighing everything to the last gram. There's going to be a bit of deviation, not every block will be exactly a quarter of a kilo.'

This was a good explanation, but if the measure was going to be wrong, surely it would be light, not heavy; drug dealers aren't going to rip themselves off, are they? Jude takes a deep breath and pushes as far as he dares. 'But Del, I've calculated the volume of the 300 blocks we saw, they wouldn't have filled the backpacks and duffel bags. Nowhere near.'

'I didn't know you were a maths genius, Jude.' Del realises his first thoughts about this new journalist are right; he's bright and persistent. 'Look, this sounds a bit far-fetched to me, but I'll check with Smithy and get back to you. Make sure *The Reporter* keeps telling the world where it's going wrong. Byee,' Del signs off in his trademark, breezy way.

Jude is worried: worried that he is going to cock up his first big proper story; worried that he is, in effect, alleging police theft of illegal drugs; and worried that he's out of his depth. This is only his third week as a paid journalist. Get this wrong and it will also be his last. He looks at Robert, hoping his more experienced colleague will know what to do next.

Robert shakes his head but at least offers advice. 'Look, let's keep quiet until we hear back from Del. Then we can decide our next moves and what, if anything, to tell Jimmy.' He picks up his black and white prints from the desk.

Jude blows out his cheeks, 'Sounds like a plan.' The new reporter sounds confident, but inside his brain is a mash and his stomach churns like a cement mixer. 'I thought being a journalist was supposed to be fun,' he mutters quietly to himself.

CHAPTER 6

THAT'S WHY...

Jimmy arrives back from the pub after some two hours and, from the slight slurring of his words and smell on his breath, he's certainly enjoyed considerably more than the single pint he'd intended. 'Right, Jude, lad, how's the great drug bust story, going?' Jude bristles at the word 'lad' and thinks Jimmy uses it more frequently after he's had a drink or two, but decides to let it pass for now. 'I've had an idea how we should run it. We've got great pics and you can write your first-hand, "fuck me this is amazing," account of the action. But many of *The Reporter's* readers know the story. They certainly will by Thursday night, when we hit the street. So, it won't go on the front – we give it pages 3, 4 and 5 and headline it "THE INSIDE STORY" with a big strap across the top "at the centre of the city's biggest drug bust." Robert, you've got those prints from the raid ready? Good. You don't need to blur out any faces of the gang members; identification or whether they were at the scene or not won't be an issue. One last thing, can you take a headshot of Jude? We'll give him a picture byline on page three.' The editor turns to look at his trainee reporter. 'Not bad for your second week, Jude? Write it in the first person; I want "I was shocked when... the heady smell of cannabis filled the room... the tough gang leader sneered in my direction." Give it both barrels, OK? Right, what are we waiting for everyone? We've got a paper to get out.' Despite deadline being days away, Jimmy's enthusiasm is infectious, and the team set to work.

Late in the afternoon Jude's phone rings. 'Evening, Jude, I thought you'd be off home by now?'

'Chance would be a fine thing, Del. I'm working longer hours that the AA, and they fix your car 24/7.'

Del laughs down the line. 'Jude, I'd be careful using phrases like the AA in your office. I like a drink but your editor…'

'Is there nothing you don't have the lowdown on, Del? Talking of which, did you find out about the "excess" from Chief Inspector Jones?'

'I've done better than that, but first you have to reassure me that this is not for publication, Jude. I'll give you chapter and verse, but you can't print it, OK? You'll understand when I explain and realise I'm being reasonable. Tell you what, if you think I'm being unreasonable, when I've explained it to you, print what I'm about to tell you.'

'That's ridiculously fair, Del. What's the story?'

'It's pathetic, really, but my boss, Chief Inspector Mitchell Matthews, explained. I don't think you've spoken to him yet; he's like you – ambitious, very straight and easy to get on with. Hasn't got my charm, of course, but who has? Anyway, before heading up the force's communication division – he moved here about 18 months ago – he was head of vice. The fact is that this force, along with every other, is judged on targets by central government. It's all spreadsheets and numbers. To make matters worse, these days half the senior officers are being fast-tracked straight out of Oxbridge and have never walked a beat in their life. No division is more heavily judged or measured than vice, partly because everything is easily measured – value of drugs taken off the street, weight of drugs seized, number of soliciting arrests, how many under-age drinkers and publicans supplying them charged, etc, etc. Basically, the politicians reckon success or otherwise can be judged on whether you hit or miss these annual targets, especially in vice. Why am I telling you all this? Obviously, the key figure for vice is the amount, the volume and value of drugs taken off the street.'

'So Chief Inspector Scott will want to have the biggest number possible to beat his target?'

'Jude, didn't you tell me that you used to be in sales, when you had a proper job, long before you trained to be a scribbler of life's miseries? Did you have sales targets then?'

'Yeah, of course, but what's that got to do with the price of fish?'

'And if you beat your targets handsomely, what happened the following year?'

'Well, you tried not to exceed the current year's target by too much, otherwise next year's target was ramped up out of sight and you had no chance of earning your bonus... Oh, hang on, I get it.'

'Good, I wondered if the penny would drop. So, one outstanding piece of police work this year could make the vice squad look bad next. It won't affect the sentences of the toerags we've caught red-handed – they'll get the maximum time inside regardless. The 'excess' drugs are quietly held back, in case there is no smuggling ship's crew to arrest red-handed next year. Then the extra cannabis is added to next year's numbers and everyone is happy. The drugs are still off the street and the pen pushers have their results. Police officers don't get a bonus, although I might suggest it to the Chief Constable next time we have a chat, but they do get a pat on the back and possibly promotion. Capeesh?'

'Del, thanks for explaining. When I was in selling to the city council, it used to do the same thing, but in reverse. At the end of its financial year, if the council hadn't spent all its budget, it would buy all sorts, sometimes stuff it didn't really need or want, knowing that if the budget was underspent, it would be cut the following year.'

'Look, Jude, I know this sounds a little odd, but at the coal-face, at the sharp end, it's playing the system a little, like this, well, that makes the system work. I think you understand. And I'm being reasonable?'

Jude pauses for a little before answering. 'I guess. You're right, it's what makes the world go round.'

'Good, I knew you'd see the bigger picture. And I've got another great story for you, well a competition. I was in Southampton city centre the other day and got a sandwich from British Home Stores. It was rubbish! Almost frozen, white bread that tasted of nothing and the cheese was so thin it was almost see-through. You should run a competition to find the city's best lunchtime sarnie. I'll even help judge it. Byee.'

Jude finds Robert in his little darkroom, and, as the red warning light in the corridor isn't illuminated, enters. 'Good to see *The Reporter* isn't wasting its money on palatial photographic darkrooms. I've seen bigger broom cupboards than this, Robert. And the smell of your chemicals...'

'That's why I use the changing bag to transfer the films into the developing containers. It's not healthy in here, is it?'

In the snug privacy of the darkroom Jude explains to Robert why the police keep the size of the drug haul low and the pair agree not to mention the mis-reporting to their editor. After work, both Robert and Jude refuse Jimmy's offer of 'a quick one' before heading home. Robert explains, 'Jimmy, I'd love to but I'm starting jogging tonight. A few of my old school chums have taken it up and say they've never felt so good. How about you Jude? Fancy looking out your old plimsolls and coming along for a couple of miles. Sitting behind that typewriter old day...'

Jude shakes his head but, on the drive home, decides to change his route and heads past the boxing gym where, 10 years ago, he was a regular member, skipping, working on the heavy bag and the speed ball, even sparring in the ring. *The New Boxing Gym* is still there, no longer new – it had been 'given to the community' by a developer desperate to persuade the city planners to pass a big redevelopment programme for a derelict part of old Southampton.

'Nothing ventured, nothing gained,' Jude tells himself as he parks his car and laughs, instantly recalling the code for the lock on the gym's door. He taps four digits on the keypad and, amazingly, the door opens to his push – the number hasn't been changed in the last decade.

The smell of sweat and muscle rub, the squeak of boxing boot on wooden floor, the thud of leather glove hitting leather bag combine to transport Jude back to another time, another life.

'Bloody hell! As I breathe, you a sight for sore eyes, Jude Devlin. How long… well, too long, that's for sure. How are you, Jude?' The man – it's difficult to put an age on him, 50's or 60's, is in good shape but grey-haired. He wears dark tracksuit bottoms and a white T-shirt with 'Ali's the Boss' emblazoned across the front in red. He walks towards Jude, smiles and thrusts out his right hand.

Jude shakes it eagerly and, without realising, returns the smile. 'You're right, Sergeant Broski, too long.'

'Inspector now, but when did you ever call me anything other than Phil?' He takes a step back and eyes Jude profession-ally. 'Well, I can see why you've come. Too much of the good life, I'm thinking. Nip into the changing rooms, there's some spare kit in my office, help yourself, it's not locked. I've got to time some rounds – regional championships at the weekend. If you're not in a rush, let's catch up afterwards?' Jude's about to explain he's only popped into the gym because he was driving past, was no longer a member and wasn't sure he wanted to be. But Brit-ish Transport police sergeant Phil Broski, now inspector, is one of the nicest, genuine and most honourable people Jude has ever known. And the inspector disappears into the main hall before Jude can protest. 'Well, I'm here, nothing else planned for the evening,' Jude thinks, 'why not?'

Some 90 minutes later, Jude is back in his own clothes, dry-ing his hair with a spare towel, and feeling more alive than he has in ages. 'Great to see you again after so long, Jude. You look like you really enjoyed the session.'

'I hadn't realised how much I missed the gym, if I'm honest, Phil. I've got blood pumping through bits of me I forgot I had.'

'And you could do with losing about half a stone of those

"bits,"' Phil laughs. 'So, where have you been, what's new? Are you back in Southampton permanently?'

'Looks like it; I started as a trainee journalist on *The Reporter,* so I have to stay for at least two years for my indentures.'

'Well, don't be a stranger here at the gym. I'll make you an honorary member for the first year; you can't be earning much as a trainee. Let's have a proper catch-up soon, Jude, I've got to dash, there's a boxing committee meeting I'm supposed to be chairing. Great to see you!'

CHAPTER 7

IT WAS ALL GOING SO WELL

Jude, for once, is first in the office and, after filling the kettle and making himself a coffee, starts the first proper job of the day: opening the post. The important thing is to find any press releases that may contain a real story. In his few weeks as a trainee journalist, Jude has worked out what makes *The Reporter* tick: advertising. It's the same for all free newspapers. Today, being Tuesday, Jimmy, the editor, will be informed by the advertising department how many pages he has to fill.

It's a simple equation: if the advertising department has sold the equivalent of 36 full pages of adverts, then news will need to fill 24 pages. It's the magic 60/40 rule. You need 40% editorial to keep the readers interested and 60% advertising to make the paper profitable. The greater the total number of pages, the more profitable the paper is. Like it or lump it, regardless of what the editor, the reporters and photographer think, the advertising team are the kings inside *The Reporter's* dilapidated building.

Actually, they were the 'Queens' of the ramshackle pile. Southern News Print, owners of The Reporter, had decided to employ an all-women sales team. Realising that the vast majority of people who buy ads, either for companies or their own businesses, are men, management reckoned that a pretty female face would win the order. The sales office consists of the four senior sales reps, who spend their days out and about, driving their company cars and visiting clients, and the six-strong junior sales team, who are office based and either phone potential advertisers or answer incoming sales calls. The advertising 'girls' never tire of ensuring the news team remember that they'd 'be out of a job if it wasn't for us.'

Normally, Jude finds the members of the sales team irritating and superficial, and sees them as a 'necessary evil'. That's until he's tries to pay for his lunch, a sandwich and can of Fanta, at the local corner shop and can't find his wallet. He goes through each and every pocket of his suit... twice. Danielle, one of the telephone sales team, is standing behind in the queue. 'Left the wallet at home? That's a really old trick, you won't con anyone with that, Jude? Mind you, I know you reporters aren't paid well, especially the new trainees.' She laughs confidently and hands a shiny pound coin to the shopkeeper.

Jude protests, 'You don't have to buy me lunch. I'm not really that hungry.'

Danielle laughs again. 'I'm not, you can pay me back, this is a loan.' For the first time, Jude looks properly at Danielle. He notices that, unusually for members of the sales team, she is dressed plainly and is wearing little make-up. She is, perhaps, a little younger than him and is surprised to find he's attracted to her relaxed self-confidence and something he can't quite put his finger on, a devilment, maybe, hiding behind her eyes. 'Yes, a loan, of course,' he mumbles and quickly heads out of the shop and back to the safety of the newsroom.

Jude reads a press release inviting a reporter and guest to visit *Hydrogen*, an old sailing barge owned by Bell's Whisky, when she visits Southampton Docks. 'Perhaps Danielle will come along, if I ask her,' the thought, 'it's about time I started to have more of a life.'

Not wishing to appear too keen, Jude waits a week, until the day before the whisky barge's visit, to catch Danielle on her own. Spotting her walking along the corridor, he dashes out of the office, his prepared script in his head. 'Danielle, here's the pound I owe you, I need to repay the loan.' Jude is well aware he gave the money to Adrian, another member of the sales office to pass on to Danielle on the same day he borrowed it, and expects her to refuse the money.

'Thanks, I was thinking of charging interest,' Danielle smiles and, well aware this is a pretence by Jude, drops the coin into her purse and starts to walk off.

Jude is thrown from his prepared script of a nonchalant invite. 'Er, well, hang on a minute. I don't suppose, you know, look, there's a sailing barge coming to Southampton tomorrow, tomorrow night. Free whisky, er, I'm not a whisky... are you, do you drink?

Danielle fights to hold back her laughter at the reporter's obvious discomfort. 'Jude, this isn't a date or anything, just a work trip, right?" she asks.

'Right, yeah, not a date or anything.'

'OK then, sounds fun, I think, although I don't really drink whisky.'

Red-faced he returns to the news room to find Jimmy in concerned mood. 'OK, the paper is full but really, "City Cat Thefts." Is that the best we've got for the front?'

Sarah fights her corner. 'The Cat Protection League genuinely say their furry friends are being stolen off the city's streets. A van is going round–'

'And The Flat Earth Society believe, well, the clue's in the name.' Jimmy isn't amused. 'Come on, we can do better than this. Look, for the last month we've been beating *The Echo* hands down. I've heard that all their 40 journalists were called to head office last week and given a bollocking because of us, because of you. That's brilliant work. Let's keep it up, chase up our contacts, see if we can land a real corker of a splash.'

The next night, still without 'a corker' in sight, Jude draws up outside a flat at the address Danielle has given him. She opens the door and Jude gasps. Danielle is wearing a mauve miniskirt and matching top, her long auburn hair, normally clipped up, brushes her shoulders and her eyes are covered by Ray Ban aviators. 'Wow, you, you look stunning.'

'Quelle surprise, Jude?' Danielle smiles broadly. 'I don't bother dressing up for work, it's too competitive in an all-female office, especially when the outside sales reps come in; they always have to look good. If I'm honest, I wasn't sure what to wear for a whisky barge, but I decided no high heels.' Danielle laughs easily and Jude thinks he's going to enjoy the evening more than he'd expected.

They drive in his little old Peugeot convertible and Jude has to speak loudly over the noisy engine. 'Danielle, I hope you don't mind, but before we go to the barge, I need to stop off. I've a story I need to cover, it won't take long. I heard a couple of guys at my boxing gym talking about it and, well, if I'm honest, we're desperate for a front page for tomorrow and this is my last hope.'

'Of course not, just as long as I get a byline.' Danielle smiles. 'OK, scoop. I'll keep the engine running for the speedy getaway.' She laughs openly and freely.

Jude parks the car outside *Queenie's Massage Palace.* 'That's probably a good idea, about the engine. Sit in the driver's seat, just in case. The clutch is really sharp. I'll be back as soon as poss.' Before Danielle could ask if he was joking, Jude was gone, the key still in the ignition and the engine running.

Some ten minutes later Jude is back, Danielle moves to the passenger seat of the Peugeot and they head off. 'Did you get your story?' she asks.

'I think so, I'm not entirely sure, but yeah, we should celebrate by drinking whisky that neither of us like.'

The barge is moored in a quiet part of the docks, rundown and desolate. But walking down the rickety gangplank onto the shiny wooden deck, they both feel they are stepping back in time. The early evening sunshine reflects off Southampton Water and inside the boat is all dark polished mahogany and gleaming brass, its air infused with whisky and bonhomie. Danielle's quick wit and confidence brings smile after smile to Jude's face and, in return, she seems to enjoy the reporter's company. They laugh often and enjoy a fun evening on board *Hydrogen,* sampling old whiskies. They're both given a bottle of Bell's finest

throat-burner to take home with them. Jude realises how sensible Danielle had been by insisting 'it wasn't a date or anything,'
at the outset. The lack of pressure meant it was easy for them
both to relax and enjoy each other's company, and dropping
Danielle back home was totally free of the big question: Should
he kiss her on the cheek or ask to be invited inside 'for coffee'.
A simple wave as she walks up her garden path is all that's required. On the drive back home to the pub he realises just how
long it's been since he's been on a date, how long since he enjoyed
the company of an attractive, sharp and fun woman. It would
have been before he started at journalism college in Darlington,
and that was almost 18 months ago. In truth, he thinks, he's not
had his old lust for life since his divorce. 'And now's the time
for change!' he says to himself loudly over the car's grumbling
engine.

As usual, Jude parks his car at the rear of The Proud Stag and
is surprised not to be greeted by Rin Tin Tin's welcoming bark.
Inside there are few customers and Gerry is solemnly pouring a
pint and doesn't hear Jude's 'How's it going?' In the pub's little
kitchen, a red-eyed Milly is finding things to do.

'Milly, what's up. The Stag's like a funeral parlour.' As Jude
speaks, he realises he should first have engaged his brain, and
blames the whiskys he'd drunk earlier.

'That's what it is, in a way, a funeral parlour. Rin Tin Tin is
dead. I was trying to get George asleep, pushing him in his pram
around the garden, when I found his body.' Milly wipes her eyes.
'He was only a baby himself, really.'

Gerry joins his wife and cousin in the kitchen, slumps down
onto a chair. 'Rin Tin Tin had foam around his mouth. I found a
half-eaten leg of lamb in the garden. The vet's pretty convinced
he was poisoned and is having some tests carried out to make
sure.'

'Bloody hell, what do the police say?'

Milly looks at the ceiling, then at her husband. 'He doesn't
want to tell them.'

Jude sits down and immediately stands up. 'Why? I mean,

we've got to.'

'Jude, just let me, us, sleep on it, OK?'

'But Gerry, you've got to, or pay them.'

'All you've done is make matters worse, Jude. So don't go fucking telling me what to do. Not if you want to stay under this roof.'

Gerry is out of order. But, Jude knows he's right. His front-page story has made the situation worse and he should be sorting it out. But how? He'd sleep on the question or, at least, try to. But, he decides, this time he won't mention this latest development to anyone at *The Reporter*.

Jude arrives early at the office the following morning and, for once, ignores the post in favour of typing furiously on his old machine. Sarah and then Jimmy arrive, equally gloomy over the lack of a strong splash for the paper.

'I'm expecting a rabbit out of the hat from one of you,' Jimmy says, more in hope than anticipation. Sarah shakes her head and looks down at her desk.

Jude dramatically turns the platen on the carriage of his ancient Imperial with one hand and pulls off the two pages and carbon sheet separating them, with the other – the promised computers have been 'delayed a month'. Taking the top sheet and adding it to two others, he stands, walks over to Jimmy's desks and presents them to his editor with a thespian bow. 'I reckon this should do the trick.'

Jimmy shows no emotion whilst reading the first page but then starts to nod, his eyes never leaving the typed pages. 'The writing's a bit over the top, all first person, and the story is downmarket for us, but it'll have to do.'

'Praise indeed,' Jude thinks.

Jimmy looked up from his reading. 'We'll need a quote from Queenie, Jude, you must have that for balance. And Robert, get a photo of the shop front, it'll need to be square – I'll leave a hole for it and insert it on the stone – Jude'll give you the address. I'm thinking "THE CITY'S MRS MASSAGE" for the headline. No, I've got it, "SEX FOR SALE IN SOTON."

The team crack on with their jobs – Queenie eventually answers her phone and, after Jude explains the story he's written and asks for a response, she tells him, 'Write what you fucking well want and I'll see you in court,' which, under Jimmy's guidance, becomes 'no comment.' The front page, the final part of the week's paper, is laid to rest, almost. Before the button is pressed for the massive metal print rollers to start turning, Alex, the company's MD, has to sign off the week's edition. This is really a formality: Jimmy faxes the front page over to Alex at head office and then, from the print room, phones him and reads over a list of the other stories in this week's paper. Alex looks for spelling mistakes and missing quote marks on the front page – sometimes Jimmy would leave out a hyphen for Alex to spot and allow the MD to believe he's contributed to that week's paper.

Sarah, Robert and Jude are playing a makeshift game of table tennis on the photographer's desk, with books standing on their ends in the middle forming a crude net. Spirits are high after again producing a great paper against all odds and the pressure is off, at least for a day or two. Jimmy enters the room briskly and Robert asks if he wants to join him against Sarah and Jude in the table tennis.

'Stop that bollocks. We need a new front page. Alex has gone ballistic – claims we're guilty of entrapment. Jude, we're taking another angle on the story and not naming anyone. The headline is "POLICE CITY CENTRE SEX CRACKDOWN" – I've already set it – so make the story fit. Speak to your new best mate, Del. Beg if you have to. We've got,' the editor looks at his watch, '*you've* got 15 minutes for finished copy on my desk, 270 words.' Jimmy sits down heavily at his desk, fumbles with his dark eyepatch. 'Robert, I don't give a fuck what or who, I just need a new, square photo of the police, that's all, in some form or other.'

Jude is stunned. He points his table tennis bat at the editor. 'Tell me this is a joke, Jimmy.'

The editor shakes his head and looks again at his watch.

'This is *bollocks*, Jimmy. That's a perfectly good story

and there was no entrapment. Halfway through the massage Queenie stopped and offered me extras. When I asked what they were, she put her hand under the towel and touched me, you know, on the penis. She said, "Well, for an extra three pounds we could make this little thing bigger." You know all this. In a shop in the middle of our city, where anyone could just walk in. How is that entrapment? The people of this city should know.'

'Have you finished, lad?'

Jude nods.

'Good. An expert in journalism after a month in the job.' Jimmy shakes his head and looks yet again at his watch. 'You've now got only 13 minutes. If you don't like it, well,' the editor nods towards the door 'Shut that behind you and don't come back. Or sit down and get me the story I've asked for.'

Like a petulant teenager, Jude sits down reluctantly and dials Del at Hampshire Police Headquarters in Winchester. Del's bright tones answer: 'Hi, I'm out of the office, enjoying a hard-earned and much-deserved rest. I know it'll be difficult, but you'll just have to try to keep the wheels of our great British media turning without my help until Friday. Byee!'

Jude realises he's buggered; no one else will give him the quotes he needs – no quotes, no story. His one contact is un-available and he doesn't know what to do. While he thinks, Jude continues to hold the phone to his ear. Then he speaks into its mouthpiece, whilst scribbling shorthand on his reporter's note-pad. 'Del, can we say there's going to be a crackdown on massage parlours? Great... thanks. And that's on the record. Really... ter-rific. Del, I owe you. Speak soon.' Jude replaces the receiver, folds clean sheets into his Imperial and starts typing, banging the old keys for all he's worth.

Jimmy stands over Jude, watching typewritten words form on the blank page. Jude is typing the third and final page of the story, finishes it and lifts it high above his head, where Jimmy's snatches it, puts it with the other two pages and heads out and down to the print room as fast as his dodgy leg will allow.

CHAPTER 8

IS THIS FOR ME?

In the office the next morning, both hands round a mug of Maxwell House, Jude despairs, trying to decide which half of his life is worse: his pub-home, where the death of Rin Tin Tin is being mourned and the likely threat of further action from the 'protection' gang hangs heavy, or the office, where they all know a good story was spiked because of the managing director's lack of balls. Jude has added to his list of woes by making up a quote from a serving police officer and now has to tell Del what he's done, before the policeman reads 'his quotes' himself in this week's paper. 'That must be a criminal offence, a month into the job and I could go to jail,' Jude thinks, 'what a great fucking journalist I am.'

'Jude, Coroner's Court, 9.30?' Jimmy's loud voice may have been phrased as a question, but it wasn't. 'There's an inquest into a teenager who's died of a drugs overdose.'

'Will do.' The trainee reporter realises he must have really pissed off his editor yesterday. Drug overdoses aren't big deals and *The Echo* will cover it, so there'll be nothing fresh for next week's edition of *The Reporter*.

Jimmy beckons Jude over to his desk. 'Look, I know a drugs overdose doesn't look promising. But we've had a few recently, maybe twice the normal number by my caculations. Try to speak to the investigating officer afterwards. And introduce yourself to the coroner, he won't want to talk, but you never know. I've just got a feeling there's something going on.'

Jude's mood lightens; perhaps there's a story after all. And it looks like Jimmy isn't bearing a grudge. Then his mood plummets – he remembers he has to phone Del and it's not a call he can make from the office. On the way to the Coroner's Court, Jude stops his car next to the first phone box he comes to. He expects, at best, a bollocking and to lose his best (and only) contact, at worse, to be charged.

Del is, as usual, as bright as a 100-watt bulb. 'Jude, or "Telepathic Trainee" as I've now christened you, who evens knows what I think, I wondered when you'd call. Not only have I seen your fine organ this morning, I've also heard you talking to yourself on the office answerphone tape.'

'Del, I can explain. Look, I'm sorry, it won't happen again, it was–'

'Jude, calm down, you'll do yourself a mischief. Now, breathe deep and relax. Yeah? Good. I was thinking of offering you a job here because, well, what you wrote was nothing that I wouldn't have said. I'm sure you knew that. Of course, we don't mind telling the bad guys we're going to crackdown on them – keeps them occupied and nervous.'

'Del, I was so worried.'

'Stand down Jude, and I'll give you my home number if case you're ever stuck again. But be careful in future, you got it right this time, but if you'd dropped me in it…'

'I get, Del, I get it.'

A relaxed and relieved Jude Devlin walks into the inquest and sits, in the press box, next to a reporter from *The Echo* he's met but whose name he can't remember.

'Right, Jude? Nothing much here for you, is there?'

'No, but nothing else is happening, so Jimmy sent me here. I think he wanted me out of the office.'

'I saw that splash of yours yesterday – a bit weak, compared to *The Reporter's* recent great run of stories.'

The conversation halts as they stand to acknowledge the

entrance of the Coroner, an obese and elderly solicitor who considers the feelings of the family of the deceased to take precedent over revealing any details of the cause of death or any other accepted procedures. At least, that's the view of all journalists who were unlucky enough to cover his inquests. Despite being a tragedy from which a family may never recover, for the two reporters present the inquest is a routine affair and, Jude realises, will not make a story for *The Reporter*. When the inquest is finished the Coroner, through his clerk, refuses to meet Jude. But the police sergeant has time for a coffee in the court canteen. He reckons the number of 'deaths by O.D,' as he labels them, has trebled over the last two years, but is reluctant to hazard a guess why. 'We leave that kind of thing, speculation, to you journalists,' he smiles.

Back in the office the trainee reporter is told the Managing Director, Alex Pointing, has arrived from head office and is waiting for Jude in the advertising's department's 'meeting room,' a classy, modern space where would-be clients are regularly schmoozed and kept well away from the riff-raff journalists. It's the first time Alex has seen Jude since he interviewed him for the job several months ago. Alex's red plastic-framed glasses are bigger than Jude remembers. The MD rages, phrases like 'entrapment, bankrupting the paper, if I hadn't been around, amateur production, must involve your editor, idiotic moral crusade' all swirl in the poisonous air. After 15 minutes, Alex's fury has all but blown itself out and Jude wonders how anyone can talk for so long without, apparently, stopping for even the shortest of breaths. 'Must be an incredible underwater swimmer,' Jude hears himself muttering.

'What? Jude, you do realise the severity of your situation. If you are sacked before completing your indentures, no other paper will take you on. But this is even worse. You are on a three-month probation period, so officially you haven't even started your indentures. You'd be lucky to get a job in Tesco... we don't even need to give you notice. But, luckily for you, here at *The Reporter* we pride ourselves on being caring employers. We're going to extend your probation period to six months, and then your indentures will start properly. My secretary will write to you confirming the details, Jude. You need to be very, very careful from now on. You may turn out to be a good reporter, but, if I'm honest, I have my doubts.'

There is no point arguing, Jude reasons. In any room Alex is in, there's only one voice he's interested in hearing. Alex waves his hand like a medieval monarch dismissing a courtier and Jude's drubbing is finished. Despite the heavy rain, the junior reporter leaves the office and walks to the corner shop, his jacket pulled up over his head. He doesn't need or want anything but it gives him the chance to get out of the building, clear his thoughts and replay Alex's monologue in his head.

'You look like you've lost a fiver and found 10 pence.' Jude looks up to see Danielle's pretty face, haloed by a chequered black and white umbrella, smiling at him.

'Sorry,' Jude says, 'I was miles away.'

'Well, wherever it was, it didn't look fun. Not like the other night; I had a great time. We should do it again, soon.'

'If I'm still around,' Jude thinks.

'Do you want to share my umbrella back to the office?' Danielle thoughtfully asks.

'No, you're alright, I need to get some things for the newsroom,' Jude lies, knowing he's missing an opportunity with Danielle, but needs time alone to think.

Danielle looks out and up from under her umbrella at the heavy rain. 'It's always the new recruits who get put upon: get given the worse jobs or blamed for things,' she smiles. 'See you later.'

Getting wetter by the minute, Jude watches Danielle walk away. 'That's it,' he thinks, 'I'm being made to carry the can, the new boy. Despite being a trainee, Jimmy is hanging me out to dry.' He looks at his now-soaking jacket. 'I could do with some drying.'

Only the editor is in the newsroom when a sodden Jude returns. 'Right, lad, get your coat, if it's worth putting on. I'm buying you a pint and then you can buy me one.' Surprised, and slightly reluctantly, Jude does as he is told and the pair settle down in the corner of *The Osborne*, order ham rolls and sup their beers.

'Jude, you think I've been harsh on you, letting you take the rap. That's not a question, it's a statement. But hear me out before making your mind up. We both know that your story was sound, it was Alex's lack of a backbone that stopped it being published. But he was never going to accept that explanation, was he?'

Jude finds himself nodding in agreement.

'I've got a mortgage and maintenance to pay the ex each month. Personnel have given me two warnings already, thanks to Alex, for stories I've allowed in the paper. A third and... Well, who's going to give a job to a one-eyed editor in his 50s who's been sacked from a bloody freesheet? Especially one who, as you know, likes a pint or three?'

Without irony, Jimmy takes a sip of his beer. 'Look, Jude, it's not fair, I know that, but it's the way it is. You're not a wet-behind-the-ears 20-something fresh out of university, you can understand.' He lowers his voice a little. 'I shouldn't have let your story in the paper. Alex doesn't think our readers should know that sex happens in Southampton. I'm sorry, but I can't lose this job, Jude, I really can't.'

And the reporter understands. That is the worst of it. He understands and pities his boss, he finds it hard to swallow his ham roll and even harder to meet Jimmy's eye.

'There is some, small good news,' Jimmy tries to sound upbeat. 'You can call back that Queenie. A woman in her position, she'll be a brilliant contact to have; think of what she must hear from the men on that massage table of hers.'

Jude looks quizzically at his editor but is relieved the topic of conversation has moved on, if only a little. 'Why will she talk to me, she'll hate me – she threatened to sue.'

'Not at all. Tell her that you listened to her point of view and decided not to run the story. Then arrange to meet her face to face over coffee or something. Look, I can teach a monkey, given enough time, how to write a story. But it's getting the story in the first place, that's everything. And there's only one way to get those exclusives, it's through contacts that you build up over the years, people who trust you. That's the difference between a good reporter and a great journalist, contacts. Never forget that, Jude.'

Back in the office, Jude takes his editor's advice, phones *Queenie's Massage Palace* and, hesitantly, suggests that it would be in his and Queenie's interests if they met for coffee. Jude is pleasantly surprised as he listens to Queenie's deep, sexually laden voice. 'OK, but it's lunch, and you're paying. The Polygon, 12.30 tomorrow.' She hangs up.

The afternoon drags: boring press releases and a phone call from one of half a dozen or so regular weirdos who phone *The Reporter* and always start the conversation with, 'I've got a great story for you.' Jude is learning that when he hears that phrase, well, the opposite is true.

Caller: 'I've got a great story for you.'

Jude: 'OK, what is it.'

Caller: Don't you want my name, first?'

'Jude: 'If you like.'

Caller: 'Matthew, Matthew Dawson. You can call me Matty, all my mates do.'

Jude: 'Matthew, er, Matty, what's the story?'

Caller: 'What's your name? How old are you?'

Jude: 'It's Jude, and I'm not sure it's relevant, but I'm 32.'

Caller: 'Jude, do you specialise in any area of journalism? I need to talk to someone who's experienced, who really knows their stuff.'

Jude: 'Matty, it's pretty hectic here. I need to know what the story is, please.'

Caller: 'OK, do you do shorthand? Trust me, you won't want to miss any of this.'

Jude: 'Yes, it's part of our training,' (attempting to ensure the irritation in his head isn't transferred to his voice), '100 words a minute, before you ask. And, yes, I have a new pen and fresh notebook right here in front of me.'

Caller: 'Right, here goes then... this incredible rain we've been having, worse on record, I know the reason why.'

Jude: 'OK...'

Caller: 'It's Chernobyl, isn't it? Exactly four months ago, to the day. All that radiation in Russia. That's how long it would take to affect our climate here in the UK. And the result? Biblical amounts of rain, biblical.'

Jude: 'That's fascinating, Matty. Can you tell me what proof you have? Is there some research you've had access to or qualifications you have to justify this, um, interesting claim?'

Caller: 'Typical, I give you a world scoop, a huge exclusive and all you can think about is qualifications or justifications. No wonder you're still working for a local, free newspaper at the age of 32.'

Jude: 'Thanks, Matty. If you get any proof, let me know, OK?

Caller: 'How long have you actually been a journalist.'

Jude: 'Goodbye, Matty.'

Caller: 'ARE you actually a journalist? What proof do *you* have?'

Jude returns the phone's handset to its cradle. Normally the call would have made him laugh, today he just sighs.

It's 5.30pm and Sarah has been listening to the whole conversation. 'Right, Jude, there's a new wine bar opening up in the centre of the city and I've got two press passes to the launch party that starts at 6pm with free champagne. I was going to take my long-suffering Dave, but you need cheering up. Let's finish what we're doing and head into town.'

The wine bar is all black, chrome and mirrors and is weird, like it was designed by someone who'd never been inside a wine bar. Instead of being warm, relaxed and inviting, it was cold, dark and clinical, like a hospital operating room with only its emergency lights glowing in the dark.

Sarah and Jude grab a glass of 'champagne' and find a quite table in the corner.

'So, how're you finding *The Reporter* after your first month. For someone who's already had a splash and a picture byline, you seem a bit, well, down in the mouth.' Sarah takes a sip from the flute she'd been given, and breathes in quickly. 'It's bloody Asti, the tight bastards. They're not going to get five stars from me, now.'

'I don't know. Alex ripped my head off today. He says he doesn't think I'm going to make it as a reporter.'

'What the fuck does he know? Biggest paper he ever worked on was the weekly Basingstoke Gazette. He realised his own shortcomings and jumped, before he was pushed, and landed in management. To hear him talk, you'd think he covered Vietnam, uncovered Watergate and yomped across the Falklands. He's never got further than Winchester.'

Despite his mood, Jude smiles. 'I didn't realise. He does think he's some sort of tycoon, Southampton's own Robert Maxwell.'

'Don't worry about him. Always remember, Jude,' Sarah raises her glass and Jude has to join her in the toast. 'To us journalists – it's us against management and the world!'

Jude drinks but then looks reflectively at the bubbles rising in his glass of Asti. 'I'll try. I just wonder, you know, if coming back to Southampton was a mistake. I know I want to be a journalist, that's what I really want to do. It's just coming back here. I thought, after 10 years away, enough water would have flowed under the Itchen Bridge – the bridge wasn't even finished when I left. I wanted a new start but, well, I'm not sure about Southampton or, after the last few days, *The Reporter*. Is this for me, really?'

Sarah ensures the Asti keeps flowing and, for reasons he can't quite explain, Jude tells her about his life, things he hasn't told anyone during the last decade. How he was once a successful sales rep in the electrical business but had to flee the city in disgrace. How he'd left his bride-to-be, the gorgeous Sue Wraith, on the day of their wedding, when she refused to disown her criminal family. The same family who'd tried to blackmail him into robbing from his employer. Since then, Jude's visits back to his home city have been numbered on the fingers of one hand.

Driving home, Jude feels a lightness he hasn't experienced in years. The sharing of the secrets from his past life is having a cathartic effect and he's sure they'll be safe with Sarah, who's been so helpful in his new job. And what had his mum always told him? 'A problem shared is a problem halved...'

CHAPTER 9

Your Royal Highness

The Polygon *is* the city's best hotel, famous for its age, expense, snootiness and discretion. Many years ago, Jude was told a story about the hotel's night manager being asked by a minor royal to find him 'a big woman' for the night. The manager had replied, 'The one favoured by your father, sir, or her daughter?'

The reporter arrives punctually at the hotel restaurant, *L'Ambiance*, but remembers he doesn't know Queenie's surname. The maître d', without asking who he is, shows him to a discreet table where Queenie, dressed immaculately in a green tartan business two-piece, is studying the menu keenly. 'Ah, Jude, didn't recognise you straight away with all your clothes on. Alain, did, of course and he's never met you before. How do maître d's do that?' she purrs.

'Queenie, thanks for agreeing to meet me. I'm sorry we got off on the wrong footing.'

'In a way I was disappointed the story didn't run; might have been good for business, some free advertising.' Queenie flashes a huge, warm smile.

'I'm hoping that I could be of help to you, Queenie, to make up for–'

The huge smile disappears. 'Cut the crap, Jude. The fact is you tried to turn me over. OK, it's your job, I get it. But you were out of order, pretending to be a punter. Me and my girls do nothing wrong, nothing illegal, and we've nothing to hide. So next time, knock on the front door and ask. Remember that and you and I will get on just fine.' Her blonde relaxed curls bounce with the emphasis she puts into her last sentence. It is difficult to put an age to Queenie, somewhere over 30, but Jude has no idea just how over. 'Now, let's order,' Queenie commands, the smile reappearing.

To his surprise, Jude has an entertaining and enlightening lunch. Queenie is excellent company: funny, frank and interested, asking 'what does *being* a reporter really involve?' and, unlike most people, takes a genuine interest in his answer. Jude explains that yesterday he'd covered an inquest into the death of a teenager who'd overdosed on heroin.

'There's too many of them kids dying that way. The government doesn't care – did you see their campaign last year? "Heroin screws you up." Come on, who's going to pay any attention to that?' She shakes her head and finishes her Martini and lemonade.

Jude explains he's keen to write a story on the dramatic increase in drug overdose deaths and that the police have confirmed that the number has trebled in two years. Queenie says that in her 'old line of work' a lot of the girls were 'users,' although she never went near the stuff, but she knows the street price has halved in recent months.

Queenie smiles. 'It's basic economics, simple Keynesian reality. Reduce the price, increase the committed-user base, then up the prices to their old levels. But, to do this, you need supply-side control, to have a near monopoly on the market.'

'Wow,' Jude is impressed. 'So, for the prices to go back up, there needs to be just one supplier.'

'That's about it, anyone with 80 per cent market share controls the market and, therefore, the price in the short and medium term, if all other factors remain the same.'

'Thanks for the economics lesson, Queenie. How do you know this stuff?'

'I'm not just a pretty face. Mostly the Open University. Anyway, economics is common sense to anyone who's ever had to live on a tight budget. Thank God we've got a woman as Prime Minister, she won't put up with 10 million unemployed for long. Maggie knows it's such a waste.'

'When I'm back in the office I'll run the monopoly drugs supply idea past the police press office. The chief inspector there used to run vice, Chief Inspector Michael Matthews, he might–'

Queenie drops the serviette she was dabbing her mouth with. 'Fucking Smarties?' Instantly she's back on the working-class streets of her youth, not the rarefied atmosphere of *L'Ambiance*. 'That shit! Don't go near that cheating, lying–' with effort she clamps her mouth shut to stop herself saying anything else, realising that other diners are turning to look. 'Jude, you don't know me, but trust me, the man is evil. We didn't even like saying his name, so we christened him Smarties, you know, Michael Matthews, M&M, the American Smarties.' Jude shakes his head, bewildered. 'It's OK, Jude, Matthews never realised Smarties referred to him either. It was our code. Look, let's just say, when he ran vice, he was ambitious but bent. And once a bent copper, always a bent copper.' Queenie looks at her watch. 'Maybe one day I'll tell you the whole story, but not today, I've an appointment.'

Jude raises his eyebrows.

'With the bank. I've enjoyed our little lunch, Jude, oh, and I've settled the bill ahead, I'm sure *The Reporter* doesn't give its junior reporters much of an expenses allowance.' Without being summoned, Alain appeared carrying Queenie's coat. She allows him to place it, film star-like, over her shoulders, smiles radiantly at Jude, glances at Alain, and is gone.

CHAPTER 10

Scouse About

The week is passing slowly for Jude; there have been no developments at the pub and, after almost losing his job, he's kept a low profile at *The Reporter*. He takes Queenie's advice, for the moment, and decides not to mention the increase in OD deaths to the police press office. But the idea for the story itches away at him. It's the following week's inquest that changes everything. Sarah should have covered it, normally they take it in turns, but she's writing a long feature about a single mum who turned her life around by setting up a successful modelling agency. The editor loves it because he can use lots of photos of scantily-clad models across the spread. 'What an industry,' Jude thinks as he drives to the inquest, 'shame Jimmy didn't give me that story, I could do with perking up my private life.'

The inquest is yet another OD, this time a lad from Liverpool, but otherwise sadly run-of-the-mill, following the recent pattern. Jude types the story up and passes the top copy to Jimmy – the Apple computers are still 'delayed' – and the editor tells him to phone the story through to *The Liverpool Echo*. 'It's lineage. If they use it, they pay us, not much, but it's saved for a decent night out for the four of us at Christmas. Sarah keeps the money; she calls it the EDIT (Editorial Dinning In Town) fund. So, speak to someone on the news desk first, *The Liverpool Echo* is a big operation.'

Jude does as he's instructed but *The Echo's* assistant news editor sounds underwhelmed. 'We've got enough of our own druggies ODing up here,' a strong Scouse accent informs him. 'What's the name, anyway?'

Jude checks his shorthand. 'It's an odd name for someone from Liverpool, sounds more French. It's Darius LePlante, with an 'e', he's 41.'

'Fuck me, yes, give us everything you've got, we'll pay. Any photos of the body? Were any of the family at the inquest? Did you speak to any of them?'

'Slow down, why the sudden interest,' Jude asks.

'Darius is, was, a real hardman, the sidekick and main muscle of Mackie Mitchell, who is the Mr Big of the drug scene in Liverpool and doesn't mind who knows it. Look, Liverpool is the centre, after London, of the country's illegal drugs, both hard and soft, and Mackie is at the centre of that. This is a huge story for us, even if LePlante died of old age, which he obviously didn't, we'd give it the spread and a single column on the front. What did the coroner record? Bollocks, there's a girl in advertising who's a distant relative of his and she's said nothin.'

Jude is furiously scribbling shorthand down on his notebook and doesn't stop whilst answering. 'Death by misadventure. There was no family, nothing, no representation for LePlante at the inquest. It was over in minutes. I've got the measurement of heroin in his blood. The coroner said it was enough to kill four people.'

'That's ridiculous, he knew what he was doing, he grew up dealing. And he's physically massive. The word was Darius never used. Mackie insisted on it. Hang on.' Down the telephone Jude hears the muffled cries of the assistant news editor shouting across his newsroom. The Scouse voice returns. 'Right, I'm putting you over to copy, give us everythin' you've got, what the weather is like, everythin', this will be the last edition's splash and spread and we'll follow it up tomorra.' Click.

Jude started to sweat; he'd never filed live copy over the phone before; he'd only even practised it once at college, phoning from the lecture theatre to the mocked-up 'newsroom,' and even then he'd cocked up, missing out three vital facts: the fictious murder victim was a 'Sir,' who lived in Kensington and was found with an orange in his mouth.

Another Scouse voice, this time female and no nonsense, comes down the line and galvanises Jude into action. 'Right, luv, off you go, they're keen on this, apparently.'

Jude stutters his way through the story, and knows he isn't doing much of a job of producing a Liverpool version of the inquest in his head and dictating it, all in one go. Finally, the copytaker says 'thanks, luv,' and the phoneline goes dead.

Jimmy laughs; he'd obviously listened to every word. 'It's stressful, filling copy live, isn't, lad? You're get the hang of it, in time. Don't worry too much, that's what sub-editors are for, turning your turgid mess into timeless prose for the proletariat. Did you give them your name and *The Reporter's* address so they know where to send the cheque?'

Jude shakes his head and redials *The Echo,* relaying the all-important details.

Jimmy limps over to Jude's desk and gives him back the inquest story. 'Right, I've been thinking. We've got our splash now: "Scouse Drugs War in City." Well, get working, you'll need to stand all this up. But one thing is for sure: this LePlante lad wasn't in our city to watch the Saints or go on a cruise on the QE2.'

Del, as usual, is helpful and stands up the story for Jude with the quote 'Hampshire Police is aware that a major drug dealer from Liverpool was interested in expanding his empire into our county. We are confident that proactive policing, the details of which obviously have to remain confidential, has made that person reconsider their plans. The gentleman's subsequent death is untimely and we extend our condolences to his family.'

Merseyside Police confirm that LePlante 'was a known associate of Mackie Mitchell'. Jude phones *The Liverpool Echo* again and gives them the quote from Hampshire Police. As a quid pro quo, he's connected to the regional paper's cuttings' room where, each day, every story in the paper is carefully cut and filed before being meticulously cross-referenced. It's an invaluable resource and a helpful member of staff reads out a few stories involving LePlante: the paper has named Mackie Mitchell as a drugs dealer, stating he'd received two jail sentences, one suspended, for supplying both cannabis and heroin. But, as he's managed to steer clear of the courts in recent years, the paper is careful to add the words 'believed to be' before 'the city's Mr Big in the drug underworld.'

By the close of play Jude has a great story. Jimmy is delighted and says he'll run it past Alex to ensure there are 'no problems' but is sure the managing director will approve. 'Remember, drug dealers don't sue newspapers, they get their own back in other ways.'

Jude feels only slightly unsettled at Jimmy's observation – Liverpool is a long way away – and is in a good mood as he rings the buzzer on Danielle's flat. She's agreed to go and watch the city's premiere of *Top Gun*. Being a trainee journalist on *The Reporter,* or any editorial job on the paper, was poorly paid but there were a few perks, and Jude presented the editorial team's 'Golden Ticket' to the Gaumont Cinema's usherette – it magically allowed free access for two people to any film at the city's Gaumont and Odeon cinemas (you had to pay to go into the Classic, the other city centre movie house, but it only showed soft porn, mostly with subtitles). In return Jude is expected to write a review for *The Reporter*, so he takes a few notes and wonders if it was such a good idea to bring Danielle to watch heart-throb Tom Cruise for one hour and 50 minutes on what he considers their first proper date. The pair enjoy the film, agreeing it's fun but corny; Danielle offers a quote for Jude's review. 'Tom saves the world and gets the beautiful Kelly McGillis. Of course, he does; I'd want my money back otherwise!' Instantly Jude realises he's just been given the intro, the first paragraph, to his film review.

They drive back to Danielle's flat, where the advertising girl takes charge. 'Jude, thanks, I enjoyed tonight. Again. Look, I've recently finished a bit of a disastrous relationship and, if it's OK with you, can we enjoy being friends at the moment? I think both of us could probably do with a few more friends right now? And neither of us need any work complications.' She leans over the gear lever, gives Jude the briefest of pecks on the cheek, and walks up the short drive to her flat. Driving back home to the pub, Jude thinks, 'Well, perhaps it wasn't a proper date, then?'

Next day, after opening the post, Jude checks the big, leather-bound red diary that, for no reason anyone remembers, lives on the corner of Richard's large desk. In Sarah's handwriting, Jude reads that, from 12.30 to 2pm, he, Sarah and Richard have an appointment, but there are no more details.. The phone rings and Jude is soon too busy to worry about it.

At 12.25 the insistent noise of a car horn sounding its displeasure lures the news team to the window. They look down to see Del, smiling broadly and sitting at the wheel of a very flash Jaguar XJ-SC petrol-blue convertible, waving up at them with one hand and pressing the other against the car's horn.

Sarah looks pleadingly at Jimmy, who nods his assent and the three run down stairs like naughty schoolchildren bunking off a lesson, laughing and shouting.

'Wow, Del, this is fabulous. No wonder the mystery appointment; you wanted to show this off.' Sarah is obviously impressed.

'Promotion, Del? This is brand new; it must have cost a packet,' Jude enthuses while Robert took a couple of photos – the photographer never goes anywhere without a camera of some sort – with Del posing proudly in the driver's seat.

'I've just collected it from the showroom so my favourite journalists will be the first to go for a spin. Shame it took someone's death to pay for it. Mum gave me the house, but as I've already got one of those, I sold it and bought one of these,' Del said, raising both hands and arms with the panache of the amateur thespian he was, to indicate the gleaming Jag. 'Hop in.'

'Er, it's only a two-seater, Del,' Jude laughs.

'That's why I love journalists, nothing ever gets pass them. Yes, it's only a two-seater but the top's down, so sit on the tonneau cover and hang on to the rail where the targa top normally sits, I won't go more than 60. Trust me, I'm a policeman!'

With Sarah in the passenger seat and Robert and Jude precariously perched on the lowered roof and hanging on for their lives, the four laugh and scream their way around the narrow country roads of the New Forest, narrowly missing cyclists, ponies and pigs as Del throws the car round twisting bends. Realising they weren't far from The Proud Stag, Jude shouts above the noise of the engine and on-rushing wind. 'Del, take the next left, I know the perfect pub! It doesn't do food but I'm sure Gerry or Milly, that's my cousin and his wife, will knock up a few cheese rolls, and the beer's great.'

As they pull up in the pub's car park the noisy bunch are greeted by the cloying smell of fresh burning. A blackened Gerry stands motionless and metres apart from Milly, who's holding a hosepipe. Neither acknowledge, or even seemingly notice, the car or its occupants' arrival as they stand in front of the smoking and charred remains of the pub's large outbuilding, its thatched roof now a memory. It had housed the pub toilets, skittle alley and storeroom, now all smoke-black and useless. Jude jumps out over the top of the car and runs to his cousin. 'Gerry, what's happened? It was fine when I left for work this morning.'

'Can't you guess?' Gerry pulls out a beer mat from his back pocket and passes it to Jude. 'It was pinned to our front door.' Jude has seen similar a thousand times – all the pub's beer mats are the same – a photo of The Proud Stag with the words 'Milly & Gerry guarantee you a warm welcome!' printed underneath. This one is different; it has a handwritten felt-tip message. 'YOU NEED PROTECTING.' Gerry takes the beer mat back and puts it in his pocket.

The others from the car join the cousins and Jude carries out stilted introductions. Gerry looks alive when he hears 'Sergeant Del Simpson' and starts a long story about how he was meaning to have the electrics checked in the outbuilding, worried that mice had been chewing through the cables. When Jude goes to interrupt, Gerry quickly shuts him down with, 'Look, you haven't come here for this, the beer is still working and we can find a sandwich or two. Come on, Jude and I will go ahead and pour the pints.' When the cousins are alone in the pub Gerry is straight to the point. 'Not one word about the protection gang to your mate Del, OK? I need time to figure this out.' Before Jude could reply, the group enter into the public bar, led by Milly, who has yet to say a word and seems in shock. The rest of the lunch is subdued with hesitant talk of insurance, builders and mice before Del asks Gerry why there wasn't a fire engine at the scene.

'There was no point calling the emergency services. The fire couldn't jump from the outhouse to anywhere. It was always going to burn itself out before a fire engine could arrive from Lyndhurst. No one was injured, there's no crime committed, so what's the point in dialling 999?' Jude thought the answer sounded a little pat, perhaps even rehearsed. Gerry really did want to keep this quiet.

Back at *The Reporter* there's a message waiting for Jude and, after work, although he's desperate to drive home to the pub to find out what's really happened, he heads for a house in Weston, a rundown council estate on the east side of the city. Daphne is Jude's other, much older cousin. The message was from her son, Craig, a smiling, gangly and likeable 18-year-old, who Jude last saw 10 years ago.

Weston has gone from bad to worse over those intervening 10 years: front gardens growing rotting sofas, racist graffiti sprayed on dilapidated fences and Union Jacks instead of curtains in bedroom windows. Jude thinks that Prime Minister Margaret Thatcher's 'right to buy,' hasn't yet penetrated Weston.

The front door still needs painting, the same as it did 10 years ago, although he notices a new piece of bare wood covers the doorframe where the lock latches. He is about to knock the door when it's pulled open. There stands Daphne, who is older, smaller and less of the beauty that Jude remembers. She still has those great cheekbones that Dad always favourably compared to Sophia Loren's. She doesn't say anything, just gives Jude the biggest hug he can remember. Inside this sad house is Craig, who is

JOHN BARRY SHIRLEY-WARREN

genuinely pleased to see his great-cousin.

After pleasantries – Daphne and her son are careful not to ask why they haven't seen Jude, remembering the circumstances that forced him to leave the city – Craig explains they'd heard a rumour he'd trained as a journalist and then, last week, saw his picture byline in *The Reporter*. 'It was Mum's idea I phone you, hope it's alright, Jude. We thought you might be able to help. It's got to be a story for your paper, even if it's only a freesheet.'

Jude looks at the ceiling; how often had he heard those words, 'only a freesheet' in the two months since he'd started working as a reporter. He let the remark pass. 'How can I help? Tell me everything, Craig.'

As Daphne makes her favourite cousin, a mug of tea, Craig reveals the full story. How, with no qualifications and 10 million unemployed, he deals a little cannabis 'to make ends meet'. Jude nods but doesn't take notes. 'As you can see, I still live at home with Mum, I don't need much.' He's kept off the radar of the local drug dealers, but in the last month a new group has moved in. Apparently, the leaders of the old crew were arrested in a big drugs raid. 'You wrote the story, didn't you, Jude, for *The Reporter*?' Jude nods. 'Well, since then, anyone dealing even a quarter ounce has been warned off. Including me. But I need the money.'

'So, you carried on dealing?' Jude asks.

'It's not dealing like you think, just tiny amounts to mates, lads from the football team, that kind of thing. Sometimes less, a joint or two I roll for them. It's peanuts.'

Daphne is standing by the sink; she's hardly spoken since the big hug she'd greeted Jude with. But she can no longer hold back. 'That's when they fitted him up!' she blurts out. Both Jude and Craig turn to look at her; she's given up all pretence of doing the washing up.

Craig nods. 'It's true. The police came round yesterday, 6am. Battered the door in, dragged me and my girlfriend Julie out of bed. Julie was naked, the coppers loved that. We come downstairs so they can search the place; they've got a warrant and everything. Then one copper comes downstairs holding a big plastic bag of weed. Says "Sarg, must be a kilo in here." And I'm handcuffed and taken to the station.'

'Craig, are you saying the cannabis... it wasn't yours.'

'I wish, a kilo? Do you know how much that is worth? I could never afford to buy that.'

'Could it have been put there? I don't know, by Julie, storing it for someone else?'

'Jude, wise up. No one would trust us with that! Neither of us would touch it, anyway. That amount is a definite custodial. It's a police stitch-up.'

'Sorry, Craig, am I being thick? If you're only dealing tiny amounts, why would the police go to all the trouble of planting drugs on you? If you're such small fry, it's not worth their risk, is it?'

'Jude, look, you've been away too long. Just think, if you're the new team supplying the drugs on the Weston estate and you warn everyone off and want to get rid of someone who is supplying even just a little, what would you do?'

'Normally you'd scare them off: sort them out down a dark alley or after they come out of a club pissed up.'

'Yeah, except in Weston people don't scare easy and have big families or mates who are going to want to get even. But if you can get the police to do your dirty work...'

'Hang on, Craig, you're saying the drug dealers can get the police to raid anyone dealing on their patch? That's a bit, well, far-fetched, isn't it?'

'Jude, look, I'm fucked, but I'm not alone. I know of three people in the last few weeks, in Weston alone. All been done for big quantities of cannabis, one even heroin, although he's never, ever dealt it. Check the records. The word is, it's happening all over the city. The way it's going people will be scared to let their mates have a drag of their joint.'

Daphne spoke again. 'OK, Jude, I know my Craig isn't an angel. I don't know anyone on this estate who is. But this isn't right; he's likely to get two years for this. You're our only hope.

Just, you know, see what you can find out, will you?'

Jude nods, gives his cousin a kiss on the cheek and promises to be in touch.

CHAPTER 11

Count the Buttons

Back home at the pub Milly is changed from her catatonic state at lunchtime and now can't stop talking. She tells Jude that she and Gerry had started to turn part of the outbuilding into a nursery. 'It gets the sun in the afternoon, and I was going to put little George in there after lunch for the first time today, for his nap. Just think, if they'd set fire to it then, rather than this morning… we've lost a building but those bastards could have killed our little boy.' No wonder she was in shock.

After closing time Gerry, Milly and Jude chat over a nightcap. Gerry is concerned that the police will get involved. 'Jude, did your sergeant mate, Del is it? Did he believe my story about the mice?'

'I doubt it, Del comes across as a bit, well, superficial, but he's very bright and been in the force for years. He never mentioned the fire after we'd left.'

Milly downs her Drambuie and slams the empty shot glass down on the bar. 'Is that all you're worried about, Gerry? Do the bloody police know? We could have lost our son! We should call the police; I'm a barrister for God's sake. My life is the law, but no, we can't call them in to help us.'

'Milly, you know why. How can the police help us stuck in the middle of nowhere like we are? We speak to the police and the whole pub will go up in flames. Let me talk to the gang, negotiate a sensible amount to pay them.'

'Number one, how will they know we've told the police, and, number two, you can't negotiate with a gang.' Milly jumps off her barstool, grabs the bottle of Drambuie from behind the bar and pours its golden liquid into her glass, only stopping when it threatens to overflow.

'Look, it's not my decision.' After downing his shot, Jude tries to defuse the situation. 'But it appears that organised crime has high-level contacts in the police in our area. You remember Craig, Daphne's boy, lives out on the Weston Estate? I spoke to him today and he's convinced he's been fitted up, that the police planted a kilo of cannabis in his room to get him off the streets and leave the pitch clear for a major gang.'

Milly's laugh is hollow. 'Sounds like he's been smoking too much of his own weed. This isn't The Bronx or prohibition Chicago, it's little old Southampton, for God's sake.'

Gerry tops up his glass and then Jude's. 'We've got to do something; these bastards aren't going away. They're going to be in contact very soon, I'm sure of that.'

'As I said, it's your decision, but I can make some discreet enquiries, just to see how big a problem this is and how many other pubs are being shaken down like you guys.' Jude finishes his drink and eases himself from the barstool.

Both Gerry and Milly nod in agreement. 'It can't do any harm,' Milly says, 'and if there's a lot of us, well, perhaps we could stand together against the gang. But we have to do something… and soon.'

'Just make bloody sure the enquiries are discreet, Jude,' Gerry says, looking intently at his cousin. Jude nods and turns towards the stairs and his bed.

The following Friday evening, Jude has the ideal opportunity to make those 'discreet enquiries.' It's one of the senior sales reps' birthdays and the newsroom have been invited to join the advertising staff on a pub crawl. Sarah has invited Del to join them. 'He's great company, the advertising lot won't mind,' she reasons.

The whole evening is a casual, almost ramshackle affair, the size of the group swelling and subsiding as friends and acquaintances, customers and suppliers, join straight from work or leave to go home. But the women from advertising know how to party and are not shy of spending their sales' bonuses on having a good time. Most of the evening, Danielle and Jude are side by side; they get on easily together and she makes the reporter laugh with her insights into the rest of the sales team. 'The reps all have similar personalities, although they all seem quite different. Normally, at the end of the day, they come into the office to sort out any queries or boast about the orders they've landed. I think they miss not having any proper workmates to chat to when they're on the road. Anyway, you know Rachael, she's the top sales rep – she calls herself "The Waiter," because "I always take the order."

'When she comes into the office I can always tell if the last customer Rachael's visited was a man or woman; I count the buttons that are undone on her blouse. If it's a man, it'll be more, to show off extra cleavage.'

Jude almost sprays his beer across the room, laughing hard. 'I'll never be able to look Rachael in the face again, at least not until I've counted the buttons.'

Del, who looks even more elegant than usual, in his white polo neck, pale blue jacket and navy pocket handkerchief, wanders over holding a tall glass sprouting a small tropical forest, and interrupts. 'So, Southampton's brightest reporter is being entertained by the beauty of sales, is he? A dangerous combination: investigation and Mammon, you'll be uncovering untold wealth together in the future. Well, Jude, aren't you going to introduce me?' And without giving Jude the opportunity to carry out his implied request, Del raises his right hand towards Danielle, 'Enchanté, mademoiselle.'

Instead of shaking his hand, Danielle raises it to her lips and kisses the back of it, in the French manner. 'C'est un honneur de vous rencontrer, Del, j'ai tellement entendu parler de vous.'

Del looks stunned and Jude roars with laughter. 'I think the only other French word Del knows is "gateau."' The three laugh; Jude knows it would take much more to embarrass Del.

A little later, when Danielle 'pops to the loo' Jude is alone with Del. 'Have you heard of many pubs or restaurants being asked to pay protection money?'

'You mean your cousin. It didn't seem like the handiwork of mice at the pub, not unless those mice used petrol – I could smell it over the smoke. I did wonder if you'd ever get round to talking about that. After our lunch the other day I phoned vice and they assured me that it's been really quiet on that front. They'd be the first to hear about it. I didn't mention your cousin's pub.'

'Thanks Del, really appreciate you not mentioning *The Running Stag*. I've encouraged Gerry to tell the police but he's scared he's going to make things worse.'

'I'm not sure he can. Once a gang starts to bleed you, they'll just keep making it worse, demanding more, until they bleed you to death.'

'I'll pass on the advice. There's something else; I've another cousin and her son, Craig, Craig Cavanni, lives in Weston and reckons he's been fitted up with a kilo of cannabis. He says he might sell the odd joint to his mates, but he's never seen so much gear in his life and could never have afforded to buy even a fraction of that amount.'

Del pulls out a small police notebook from his jacket pocket and makes a note. 'Cavanni, strange name on the Weston Estate, Jude?'

'Isn't it? Our Daphne married an Italian ice cream seller. When she got pregnant, he fucked off back to Italy and she never heard from him again. You can't believe the stick she got on the estate over the years: "ice cream sellers don't normally leave a bun in the oven", "should have stuck to 99s, not 69s."'

Del is putting his notebook away as Danielle returns and says she doesn't understand what's just happened to her. 'In the toilets, I've just been asked if I want to score. When I said I didn't play football, the girl looked up to the ceiling, shook her head and marched out of the loo.'

Del and Jude are convulsed with laughter. 'Do you want me to go and arrest her?' Del manages to squeeze out the words and uses the silk pocket hanky to dab his eyes.

The pair explain to Danielle that she'd been offered drugs and she joins in the laughter, which, eventually, subsides to giggles. They all sup their drinks, Del through a straw, before Jude admits that he was approached earlier in the pub. 'That's twice tonight I've been offered dope, and not very secretively, if you know what I mean. Del, you need to have a word with your mates in vice and get them to pull their fingers out.'

CHAPTER 12

End of the Palace

The atmosphere in *The Proud Stag* is so tense that Jude starts to wonder if, maybe, the time has come to start looking for a flat of his own. But he realises he can't leave Milly and Gerry – who've both made him so welcome – until the trouble with the protection gang has been sorted, one way or another. Anyway, he realises that the most he'll be able to afford on his wages is a bedsit. When he isn't working, the weekends drag and, to escape the tension of the pub and his boredom, Jude is a regular visitor to the boxing gym. This Sunday's post workout shower is a relaxed affair; the boxers all enjoy showing off their physiques under the powerful water jets and chat uninhibitedly; today the conversation is about earning some extra, easy money working as a bouncer.

Jude has sparred with one of the lads, Ronnie – it was more like being a punch bag for the well-built middleweight – and the reporter, given his stricken financial position, asks what would be involved.

'Hey, lads, Jude wants to become a bouncer. What do you think?' Ronnie shouts over the noise of the spray. From out of the steam comes laughter and shouts of 'he's too pretty' and 'maybe in six months, if he comes here every day and works the weights.'

Ronnie smiles and lowers his voice so only Jude can hear.

'There's only one business that supplies bouncers, door minders, as they call them, to the discos and clubs in Southampton. They're a tasty family who own it, so they don't have any competition. They're taking on a lot of new premises, pubs and wine bars, and are looking for more bouncers. There was a flyer on the notice board until Phil saw it and took it down. Said that family weren't welcome anywhere near his gym.'

'What's the pay like, Ronnie?'

The middleweight pours shampoo into his hand and rubs it into his scalp. 'I don't think it's for you, Jude, although the pay is pretty good. And, for the new places, it's even better, because you may never visit the premises, you're "on call". So, you can be the bouncer for like, or four or five different pubs and never once have a drunk take a swing at you. Result in my book.' He puts his head under the shower to rinse out the shampoo.

'Sounds good to me, and I do need the cash. So, Ronnie, why don't you think it's for me?'

'It's not for you, Jude, because the first rule of being a bouncer is that you look fierce, big. That way, nine times out of 10, you stop any trouble by just looking scary. The other time, the troublemaker is likely to be so pissed they don't realise how much bigger and stronger you are. So, if it does kick off, well, a sober boxer will always beat a pissed-up idiot, regardless of size.' Jude wonders if he should be upset or pleased that he hasn't got what it takes to be a 'scary' bouncer.

Over what's left of the weekend, Jude mulls over what Ronnie has said. If he and the rest of the boxers are right, well, it throws into question what vice have told Del about there being no recent growth in protection rackets in the city. The only other explanation is that all the landlords have decided they want to pay for bouncers who never visit their pubs! He resolves to call the local Licensed Victuallers Association, the LVA, a trade association that represent landlords and who normally know what's going down at the grassroots.

In the office, Jude doesn't get the chance to make the call; as he enters *The Reporter* office his phone is already ringing. He picks it up but doesn't get a chance to speak.

'Where have you been, I've been calling for an hour, Jude. It's Queenie – get you and your photographer's asses down to my place, right now!' The phone line goes dead. Jude looks out the window and sees Robert taking his camera bag out the boot of his car. The reporter opens the window and shouts, 'Leave that in the boot, we've got a job,' closes the window, grabs his notepad and runs downstairs.

A few minutes later they pull up outside of, what was, *Queenie's Massage Palace.* Now it's a charred frame, with half the roof and one wall already collapsed and the rest looking unsteady. Beside the all-pervading stench of burning, there's the unmistakable smell of petrol. A few firemen are still, half-heartedly, damping down the blackened embers from a safe distance, their yellow helmets contrasting with the pitch-dark devastation.

Robert bumps the car onto the pavement, grabs his camera and immediately starts snapping. Jude sees Queenie talking to a police constable and heads towards them. 'Sorry to see this, Queenie. Don't let me interrupt.'

She turns slightly away from the uniformed policeman and talks uninhibitedly. 'You're not interrupting, *he* won't do any bloody good, that's for sure.'

The policeman 'tuts' loudly but doesn't move and pretends to write in his notebook, ham-fistedly trying to overhear Queenie and Jude's conversation. Jude realises it's obvious to even this constable that he's a journalist. Jude and Queenie walks far enough away for privacy.

'There's only two people, well three, who are going to help me, Jude: you, your photographer and the insurance assessor. Right, get your notebook out, let's see how good your shorthand is. Ready?'

Jude nods and Queenie launches into her story. 'I was approached by two men who came into *Queenie's Massage Palace* last week and demanded protection money, £100 every week. I told them "to sling their hook," maybe my words weren't as polite as that. I've been running the *Palace* for almost 10 years and never paid a penny in protection money, not to anyone, and I'm not about to start now. Then I get a call at home at five o'clock this morning, telling me I didn't need to pay for protection anymore as there was nothing left to protect. I knew what those bastards meant, so I called 999 straight away. Then I jumped into my Mini and came here; the place was blazing, flames leaping into the air, the heat was unbelievable. The fire brigade arrived but it was as much as they could do to stop the fire spreading to the shop next door.'

Jude scribbles furiously into his note book, stops and looks up. 'Queenie, what makes you so sure the blaze was a result of your refusal to pay protection money?'

'If not, it's one hell of a coincidence. Oh, and that smell of petrol isn't coming all the way from Fawley Refinery across the Solent, now, is it?' Robert is surreptitiously trying to get a photo of Queenie with the burnt building in the background and fails. 'Jude, what's your photographer's name?'

'Robert, why?'

Queenie shouts towards the photographer. 'Robert, stopping pissing about. You want my photo, no problem; I've got my lipstick on. Go over the other side of the road, then you can get the whole building in as well. I'll stand halfway between you and the building. Jude, you need to move out of the shot.'

An embarrassed Robert clicks away until Queenie brings the proceedings to a halt. 'Right, that should do you. I've got to go, that's the insurance assessor arriving, I'm pretty sure. I put a fire under his boss before I spoke to you, Jude. Give me your notepad and pen.' She writes down a Southampton phone number. 'That's my home, call me tonight and I'll give you the full background, not for reporting. Everything else I've said is on the record, OK?'

'Queenie, are you sure? What you told me, it's not going to get you into any further trouble with this gang, is it?'

'Jude, trust me, before you arrived, I had time to consider every word. I know what I'm doing.'

'I'm really sorry about this, Queenie, it must be a nightmare. How are you going to cope?'

'Jude, that's sweet, but I'll be OK. The insurance agent is an old customer, so I won't have any problems there.'

'And you'll open up somewhere else, as soon as you can?'

'No, you can report that this is the end of *Queenie's Massage Palace.*'

Back in the office Robert develop and prints the photos but before Jude starts writing the story, he remembers to phone the local LVA. Half an hour later he's called back by its chairman, who said he'd only talk 'off the record' as things were 'pretty hairy' at the moment. Jude agrees and the chairman, the land-lord of 'The Saints,' a huge boozer on the Millbrook council estate, told him that while city centre pubs regularly employed doormen – he didn't like the phrase 'bouncers' – his members further from the city centre had recently started being offered their services.

'The approach isn't subtle. "Use our doormen and that'll stop any trouble happening, even those fires you keep hearing about." That kind of thing.'

'Have you been offered protection or doormen at The Saints?' Jude asked.

'Not yet, but everyone knows everyone in my pub; it's the heart of the community and the regulars are tough: dock work-ers and shipbuilders. They wouldn't take kindly to anyone mak-ing me putting up the price of a pint to pay for protection. Any-one coming in and demanding money at The Saints would face a proper scrap.'

Jimmy loves the story, says that, as the massage parlour is now shut, Alex, the MD, will be happy for the report to appear in the paper. 'I'll give it, young Jude, the whole of page five, under the headline "MASSAGE PARLOUR PETROL BOMBED," and a strapline "protection racket closes den for good." Clever play on words, hey? For Good? Anyway, when can I have the copy?'

Jude has only told his editor about the story and is still to type a word. 'Jimmy, let me speak to Queenie tonight, she might have something important to add. I'll come in early tomorrow morning and it'll all be written and finished by the time you get to your desk.'

Reluctantly, Jimmy agrees. 'I'll break the habit of a lifetime and lay out the front page now, instead of first thing tomorrow, and get that down to the typesetters. Give me 370 words exactly and I'll leave the space to fit.'

Later that day Del phones from the Hampshire Police press office and tells Jude that he's spoken to the arresting officer in vice about his relative, Craig Cavanni. 'Bad news, Jude, as I suspected. Your Craig is banged to rights. Two officers found the stash under his bed; he'd hardly bothered to hide it. Apparently, they'd had him under surveillance for weeks. He's in it up to his eyebrows.'

'But Del, he's adamant that he's innocent. He says he deals a little to mates in his football team, that's about it, just to supplement his dole money.'

'Jude, get real. I've been in this job a bloody long time, perhaps too long. Do you know how many drug dealers I've met who confessed, even the ones who were caught red-handed? I'll tell you; I could count them on the fingers of my left foot. Sorry, speak soon... Oh, and be gentle with that lovely Danielle from advertising, she's much too stylish for you! Byee.'

Jude grins and puts down the receiver. 'Even when he gives you bad news, Del still has a way of making you smile,' he thinks.

That evening, Jude phones Queenie and she confirms what had been forming as a theory in the journalist's head. The gang expanding the protection racket is the same family behind the drugs: The Quirks. During the call Jude realises that Queenie would make a world-class journalist: she's tough, intelligent, knows how to listen and when to ask the pertinent question. And running a massage parlour puts her in a unique position to know what is happening in Southampton's dodgy underworld. If the punters don't talk to her, they talk to one of her girls, trying to impress them, and the girls tell Queenie everything they hear.

'Jude that big drugs bust you covered, when all the gangs except the Quirks were arrested? Well, it's worked in the family's favour. They've taken over the territories of the other firms. Only the head honchos and their minders were arrested and the Quirks have employed a lot of the members of the other gangs; most were running around like headless chickens since their bosses and the real muscle went inside, and were desperate for cash. Anyone with any ambition has been given the chance to prove themselves. And anyone who has stood up to The Quirks has been quietly "sorted." That's the word.'

'Bloody hell, Queenie, that's amazing.'

'It gets better. The Quirks are ambitious, they're not content with just the drugs. It was the Quirks who torched my place and are behind all the protection stuff. I knew one of the lads they sent round to threaten me. I didn't let on; it wouldn't have been good for my health. But I knew him when he was just a teenager, and I was a working girl. He's one of the Quirks' right-hand men now, a big mate with the youngest son, Darren, always has been.'

'This is great, Queenie, are you sure it's all kosher?'

'100 per cent. This needs to get out there, Jude, but it can't come back to me, OK? We'd both be in the shit, big-time, if it does.'

'I get it, Queenie, it won't. Earlier today you said you weren't going to reopen. What will you do?'

'I'll be fine. I've done alright over the years, invested a bit and then there's the insurance money. I'm going to work from home, just me; my place is discreet, no close neighbours. When I'm ready I'll open up my Filofax and call my regulars, they'll be back quick enough. It's my girls who'll need to find somewhere new to work. I can help them out for a bit, but don't be surprised if the Quirks move into my line of business. Just make sure, in that article of yours, you say I'm shutting down for good. That'll keep the Quirks out of my hair, at least for a while.'

CHAPTER 13

Hold the Front Page

As promised, Jude has finished writing the article and it's waiting on Jimmy's desk, ready for when the editor arrives at 9am. Jimmy immediately realises it's twice as long as the 370 words specified but, instead of moaning, decides to read the whole story.

'Bloody hell! This is dynamite, Jude. How sure are you?'

'It's all from Queenie and her girls, everyone is talking about the Quirks; they've taken over the city in one fell swoop. I've not named them, of course.'

'No, I see that, and I'm going to take out the word "family" and replace it with "gang," otherwise we'll be pointing the finger at them without enough proof. But otherwise, the story is good to go.' The editor shakes his head. 'You do cause me problems, young Jude.'

'What do you mean, Jimmy. It's a cracking story.'

'It is that. So, I'm going to hold the *Dog Muck in City's Parks Furore* front page story; we can use it next week and run this on the front and carry it on into page five. That'll cost us money to replate the print rollers and piss off the printers and their union.'

Robert stops polishing a camera lens. 'Is that wise, Jimmy? I've got a mate whose dad is a photographer on *The Times*. Since Rupert Murdoch told the print unions where to go and moved the paper out to Wapping, his life has been a nightmare.'

Jimmy ignores Robert question, lost in his own plans. 'It'll mean we're late off the presses and upset the delivery drivers – their union will probably demand a bonus. The youngsters who drop *The Reporter* through the city's letterboxes will have to wait a while. But the headline "CITY'S DRUG GANG MOVE INTO PRO-TECTION RACKET" with a 72-point red *Reporter Exclusive* will be worth the ear-bashing I'll get from Alex; this is a real fucking story. Right, man the phones so I don't get disturbed for the next two hours.'

Jimmy buzzes down to the head printer, tells him to hold the presses and slams the phone back on its cradle before the department head could moan, disagree or plain refuse – there weren't many editors brave enough, or stupid enough, to put the phone down on a card-carrying member of the National Graph-ical Association.

Re-design finished, Jimmy gathers up assorted bits of paper from his desk, limps towards the door, shouts, 'Wish me luck with the printers!' over his shoulder, and heads down into the building's bowels to the print room.

Three hours later, Jimmy reappears in the newsroom, laden with a case of Grolsch – a trendy new lager in a fancy bottle with a whacky top – four portions of fish and chips, the printer's proof of the front page and a broad smile. 'Don't get carried away, but well done everyone, great stuff. We're giving the Echo a run for its money!'

Sarah jumps up to relieve her editor of the Grolsch, pops their tops and quickly hands a bottle to everyone. 'I thought the next time I'd see you would be during visiting hours at The Gen-eral Hospital. How did you manage to convince the printers to co-operate?'

'Funnily enough, Sarah, it was easier than I thought. I'm ar-guing with the printers when Old Jones is sweeping up with that old broom of his. He interrupts and says his granddaughter's best friend was raped by the youngest of the Quirks. The police questioned her but as soon as they found out who was respon-sible, they suddenly reckoned there wasn't enough evidence to get the lad convicted. Well, when the print boys heard that, not only did they start to co-operate, they offered to work through their lunch break. If Tony Dubbins at Union headquarters finds out, they'll be expelled from the NGA faster than you can say "picket line."'

The four journalists tuck into the lagers and fish and chips as Jimmy wipes his hands and then holds up the front page of the paper. The big headline and photo of Queenie's burnt-out *Palace* make a strong and impressive splash, but Jude feels disappointment that he hasn't been given the ultimate journalistic accolade: a photo byline. The editor reads the journalist's thoughts. 'I was going to put your headshot on the front, Jude, but I've done you a favour by not doing so; you don't want to be recognised by too many people right now. There may well be repercussions from this story, so you'd do well to keep your head down for a bit.'

'And we don't want to scare the readers,' Sarah laughs, and all four colleagues toast 'Jude's great exclusive,' drinking from bottles of Dutch lager, allowing the swing-top porcelain lids to bounce off their noses.

That night, over dinner, whilst Milly serves in the bar, Jude proudly tells Gerry about his front-page exclusive. Gerry doesn't share his cousin's delight.

'Jude, do you take lessons in being stupid and ungrateful, or is it hereditary? How can you live here, with us, and continue to write stories that will only inflame the people trying to scare us? Aren't you happy enough that they've killed our dog and burnt our building down? Do they need to abduct George before you accept your actions have consequences? Fuck you, Jude.'

'Gerry, calm down. No one knows I live here with you guys. They're never going to find that out.'

'Your police chum, Del, knows; your reporter colleague, Sarah, is it? She knows. And the whole of your bloody office might know. But that's OK, you carry on, putting us at risk, just as long as you get your fucking story. You know I was trying to keep this all quiet.' Gerry gets up and grabs the doorhandle to the bar.

'Gerry, calm down. You and the pub aren't mentioned in this story.'

Gerry turns abruptly around. 'So, the gang still haven't got the copy of *The Reporter* with the photo of *The Proud Stag* on the front, saying we'd be threatened? You know, the story with your name on the front page.'

Jude's elation starts to abate. 'Yeah, I suppose they may have a copy.'

'And did you mention in this new article of yours that a pub in the New Forest has been a victim of attacks after refusing to pay protection money?'

'Only at the very end of the piece. How did you know that?"

'Because, Jude, I knew you wouldn't be able to fucking resist it!'

'Gerry, hang on. Don't dash off, let's talk.'

'I don't have time to talk to you, Jude. I've got to go and make a phone call, and tell a criminal gang that I'm going to pay them protection money. Hopefully I'll get them before they read your paper.'

'You shouldn't pay them, Gerry, you should go to the police.'

'This story of yours has just taken that option off the table. I can't risk them working out that my cousin, who's living under my roof, is stirring the shit and making their lives a misery while I'm holding out paying them money.'

Gerry slams the door behind him. Luckily it doesn't wake George, soundly asleep upstairs. After 10 minutes Milly comes into the dining room/kitchen and takes her dinner out of the oven, where it's been keeping warm. As she eats, Jude asks her if Gerry is OK.

'He's pretty pissed off with you. He says you've been reckless with our family's safety. Sounds dramatic. Is he right, Jude? Have you been?'

'No, at least I don't think so... didn't think so. Now, I'm not so sure. I haven't named you or the pub or anything. Perhaps me just living here is a threat to your safety. My editor said this story might "have repercussions".' Jude put his head in his hands.

Milly gives Jude a smile. 'Well, my old mum used to say, "Don't cry over spilt milk," so buck up. It sounds to me that if you keep putting pressure on this gang the police will have to step up their efforts to catch them.'

Jude thinks the time has now come to move and take any heat off the only remnants of his family that he really cares for. 'I'll start looking for somewhere to live. It's the least I can do.' He forces a smile.

'Don't be in a rush; Gerry likes having you back around. And so do George and me. He'll calm down soon enough. And don't forget you're covering for us in the bar next Tuesday night – Gerry's taking me out for the first time in ages. So don't be in too much of a hurry, especially on your terrible wages.'

CHAPTER 14

Show at the Boat Show

At work, Jude can't settle. He moved from making coffees, to reading the papers, to phoning Del to making more coffees. Sarah can't concentrate with the skinny six-footer's non-stop movement. 'For God's sake, Jude, try and sit down for five minutes. You're suffering from SAD: Story-After Disorder. You've found a great story, written it and, guess what, the next day, nothing has changed. It's the low after the high.'

'Really, I've never heard of it before,' Jude admits, sitting down and feeling slightly embarrassed.

'Neither have I,' Jimmy joins in the conversation, 'and I've been in this business for, well, too many years. Everyone feels a little down when they've achieved something special. You think it's going to change the world but the following day, well, the sun still rises and still sets.'

'You've never heard of it because I'm the first person to give this condition a name. Perhaps it should be named after me: SSAD, spelt with two Ss, Sarah's Story-After Disorder.'

'How would you know, you need a great front-page story first,' Robert laughs and ducks when Sarah throws a ball of elastic bands, probably playfully, at him.

Old Jones joins the happy band and, for once, instead of his broom, he's carrying a small pink parcel, wrapped with a gold ribbon, and hands it to Jude. 'This has just been dropped off at reception by a bloke on a motorbike. I think it was a bloke, you couldn't really tell, he didn't take his crash helmet off,' the old retainer wheezes.

The parcel is marked private and personal so, of course, the whole office surround Jude's desk to watch him unwrap it. 'Soiled underwear from an admirer of your journalistic talent,' Robert offers. 'Inflatable doll,' is Sarah's suggestion. The banter makes Jude feel he's a part of the editorial team: a journalist accepted as an equal; 'one of the lads.'

Jimmy is first to recognise the distinctive smell, even before the unwrapping is finished. 'Get that out of the office, now!'

Jude's curiosity makes him pull away the last piece of plastic wrapping paper and lifts the lid of a cardboard box. Inside is a huge, dark-brown and very fresh human turd. Its smell immediately engulfs the office.

Sarah runs to the loo, shouting, 'I'm going to throw up.'

She almost bumps into Danielle and two other women from advertising who are tentatively putting their heads round the door to the newsroom. 'Is that smell what I think it is?' Danielle asks.

With one hand holding his nose, Old Jones uses his other to empty the contents of an olive-green metal wastepaper bin onto the floor. Then he slams the bin over the parcel with one hand. It makes little difference to the smell of fresh shit that is strangling the office. 'Open the bloody windows, then,' he orders to no-one in particular.

Jude feels he needs to take responsibility; the parcel was sent to him. 'Robert, we need something airtight – pass me that Tupperware box with your sandwiches in.'

'Bugger off, get your own Tupperware, I'm not having shit in mine.'

Fighting back the need to gag, Jimmy finds a plastic bag in the bottom of a draw and thrusts it into Old Jones' hand, who heroically lifts the wastepaper bin, puts the parcel, complete with turd, into the bag and makes it airtight with a knot. 'I'll go and burn it with the stack of leaves I've got in the yard,' he says and, holding the bag at arm's length, shuffles out of the office, ignoring Jude's comment of 'or you could just dump it down the toilet.'

The smell in the office is, according to Jimmy, worse than 'the Mogden Sewerage Works, and that caters for the shite of more than a million Londoners every day.' With all the windows open the smell slowly, very slowly, starts to dissipate.

'Who do you think sent you that, Jude?' Jimmy asks.

Instead of answering, the reporter picks up his ringing phone: 'Jude Devlin, how can I hel–'

'Just listen.' Jude is interrupted by a threatening voice, owned by man who's definitely from Hampshire and probably aged in their early 20's. 'We don't want to be in the news, not for any reason, not now, not ever. Other papers, other media understand this, you need to understand it at *The Reporter*.' The line goes dead and Jude is left holding the handset, bewildered and slightly scared. He tells his editor.

'You've rattled some cages, that's for sure, young Jude. Let's think about this and talk later.' He looks at the office diary on Robert's desk. 'Right, Sarah's got her interview with the mayor so, Jude and Robert, it's Southampton Boat Show for you. There's a young woman, a Tracy Edwards, to meet at the Guinness Pavilion at 10.30. I've got a press release and entrance passes for you somewhere. Apparently, she's planning on competing in the Whitbread Round the World Yacht Race with an all-women crew; it'll never happen, of course, but you'll get some good pictures. I wouldn't mind getting out of here and having a look around the show, I'll come with you. Let's go now, I know it's early but it'll get us out of this bloody office, it reeks like the toilet of a cheap curry house late on a Friday night. Leave the windows open.'

The annual boat show, held next to the city's Royal Pier, half on dry land and half on a temporary floating flotilla of pontoons bouncing on The Solent, is Britain's largest nautical shop window and a Mecca for sailors and yachties from around the world, showcasing multi-million-pound gin palaces to DIY Mirror dinghies, and everything in between.

Robert parks and Jimmy limps off to fantasise about the boat he will, one day, own. The photographer and reporter head for the Guinness Pavilion – a big, open-sided tent already full of, mostly, men attacking their second or third pints with gusto, despite it being only 10.30 in the morning. Outside stands a petite, dark-haired woman in her mid-20s who looks like a strong wind would blow her into The Solent.

Jude has read the press release and, after the introductions, tries not to sound incredulous. 'Tracy, are there enough women sailors, you know, experienced, to form a crew for the yacht, what will you call it, *Maiden*?'

'Jude, you do know who our prime minister is, don't you? Look, there are certainly a lot of talented female sailors out there. But, if needs be, we can train them during the preparations, as long as they're fit, keen, intelligent and aren't easily frightened.'

'Isn't this going to cost a bomb? How much money do you currently have?'

'It's not cheap to compete in the Whitbread Round the World Race, especially if you want to be competitive. That's why I'm here today and speaking to you, really. I think we can not only find a great crew but we can win the–'

'Hang on Tracy, no disrespect, but it seems to me that you don't have any money, don't have a boat or a crew and you really think you can win the race, beat 200 or so men sailors but all you have at the moment is the name of your boat.'

'Jude, we have one other thing you've forgotten about. Me, Tracy Edwards. I've sailed in the race and I'm a top skipper. We can compete and, with a little luck, win this toughest of races. What a fantastic opportunity for a company to sponsor *Maiden*, to have its name flying on our spinnaker. As an all-women crew we are going to get amazing publicity and, if we win, *Maiden* will be on every newspaper and TV screen on the planet.'

'Thanks Tracy, they're great quotes. I'm sorry I'm just writing this for our little freesheet, not *The Financial Times*. That's where you need your story told.' Jude actually thinks Tracy has more chance of getting an all-women crew safely around the world than seeing the story in the pink pages of the FT, but keeps that to himself.

Robert has been itching to take the attractive sailor's photograph. 'Tracy, if it's OK, we'll go out onto the furthest pontoon and get The Solent in the background, it'll make a great pic, the sun is in exactly the right spot.'

The three troop off, walking single-file to allow two-way traffic along the narrow pontoons, Robert, despite his heavy camera bag, leading the way at a good pace, followed by the short sailor and Jude bringing up the rear.

The show is busy and heading towards them is a tight knot of people, led by a short, balding but elegant, tanned man in suit and tie, which is unusual on this lovely day and at this relaxed venue. He's closely followed by a beautiful, sophisticated woman, taller by a foot and young enough to be his daughter. Jude doesn't get a clear view but the smell of money and privilege exudes from the group like an expensive perfume. As they draw level, Tracy says something and then reaches over towards the dapper man. Before she can touch him, a hand from a very well-built and fast-moving flunky chops down on her arm. She staggers and Jude grabs her quickly, stopping her falling off the pontoon and into the sea. The flunky, obviously a bodyguard, is uninterested in Tracy's welfare; his right hand reaches inside his jacket and holds something, ready for more action. He plants his huge body firmly across the pontoon, in front of and hiding the diminutive tanned and suited businessman.

The suave leader of the group says 'good job' to the bodyguard before dismissing him with a tap on his shoulder, and then then steps towards Tracy. Smiling benignly, he takes her hand in his and asks if she is OK. Jude notices the man has a trim moustache and looks familiar. A second bodyguard quickly ushers the reporter out of earshot in a way that brooks no argument. And then the whole event is over, almost in a blink of an eye; the man, his daughter and the bodyguards disappear into the crowd.

Jude is stunned, not sure what he's just witnessed. 'Tracy, what *was* that all about? I saw it with my own eyes but haven't a clue what happened.'

'It's no big deal. That was King Hussein of Jordan and his wife, Queen Noor; you must have recognised them?'

'Er, not really. Bloody hell.' The reporter looks along the pontoon for his photographer, whose wondered off ahead, missing the whole incident. 'Robert, Robert.' Jude's shouts are in vain.

'I've sailed with him, well skippered for him in the Med. He asked what I was doing here and when I said, "Looking for money to fund an all-women crew to compete in the Whitbread," he laughed and said, "Well, you may have just found it." Then he apologised for the actions of his bodyguard. It was King Hussein who encouraged me to compete in my first Whitbread back in '85.'

Whilst Robert takes photos of Tracy, Jude shakes his head and wonders how he's just missed out on an exclusive interview with a King. 'How many bloody kings, real kings who rule a country, are there in the world? He was close enough to touch, let alone interview and I didn't even recognise him,' he berates himself silently. The reporter looks over to the smiling sailor having her photo taken. 'And, maybe, I've underestimated this Tracy Edwards character.'

The journalists say their goodbyes to the mariner and head back to the Guinness tent where they've arranged to meet their editor. Jimmy, an almost empty pint glass in hand, immediately collars Robert. 'Well did you get the photo?'

'Yeah, really nice, on the pontoon, yachts in the mid-distance, great light and she's photogenic.'

'No, not the sailor, you fool, King Hussein and his wife, no one's talking about anything else.'

Robert gives Jude a knowing look before answering. 'No, sorry Jimmy, was he here, at the show?'

'Bugger. OK, you two head back and have the story and photos on my desk by lunchtime, I'll hang on here for a bit, see if

I can dig up a real story… I'll make my own way back to the office, later.'

Which means, Jude reckons, that Jimmy will appear late in the afternoon, pissed on Guinness. Robert drives them back to *The Reporter's* office. 'Jude, thanks for not mentioning that you saw King Hussein.'

'Yeah, but it ruins my interview. The real story is "King Hussein Set to Fund All-Women Crew" – even the nationals would want that. Now all I'm left with is "Woman Sailor Dreams Big." I save your skin but lose a great article.'

'I owe you, Jude. Thanks.'

Jude stares at the road, thinking 'or do you.' He hasn't decided which story he's going to write, one with or without the King. It seems Robert is convinced his colleague is going to 'do the right thing.' The reporter has a moment of inspiration. 'I can use Tracy's quotes, just make it appear that she spoke to the King of Jordan prior to us meeting her. I'll tell Jimmy that, as far as we know, the King sped off before we arrived.'

CHAPTER 15

A Glass and a Half

'*Royal Maiden Deal Sealed at Boat Show – A Reporter Exclusive,*' the Tracy Edwards and the King of Jordan story is the sports back page lead. On the Thursday, before *The Reporter* is pushed through every letterbox in the city, Jude spends an hour phoning the story over to each of the national papers, except *The Guardian,* whose news desk listen to the reporter's summary before explaining that it 'doesn't pay for lineage.' The Guardian still run the story the following day, along with every other national newspaper, but the rest send Jude a cheque for his efforts, which all go into Sarah's EDIT fund. Although Jude has filed identical copy to each paper, the following morning the story looks completely different in each publication. Some have added figures for the planned Royal sponsorship, varying from £15,000 to a quarter of a million pounds, while others have spoken to Tracy directly and, thankfully, she hasn't denied Jude's story.

For the rest of the week Jude spends much of his time trying to find out all he can about the Quirks, the family who now have a monopoly on supplying the city's illegal drugs and are rapidly expanding into extorting money under the guise of offering 'protection.'

Sarah's police contacts are much broader and longer-standing than Jude's; she seems to know the desk sergeant in every nick in the city, and it's the sergeants, same as in the army, who really run the show. Sarah is surprised that her contacts know little about the Quirks. 'Sorry I can't be more helpful,' she tells Jude.

He's convinced it was one of the family who sent him the shit wrapped up as a gift and then phoned to warn him off. Jimmy reckons Jude should stay clear of the Quirks for the next few months and look elsewhere for his stories. After his research unearths little about the crime family, the reporter reluctantly agrees. He's learned that Deborah Quirk or Debbs, as her friends call her - and everyone wants to be her friend, or at least no one want to be her enemy - is the matriarch of the family. She has three sons but their dad is dead or missing, no one knows or ever talks about him. Debbs got her boys into boxing at an early age to 'keep them off the street and out of trouble' according to Inspector Phil Broski, Jude's old boxing pal. Eventually Broski found out the lads had started selling anabolic steroids at the gym he still runs, and kicked them out. After talking to Phil, Jude is left with the uneasy feeling that the inspector isn't telling him everything he knew about the family. 'No one goes to your gym for years without you learning an awful lot about them,' the reporter reasons.

The three Quirk boys, Bill, Ben and Brian, all developed into big, strong lads, eventually working as bouncers at nightclubs. Apparently, under the supervision of their mum, they took over the city's door-keeping business a couple of years ago. They made sure, by the use of muscle and brain, that if you needed a bouncer, it was a Quirk or one of their employees on the door. The city's biggest nightclub, the huge *Bojangles*, held out against The Quirks; the owner insisting he'd employ his own staff. The police mounted a major raid on *Bojangles* on a busy Friday night, and ridiculously large quantities of Class A and B drugs were recovered, most found dumped on the nightclub's floor. The club owner lost his licence and quickly went bankrupt.

The new owners of *Bojangles?* The Quirks. Overnight it became the policy in all the city's nightclubs for the bouncers to search potential clubbers for drugs. The punters had no choice: if they wanted a night out, they would be frisked at the club's door. No owner was prepared to risk a police raid and bankruptcy, like the old owner of *Bojangles* had suffered.

Although no one is prepared to go on record, the consensus is that this is the Quirks' masterstroke. All the drugs the bouncers – all Quirk staff – confiscate on the doors of the city's nightclubs are kept by, of course, the Quirks. The family then moves into the much more lucrative game of selling drugs. Why wouldn't they? They had the muscle, were streetwise and got much of their supply for free. Queenie would say it was a 'classic business move: organic expansion based on supply-side advantage,' the sort of scheme normally hatched in the boardrooms of Unilever, IBM or Ford.

The word is that Debbs is the brains of the family. The two eldest sons, Bill and Ben – Jude wonders what sort of parent would name their sons after the TV 'flowerpot men' puppets – have never been charged by the police. But the youngest son, Brian, was arrested for assault, although the charges were eventually dropped when eye-witnesses 'forgot' what they'd seen. Brian is generally considered 'a tearaway' and a couple of people used the word 'thug' to describe him to Jude.

It's almost a month later when Inspector Broski comes up trumps. He calls Jude at *The Reporter* offices, something he'd never previously done. 'Ah, the reporter at The Reporter, bet you've never been called that before, have you, Jude?'

'Not more than a hundred times, Phil. I'm honoured; it must be important if you're wasting that limited police budget you're always moaning about, to call the press?'

'No, not really, just wondered if you were coming to the gym tonight?'

'I hadn't planned on it, Phil. I've got an exciting evening of washing and ironing lined up.'

'Do try and get along, Jude, for 7. I've some sparring organised that you won't want to miss out on. OK, got to go. See you later.' The inspector hangs up before the reporter can protest or even say goodbye.

Jude isn't overly keen on sparring; the other lads are more experienced boxers and the journalist only really uses the gym to keep in shape. But he thinks it unwise not to take Phil's advice and arrives to find he is alone with the policeman; the post-work crowd has disappeared and the 7.30pm training session-goers are yet to arrive. Despite their difference in age, Phil and Jude enjoy each other's company and, after the usual greetings and jokes, the inspector looks serious.

'Jude, you know you were asking after the Quirks a few weeks back? Well, get yourself down to Southampton Magistrates Court tomorrow morning, early. Brian's going to appear; two nights ago, he glassed someone at The Centre Inn, downstairs in the nightclub. He's really in trouble this time, he was there checking on the Quirks' own bouncers, so it's serious alright – he could get five years. Instead of stopping the trouble, he's created it. It'll have to go to Crown Court eventually, tomorrow is the first time the case comes up.'

'Wow, that is a story, thanks for the heads-up, Phil. How did you hear about it?'

'An old mate from Central nick called me – he knows the Quirks used to be members at the gym until I had to ask them to leave. Just don't say anything to anyone else here, a few of the lads are still their mates and some earn a few quid extra working a door on a Friday and Saturday night for the Quirks. OK?'

Jude nods but before he could speak, they both hear the buzz of the lock on the gym's front door opening. Phil raises a finger in front of his lips and looks in Jude's direction, before starting to speak loudly. 'Right, get your gear on, I want you and Dave, Des and Mike to do a round-robin session, two rounds of two minutes each, sparring with each other. By the end of the evening, you'll all have done six rounds, 12 minutes, sparring and be totally knackered.'

Early next morning, Robert stands outside of the magistrates' court and, as discreetly as possible, which wasn't very, given the open concourse outside of the busy court building, photographs every white male aged in their early 20s arriving at the court. For his troubles, Robert has his parentage questioned, was spat on and threatened that his camera would be inserted into a specific orifice and never see the light of day again.

Normally, if a photographer doesn't know what the accused looks like, they'll slip into the back of the court during the hearing to have a good look at their 'target' in the dock. But this runs the risk of spooking the accused and have them come out of court with a blanket or jacket over their head, or slipping an usher a few quid so they can leave by a back door.

Eventually the bellowing black robes of a court usher appears and the jobsworth demands Robert stop taking photographs. 'A juror going into Crown Court has claimed you've taken his photo in the precincts of the court. Judge Hornblower has told me to instruct you to stop and hand over the film, or face being in contempt and risk a potential prison sentence.'

Robert was remarkably cool. 'Please inform the Judge that I've stopped taking photos, although I strongly dispute that I'm in the precincts of the court and require a delineated map to prove otherwise. We will not publish any photos of jurors at any time. As for the film, unless you produce the relevant legal document, it's the rightful property of *The Reporter* newspaper and neither you nor the judge have any right to it.' Robert stands erect, even jutting his jaw in the direction of the court official. The usher is about to reply but, instead, clamps his mouth shut, turns on his heals and scurries up the steps back into the huge, white limestone court building.

Jude arrives in time to witness the exchange, every inch of his body still aching from the previous night's sparring. 'Robert, well done, that was impressive. Though I didn't believe a word of what you were saying.'

'You see, Jude, you take the piss out of my public school education, but it does teach you how to stand up to authority and, more importantly, to appear ridiculously confident when you tell a bare-faced lie. Why do you think that, pretty much, all politicians of both parties were public school educated? Right, I'm off back to the darkroom before that usher returns with a note from the judge telling me to surrender the film. I'll dev the roll and print them out so you can identify young Quirk when you get back to the office.'

Regina v Brian Quirk is the first case up in Court 3 that morning and Jude is the only journalist sat on the Press Bench when the accused is led into the dock. 'The Echo will be fuming,' the reporter thinks, as the 21-year-old is asked to confirm his name. Brian is charged with Causing Grievous Bodily Harm, under the Offences Against the Person Act, 1861, but is not asked to enter a plea as the case will be heard on a 'date to be set, at Southampton Crown Court'. It's all over very quickly but, as Brian is about to leave the dock, he stops, looks at the press bench and stares at the lone reporter for what seems like minutes. Jude feels a cold tingle run down his spine.

Back in the newsroom, Jude calls Del, who says he knows nothing about the case. After some digging, Jude gets the name of the victim and Del phones back to say he's got a photograph of Roy Bruce, the 19-year-old Brian Quirk is accused of attacking with a pint glass. The photo was taken by the police photographer immediately after the youngster had had 43 stitches inserted to hold his face together. Robert drives to the police press office in Winchester and collects the photo. When he's returns, Jude has finished writing the story and can clearly identify Brian Quirk in one of Robert's photos taken outside court.

Jimmy is delighted with the pair's work but is reluctant to use the photo of the victim. 'God, it's so raw and horrible. You couldn't do that with just one glass, it's unbelievable.'

Sarah chirps up. 'Call him the "Cadbury's Attacker" – a glass and a half in every bar. Oh, it wasn't a bar, was it? It was a nightclub.' She laughs coolly.

'Seriously, what will the old dears do when they open *The Reporter* and see that photo?' the editor asks rhetorically. 'They'll spill their afternoon cuppa and have a heart attack.'

Jude fights his corner. 'Jimmy, we should have the photo lifesize on the front of the paper. Show what this bastard and his family are capable of. The old dears will love it; some vicarious excitement to liven up their Thursday afternoons.'

'Look, great work, you two, the Echo will be fuming that they know nothing about this.' The editor stops to think for a moment before coming to a decision. 'We'll use the victim's photo, but inside and small, with Quirk's photo on the front. I've got the headline: "NIGHTCLUB GLASSING: BOUNCER FAMILY ACCUSED".' Jimmy is excited and energised and ignores Sarah's offer of, 'How about, "A Quirk of Fate."'

While Jude is delighted with his story, he realises that he's inexperienced and the training in journalism law at college wasn't extensive. 'Jimmy, you're the expert, but legally, are you happy with what I've written; that we can say the accused is a member of the Quirk family who provide all the city's doormen?'

'Jude, it's thin ice as proceedings are active, but we're allowed, prior to the trial, to say what Brian Quirk's job is and it's unreasonable not to make the connection between what his family do for a living. It has to come out at trial, so can't be prejudicial.'

'That's what I thought, what they taught us at college, I just wanted to be sure, especially as I can't afford to upset Alex again, not after he extended my trial period.'

'Our managing director will be happy with this story – it's "sleazy stories" Alex struggles with. But, young Jude, you do need to watch out, not for Alex but for the Quirks. They'll be upset but, if they've any sense at all, they'll have to lie low for a while. Right, I'll lay this out in the morning. Come on everyone, *The Osborne* is open and the first one's on me.'

CHAPTER 16

Getting the Finger

Danielle has agreed to go for a pizza with Jude so, after two pints, the reporter makes his excuses and leaves the rest of the news team, who look like they will be in *The Osborne* for the rest of the evening, and collects the newspaper's sales assistant from her flat.

The pair go to La Margherita, one of Southampton's many Greek-owned Italian restaurants, and have a fun night, laughing and discussing the week's paper as well as Danielle's possible promotion. She says, 'When Alex visited us this week, he took me out to lunch and said he's planning to expand the paper's circulation in the east of the city. He wants a new sales rep for that area and offered me the job.'

Jude laughs out loud. 'That's a bit different to when I last had a one-to-one with him: he offered to take my job away by sacking me; we compromised and he ended up extending my probationary period. You'll take the job won't you; more money, company car?'

'I should, shouldn't I? But all our sales reps are the same type: pushy, self-centred and hard-nosed. Don't get me wrong, I like all of them in different ways but I'm just not sure if that is me, or the person I want to be. And I'd miss the fun we have in the office.' Danielle sips from her glass and then gazes into it, lost in thought.

Jude tops up the glass from a chianti bottle half-covered in a straw weave. 'Maybe you could do the job your way, not like the other reps. Be yourself: straightforward and honest – I'd certainly buy my advertising from you. Great opportunities don't come along too often; think long and hard before you turn this one down.'

At the end of the meal Danielle insists on paying half and, although Jude protests, he's secretly relieved; money's tight and he knows his date earns quite a lot more than he does. The pair walk through one of the city centre's large parks, past the large open-air aviary enjoying the warm evening and each other's company. Jude realises he's lucky to be spending the evening with someone who's attractive, fun and easy to be with. With Alex expecting an answer to his job offer in the morning, Danielle needs time to decide. Jude drops her off at her flat and is rewarded with a peck on the cheek. During his 20-minute drive home he wonders what he needs to do, to up the temperature of the relationship without seeing it go up in flames.

Opening the post the next day, among the usual press releases, is a small parcel addressed to Mr J. Devlin. Sarah shakes it and something knocks lightly inside the box. 'Don't worry, Jude, there's no fancy wrapping paper this time – and turds don't rattle.' Everyone laughs but before Jude can open the little package the phone on his desk rings. It's Del, who informs the reporter that Roy Bruce, the lad horribly disfigured by the broken pint glass shoved in his face by Brian Quirk, has agreed to talk to Jude from his hospital bed. 'He's a bit jumpy but a nice lad. Now that Quirk has been charged and appeared in court, he feels a lot safer.'

'And a photograph, Del?'

'Yep, tell Comrade Robert to try and get one that's not blurred, for a change. Roy's in the new West Wing, level C of the General. Byee.'

Jude and Robert immediately head for Southampton General Hospital, before Roy changes his mind or has it changed for him. The ground floor doors to the lift open but both reporter and photographer have to stand back to allow an elegantly dressed woman in her late 40s, hair up and clutching a large handbag, out of the lift. She's followed by a man, aged some 25 years younger, who, given the resemblance, must be her son, although he's twice her size and all muscle. The woman glances at Jude and shows a flash of recognition before quickly looking away.

Roy Bruce is sat up in bed in a private room on Level C, his one good eye staring aimlessly into the distance. His head is swathed in bandages, hiding the chain of stitches around his face. There are holes for the remaining one good eye to see out, and for his nostrils and his mouth. Robert pushes past Jude and sticks out his hand towards the patient. 'Hi, Roy, I'm Robert, I thought I recognised the name; I took your photo last year, you were "Player of the Season" for the university football team, weren't you?'

'I'm surprised you recognised me through the bandages,' a croaky, uneven voice speaks, although most of the lips are hidden from view. 'My head looks like I'm going to a fancy-dress party as a mummy.'

'Good to see you've kept a sense of humour. Your ginger curly hair sticking out of the bandages was the giveaway,' Robert explains and smiles.

'I'd a good season – a couple of years ago I dreamt of turning professional, but I wasn't good enough, so I ended up studying aviation design at the uni. That was a decent photo you took. My mum phoned up and asked for a copy and, Robert, you sent her one. She was chuffed, even got it framed.'

Robert nods in appreciation of the compliment and then introduces Jude, who shakes the patient's hand gently. 'Thanks for agreeing to see us, Roy. Really sorry about the attack. I was in court yesterday and Quirk looks a nasty piece of work.' Jude pauses, expecting a response. When none comes, he tries again to establish a connection with the victim. 'Did the police tell you that the family run the doors to all the city pubs and clubs; they've got a monopoly.'

'Look guys, I'm sorry to disappoint you, but I've got nothing to say about the incident.'

Jude looks bewildered; normally he's good at reading body language and facial expression, but he's no chance to seeing what is going on under the bandages. 'Incident, Roy? A bloke who's in charge of the bouncers, who's supposed to be responsible for keeping everyone safe, glasses you, causing injuries that need dozens of stitches, and you call it an incident?'

'Look, Jude, did you say? I know you mean well. And Robert's a good guy. But I don't want to talk about it, OK.' The patient looks at Robert, who's raised his camera and is focusing the lens on Roy. 'Would you mind, please, no photos.'

'Sorry, Roy. Me and Jude can come back later if you're not up to it at the moment.'

'Don't waste your time. I'm never going to talk about what happened that night at the club.'

Jude runs his hand through his hair, perplexed at Roy's change of mind. 'Look, even if you'd had a few, were a bit mouthy, pissed up even, well, that's no excuse for someone putting a glass in your face.'

'I wasn't pissed up – I don't drink, never have, part of trying to make the grade as a professional footballer, I suppose.'

Jude throws his notebook down on the hospital bed. 'Roy, look, I don't get it. You could have lost an eye or worse.'

'I have,' Roy says. 'My left eye, the surgeons tried to save it, apparently. I'll be wearing an eye patch, at least at first. Maybe a glass eye later; they're supposed to be very good, really lifelike.'

Jude's voice is involuntarily raised. 'Fuck me, Roy. You've lost an eye? And if that bastard had been a little bit lower, he could have severed your windpipe or cut an artery. You could have died. Now it's just an *incident*.'

Roy takes a sip of water from his bedside table. 'There's other stuff going on, stuff you don't understand. So, no story, no prosecution.'

'What? Roy, you're an intelligent university student, studying aviation. You can't let a thug like Quirk get away with it. If he gets away with this, he'll be free to attack whoever he feels like–'

Robert interrupts his colleague. 'Roy, excuse Jude, he's keen for justice. I see you've made your mind up and we won't report anything you say. Can you help us understand what's made you change your mind?'

'Robert, I trust you, so I'll explain. But, Jude, this isn't for reporting. You both agree not to tell a soul, not to report any of what I'm going to tell you.'

Robert agrees and Jude nods. 'No, Jude,' Roy says, 'you have to say you that you won't publish a word.'

Jude nods again. 'We won't publish a word, scouts' honour. Roy, I don't know how you can explain this.'

Roy looks towards his bedside cabinet. 'Just open the door and look inside. That's all the explanation needed.'

Jude does as instructed: there's a small, black Adidas holdall inside. Jude discreetly pulls it out and unzips its, expecting to find a toothbrush or change of underwear. Instead, it's full of bundles of £20 notes and there's a small plastic bag of white powder. 'What the fuck!' Jude exclaims.

'There's cash and the coke is an extra little present, apparently it's better than Aspirin at pain relief. They're gifts from Mrs Quirk, just before you came. She and another son, Ben I think, left it here. She said there would be the same amount again, once all charges were dropped against Brian and I was back home.'

Jude slumps down onto a visitor's chair by the side of the bed. 'What, they're paying you off? And you're taking their money? You can't be—'

Robert again interrupts Jude, desperate for the patient to continue his explanation. 'That looks like an awful lot of money, Roy.'

'Five grand. And she's honest, Mrs Quirk. She told me what the surgeon has told me: that the scars to my face will fade a little over the years, but I'll always have them. She said that modern cosmetics are good but they take time and skill to apply and still won't entirely hide the scars. You saw the photo – you published it in your paper. I'm always going to look scary to other people. Mrs Quirk said that children will be afraid of me and women will run a mile rather than go out on a date with me. She said that getting a job has become 10 times harder, just because of how I look, how I'm always going to look.'

Jude couldn't believe what he was hearing. 'Wow, she told you that.'

'She didn't pull any punches and I'm glad of that. She said her son was responsible. He was wrong, she said, but asked what good it would do me if he went to prison. But if I co-operated, she would ensure I'm helped and what's in that beside cabinet is the first payment. Her exact words were, "Roy, you're going to need friends in the future, powerful friends. Go ahead with the case and you'll have powerful enemies. Refuse to testify and we will help you, now and in the future." That's what I'm going to do, refuse to testify.'

Jude blew air through his pursed lips. 'And Brian Quirk walks away scot-free. How is that right? How is that fair? How is that—'

'I'd do the same, Jude.' Robert interrupts the reporter for a third time. 'Roy, you've got a tough time ahead and you'll need a nest egg. Come on, Jude. We should be getting back to the office. Thanks for your time, Roy.' The photographer grabs the reporter's arm and all but pulls him out of the private hospital room.

They stop halfway along the corridor, when out of Roy's earshot. 'Jude, the lad's been through enough. He's not going to change his mind, at least not today.'

'But it's wrong, isn't it? He could put that bastard Quirk behind bars for years.'

'You don't get it, do you, Jude? Roy's been given his own life sentence: no one, not even his own family, are going to look at him in the same way again. Not ever. Instead of seeing that intelligent, good-looking bloke I photographed last year, everyone is going to see a scarred, disfigured scary man and want to look away. We live in a society that puts beauty above everything else.'

It's a dismal drive back to the office. Jude tells his editor that Roy is going to refuse to testify or co-operate with the police, but that he has a great story. 'Jimmy, the headline is, "ATTACKER'S FAMILY BUYS OFF GLASS VICTIM," or something like that, you're the one who's good at headlines. We saw piles of £20 notes, and Roy said he'd been given five grand and some white powder, probably cocaine, by Mrs Quirk.'

'Hang on, Jude.' Robert shakes his head and walks over to the editor's desk, where Jude is standing. 'We can't publish any of that. You gave your word to Roy that we wouldn't use it.'

'Yeah, but look, this is such a big story. We can't let–'

Jimmy stands up and looks at Jude intently, fingering his own eye patch. 'Is that right, did Roy ask for the conversation to be off the record and not for publication?'

'He did, Jimmy. But, look, he's a young lad, and probably still under the effects of the drugs the doctors have given him. He didn't mean–'

Palms open, the editor raises both arms. 'You know we can't use it. OK, we know she's given him the money. But, unless we can prove it without involving Roy, we can't use any of it. You may be a trainee, Jude, but this is serious and you should know better. If you give your word, stick by it, for fuck's sake. You've got a few days before deadline, check in with Del, tell him that Roy won't talk and ask how the other witnesses are standing up. He'll know exactly what you mean. Come deadline on Thursday I bet we end up with the story, "Bouncer Accused of Glassing Walks Free."'

Sarah has heard every word and watches Jude dejectedly walk back to his desk. 'I'll make tea, that's what we all need, a nice cuppa. Jude, that little parcel's still on your desk. Open it, maybe it'll cheer you up.'

Jude falls into his chair and, without the spirit to do anything else, takes a pair of scissors and cuts the string around the package. He lays the cardboard box on his desk and lifts its lid. Packed loosely in tissue paper is a plastic 'human' finger, the same as you can buy in any joke shop. But instead of the flesh being a beigey skin-colour and the nail being bright red, the whole thing is grey with dark crimson splashes. 'It's not a very good quality imitation,' the reporter thinks, and gives it a prod. He jumps up out of his chair, rushes to the loo and is noisily and violently sick.

Sarah maintains her calm, saying, 'Guess that's just three mugs, then,' before going over to see what Jude was looking at. She screams loudly and is joined by Robert and Jimmy at Jude's desk. The three realise the finger is real; it's grey colour and congealed blood leave no doubt in their minds. Jimmy puts the lid back on the box and tells Sue to call 'the nearest police station and tell one of your desk-sergeant mates what we've got.'

CHAPTER 17

The Grown-Up Truth

The following day the newsroom of *The Reporter* is a sombre place. The police take the severed finger for tests and promise to report back. The sergeant warns all the staff to watch out for any packages that come in. He singles out the news team to be particularly careful with their movements: 'Don't go out alone, especially to any isolated or dark locations.'

Mid-morning, Alex arrives from head office and calls a staff meeting for lunchtime and then asks Jimmy and Jude to join him in the sales' meeting room. The managing editor is his normal sympathetic and caring self. 'What is it about you two? Who gave you permission to change the name of this fucking paper from *The Reporter* to *Southampton's News of the World*?'

Jude experiences a weird, out-of-body moment, disconnecting with the conversation, and, instead of worrying about his imminent dismissal, finds himself wondering why Alex always speaks and acts as if every word was being captured on film for posterity? Was it so he could recount the story, verbatim and complete with dramatic movements, at his next soirée with Hampshire's glitterati?

'Jude,' the day-dreaming reporter snaps back into the present at the mention of his name, 'you're not the Watergate reporter in Washington, that Carl Whatshisname–'

'Bernstein,' Jimmy helpfully adds.

'Carl Bernstein, thanks. You're a trainee on a freesheet in Southampton. What is this crusade against the city's crime that the pair of you are running? Do you think that's what our readers want to hear?'

Jude's brain wonders off again, a 'Surely, he means read?' thought scrolls across his forehead as if it's an illuminated signs in London's Leicester Square.

Jimmy tries to lower the temperature of the meeting. 'They've been good, no, outstanding stories, Alex, you must agree with that. Jude has done a great job bringing those stories to the paper.'

'OK, you top investigative pair of hacks. Here's a clue to what *The Reporter* series of newspapers is really about. They all freesheets. In case you missed the clue, I'll make it easier. It's the word *free.*' With his fat fingers Alex takes off his red plastic-framed glasses and lays them on the desk for effect. 'I will deny every saying this, but here's the truth. I don't give a flamingo's fuck what stories go into our papers. Why do we sell so much advertising, which, by the way, is up again, year on year, eight per cent? It's because we're free. It's not the stories inside. Do you think the advertisers give a penguin's penis what the stories are?'

Jude can't stop himself wondering what animal's sexual organ or activity Alex is going to alliterate next. 'Perhaps a tiger's tit. Or an alligator's arse. No, an arse doesn't quite qualify,' he muses.

'No, they don't. Our advertisers just care that, every Thursday afternoon, their ads are pushed through the letterbox of every home in this city. And then the people of Southampton, as gormless as gorilla's gonads, look at our paper, I won't say read, and spend money with our advertisers. It's a virtuous cir– Jude, why are you smiling? I don't think this is, in anyway, funny.'

Jude quickly puts his hand in front of his mouth and coughs. 'I wasn't smiling, Alex, just, um, trying to keep down a cough.'

'Right. It's a virtuous circle. The advertisers get our readers' money and then advertise with us again the following week, allowing me to pay your generous wages.'

Alex nods towards the door, regally dismissing the pair from his presence. The journalists return forlornly to their empty office – Robert and Sarah are out on a job about a bespoke dressmaker opening a new shop. As well as promising the paper lots of advertising the dressmaker has offered Sarah a made-to-measure creation, as long as the paper does a photoshoot of the stages in the dresses' production, from initial measurements to Sarah modelling the finished item.

Jimmy, for once, makes the coffees and passes a mug to Jude. 'It could've been worse. We've still got our jobs.'

'Why does Alex always talk as if every word is being recorded, as if he's talking for posterity?'

'More like talking out of his posterior.'

'This is so fucking depressing, Jimmy. "I don't give a flamingo's fuck what stories go in our paper?" I wish I'd recorded that and given it to *The Press Gazette*. Alex would've had to resign.'

'It's unusual for him to be so bloody candid. Did you notice, he didn't ask how you were or warn you to be careful. He was once a journalist but now it's just about the money and his fucking ego.'

'And he's lying about the advertisers. They're not stupid: they know better stories mean more readers. If it's full of crap, who's going to bother to turn over the front page? No one. Danielle's told me that, in advertising, the phone rings more after a good edition – that's the real virtuous sodding circle.'

'Jude, Alex will never admit that; he'd have to pay us more.'

The pair are distracted and depressed the rest of the morning. Danielle pops her head around the newsroom door to remind them about Alex's staff meeting. When neither move she charmingly ushers them out of their chairs and into the big meeting room. The paper's 20 other employees, including Sarah and Robert, are already in the room when Jimmy and Jude walk in to join them. Alex, from behind his little podium, takes off his red glasses with one hand and points his specs at the two journalists. 'Here they are, everyone, our fearless editor and reporter.

Let's give them a big hand.' Alex leads the embarrassed group in a short round of applause.

'I want to say to you guys, Jimmy and Jude,' Alex raises the volume of his voice during the course of the sentence, 'and the rest of our great editorial team – Sarah and Robert are included in this – just one thing.' He dramatically stops, lowers his arms, hands and head, pauses, then continues in a theatrically hushed tone. 'You're doing a great job, keep it up.' Alex then leads the room in another round of applause. Jude thinks that the company's managing director must have attended the same school of public speaking as born-again preachers from the American deep South; all that's needed to turn the staff meeting into a revivalist rally is a few gospel singers, an organist and a white-suited Alex to threaten the journalists with 'an eternal burning hell' if they don't repent of their ways.

There's no stopping Alex, who quickly moves on to 'the people who make *The Reporter* what it is – our great sales team.' He urges his 'troops to stay strong in the marketing march' and to 'keep destroying our advertising adversaries.' He moves to wind the meeting up. 'You may have heard that a body part was delivered to our building, to the news team. Well, whatever it is – and it's still being analysed, so let's not jump to any conclusions – you have my personal assurance that the safety of each and every one of you is of paramount importance to me and the owners of *The Reporter*. So, from now on, Old, I mean, Mr Jones, will be in charge of security, bringing his extensive military background to the service of this paper. He, and he alone, will open up the building each morning and lock it up each evening. Please all be sensible when you are outside of the office. Thanks for giving up your lunchtime and perhaps you'd all be so kind as to join me in the next office where a selection of sandwiches has been generously provided.'

The four journalists congregate around a sad plate of stale white-bread triangles, their edges so curled that they reveal a congealed egg and cress filling. Old Jones, his bearing a little more erect than usual, marches towards them. Sarah laughs, salutes the caretaker and defies salmonella poisoning by biting into a triangle.

'You can laugh, young lady, but I was a Desert Rat, you know,' wheezes the old boy.

Robert grabs Old Jones' broom, lays its handle across his own left shoulder, cups its brush in his left hand, and marches around the room. Sarah starts singing the words from the theme tune to *Dads' Army:* 'Who do you think you are kidding, Mr Hitler,' and the women from advertising immediately join in, 'if you think old England's done?' Alex is unimpressed but realises he can't restore order without looking a total idiot, so picks up his plate, mumbles about having an 'important meeting' and leaves the room.

Old Jones sees the funny side and sings and laughs along. Jimmy looks at him straight. 'So, tell me, Old Jones, how much extra is Alex paying you to risk life and limb as our new head of security?' When Old Jones doesn't answer, Jimmy nods. 'That's what I thought. Nothing. He's a tight bastard, that one.'

Del phones later that afternoon with bad, good and terrible news. 'Jude, it was a human finger, but the poor bugger who lost it had been dead for some time before it was removed. The blood was added later, for effect. The pathologist reckoned it's probably come from a funeral home; after the finger was removed the coffin lid will have been screwed back on and no one will ever be the wiser. Now, rotten news. The witnesses to Brian Quirk's glassing of Roy Bruce have all bottled it. Apparently, they've suddenly remembered it was dark in the club and they can't be sure it was young Quirk who wielded the pint glass. With Bruce changing his statement and refusing to testify, well, the new Crown Prosecution Service reckons there isn't a case and have dropped the charges against Quirk. We've had no option but to release the toerag.'

'Del, you know he did it, everyone does.'

'What's your point, Jude? That it's an unfair world or that the powerful normally get their own way, by hook or by crook?'

'Isn't there anything you, the police, can do? Can't you offer

Roy protection or relocation?' Jude realises he's almost shouting down the phoneline at Del.

'Jude, do you want the press office answer or the grown-up truth? Because the press office answer is, "we will work to ensure the victim's safety, and explore the possibilities of a new identity away from the area."

'What *is* the "grown-up" version, Del?' Jude's voice is metallic hard.

'Well, let's promise him the earth and when he comes home to see his ill mum, just the once, let's see what happens to him, shall we? Or shall we be honest and say, "Life is going to be difficult for you, unless you're prepared to give up your whole current existence and identity, go to a new city and try to start again. Oh, and this time you've got one eye, your face is disfigured for life, the scars will make you easily recognisable, you'll have no mates and will only be able to get a shit job that pays subsistence wages." What would you do, Jude? What would you advise Roy to do, if he was your son?'

'That's, er, difficult, Del.'

'It doesn't end there. We're then we're faced with getting the Chief Constable to agree to the huge costs involved for what is a run-of-the-mill glassing in a gay fight in a nightclub. There's no connection to any other criminal activities.'

Jude finds himself nodding, reluctantly conceding that Del has a point. 'Hang on, Del, a gay fight? What do you mean?'

'More mistaken identity, really. According to Roy's statement, Brian made a move on him, thinking he was gay. Brian, whose toxicology showed he'd been snorting a significant amount of coke, didn't take too kindly to being rejected by Roy, so he grabbed the pint glass...'

'Roy told us he was sober, he doesn't drink.'

'I think that's true. Look, Jude, a word to the wise. Brian is now back on the street, even if his mum tries to rein him in, he's now going to believe he's Superman and untouchable. Just be careful, OK? Maybe lay off the Quirks for a while. Be sensible. Catch up soon, byee.'

The following Thursday's front page splash is 'GLASS AT-TACKER WALKS FREE'. Jimmy is sailing close to the wind with the headline. But he's banking on the Quirks not wanting the publicity of going to either court or the Press Council to complain, and Alex's hazy knowledge of journalism law lets the headline slip through his censure. Jude's article tells how Brian Quirk has been released after all witnesses either changed their stories or refused to testify. It said that Brian works with his mother and two older brothers in the family business, which has a near monopoly on the city's nightclub security, supplying the vast majority of bouncers and doormen across Southampton. The article finished with a quote, helpfully supplied by Del, 'Hampshire Police are not looking for anyone else in connection with the attack.'

CHAPTER 18
Bitter Cold and Cold Bitterness

Each week Jude has to fill half a page of the paper with a vox-pop – he asks 10 people, chosen at random in the city's High Street, their views on a particular subject and Robert photographs them. As there's no obvious place to go with the Quirks' story, Jude chooses 'safety in nightclubs' as the week's topic for the vox-pop and has to talk to more than 80 people before he finds 10 to agree that they're 'scared to go out to local clubs' and he even has to steer these towards mentioning the recent glassing. He realises it's probably pointless, but if he can start a movement that stops people feeling safe in the city's nightclubs, their revenues will decrease, which will mean less money for the Quirks.

Back in the office, Jude takes two phone calls within an hour of each other. The first is the unusually serious tones of Del. 'Jude, don't ask me how I know this, but trust me, I know this. The Quirks aren't happy with you. They're unhappy that they've be named. Apparently, they're pretty keen on their privacy. Now the case has been dropped and Brian is free, well, be sensible. Make sure *The Proud Stag* is properly secured at night. Don't go out alone during the day and don't go out at all at night. OK?'

'That might prove a bit difficult, Del. I'm sleeping rough, probably in the park tonight, with the alkies. I'm doing a first-hand piece on the provision of care for the city's rough sleepers.'

'Not a good idea, really, Jude, is it? I suspect I can't get you to change your plans?'

'I can't change them, Del. This has taken over a month to set up, to win the trust of St Dismas, the hostel for the homeless. It's an important story.'

'OK, that's what I thought you'd say.' Del thinks for a moment. 'I'll have a quiet word with the sergeant down at Central nick, he's an old mate. See if he can increase the foot patrols; he knows where the rough sleepers go better than anyone.'

'Thanks, Del, you're a pal.'

Although writing a first-hand account of 'life for the city's rough sleepers' was Jude's idea, the reporter is having second thoughts even before Del's phone call, concerned about the volatile nature of the people he'd be spending the night with.

Sarah has obviously been listening to the call. 'Jude, you do realise it's going to go down to minus three tonight? You must be mad, it's already the coldest October for years; I'm writing something about it now. If I were you, I'd put it off until next July? Who's for coffee?'

Jude nurses his hot mug, wondering if his ski trousers and thermal underwear, a few jumpers under his big coat, gloves and his Saints' bobble hat would be enough to keep him warm that night. His thoughts are interrupted by a ringing phone. It's his. The charming voice on the other end is that of woman, not young or old, but considered and confident. 'Jude, you're not very bright for a reporter, are you?' She is speaking even before Jude can say hello. 'You don't learn your lessons, do you?'

'Who is this?' Jude tries to interrupt but, serenely, the caller continues.

'Be careful, Jude or you'll end up inside; perhaps we can arrange for you to share a cell with your cousin's son, Craig. Or you may find yourself somewhere worse, much worse. This is your final warning. I do mean, final. If you don't want to hear from us again, and I promise you, you don't, keep out of our business. Write about your donkeys or The Saints. No more warnings, no more faeces or fingers. Bye, Jude.' The line goes dead.

Stunned, Jude replaces the handset. A hundred thoughts sprint around the racetrack of his brain...They know Craig is my cousin Daphne's son. They must know where I live, about Gerry and Milly and little George and the pub. Are they safe? Just by living there I'm putting them in danger. Was that Deborah Quirk herself on the phone? What the fuck have I got myself into. Should I tell Jimmy? Or the police? Call Del? Jude thinks his head is about to explode. He takes a deep breath, stands and raises his voice. 'Anyone want anything at the shop? I'm nipping out for five minutes.'

By the time he returns from the local corner shop, Jude has decided to keep the call from Deborah Quirk, if that was who it was, to himself, rationalising that there is little point in spreading his worries. And now he *is* looking forward to his night of sleeping rough, hoping and praying it'll be a welcome distraction from everything else going on in his life. The rough sleepers will have no connection with the Quirks, so at least he'll be safe, comparatively, in their company, he reasons. Back home, at the pub, he changes into his warmest clothes and decides to take just a £10 note with him, before slipping an extra fiver down his left sock for emergencies. He half expects his evening companions will want him to furnish them with drink in return for sharing their stories with him, and wonders about the morality of giving strong alcohol to people who are already addicted to it. But if he wants the story – for the winos to talk to him, Jude suspects he'll have no choice.

The manager at St Dismas repeats the 'cardinal rule' to Jude to not buy any of the men alcohol, before introducing the reporter to some of the hostel's residents. Soon the reporter is enjoying their company in Hoglands Park, where an adult football team trains without conviction under the last of the October evening's light. Jude is in the 'safe hands' of Des and Mick, two habitual drinkers and rough sleepers from the hostel. They, like all those who stay at the hostel, have to leave each morning by 8am, take all their possessions with them, and are forbidden from returning before 6pm that night. When they do, there's no guarantee a bed will be available for them: it's first come, first served and a queue starts forming from mid-afternoon along the street outside the hostel building.

Mick opens his grubby old backpack and pulls a can of Carlsberg Special Brew, opens it and takes a good drink. Then he takes out another can, gives it to Des and, less enthusiastically, produces a third for Jude. The reporter knows this not only welcomes him into the little group but also infers the burden of having to 'buy a round' in return. 'It's not cheap, Special Brew, but it's 9% proof, so work out the mathematics,' Mick said in his Irish lilt. 'It's the best bang for your buck, as the Americans say.' He takes another long swig from the can.

Den, originally from Aberdeen, says the pair come to this park most nights. 'But we don't drink too much. They lock the door at 11 at St Dismas, so you go there early, by six, to try and reserve a bed and then you can leave your gear there. But you have to get back before they bolt the door. If you turn up pissed, they won't let you in. It's a good rule, you don't want to share your night with someone screaming, crying or looking for a fight, do ya? There's 16 beds in the one dormitory, it's hard enough to get a good kip, especially if you're sober.'

When the cans are finished, Des opens his plastic bag and hands round purple tins of Tennent's Super. 'It reminds me of home, and it's still 9 per cent.' Jude learns that most of the rough sleepers have drink issues and none, as far as he can make out, are from the Southampton area. 'You don't want your mum or your son seeing you looking the way we look, now, do ya,' Des laughs, revealing a mouth where toothless gaps greatly exceed the number of teeth. 'Put that in your newspaper. And tell your readers how the thugs come into the park in the summer and try to give us a kicking, just 'cause they can.'

The cans of Tennent's Super are soon empty and the reporter is told, in no uncertain terms, that it's his round. Jude explains he doesn't have any drink with him and Des says 'Nay bother' and, with Mick, escorts the journalist to a small, unpretentious supermarket nearby. The old Indian owner, eagle-eyed from behind the till, greets both Des and Mick like long-lost friends while his hand quietly searches under the counter for the insurance of a baseball bat. Mick takes charge of the shopping, selecting as many cans of the strongest beer as he can carry, 'Let's have a proper party, eh?'

The evening is an education for Jude: the mood starts with suspicion, moves to great good humour and bonhomie until, when the alcohol runs out, it turns much darker.

With all the cans empty and the beer drunk, the two friends turned on Jude, demanding he get out the rest of his money. It is 10.40pm. 'Lads, that's all my cash gone. Don't you need to get back to St Dismas, before they lock the door.'

Des does his best to turn on the charm. 'Don't you go worrying about us, laddie. Maybe we won't bother with St Dismas tonight. Let's have another wee drink instead. Ya may no' have cash, but you'll have one of them credit cards. Old Gupta's a good lad, he'll take that.'

'No, no I don't. Well, I do, but I didn't bring it with me.' Jude explains, worrying that while he and Des sit on the park bench, Mick is out of sight and his alcohol-infused breath is now hitting the back of the reporter's neck. Jude pretends he can't get his hand in his pocket properly whilst sat, quickly stands up and, as he does so, turns. Behind him he sees Mick furtively putting his hand back inside his old overcoat. Jude pulls two grubby one-pound notes from his pocket. 'I've got two quid left. I need to make a phone call; you two go to the supermarket and I'll catch you up.' He holds out the notes and Mick quickly grabs them. Jude notices that Mick's trousers are stained around the crotch area; he's obviously pissed himself, and the reporter wonders if it's a regular occurrence.

'Sees you later,' Mick calls as the two hurry off towards the supermarket.

Jude believes he's as cold as he's ever been in his life. Despite the layers of clothing, he struggles to feel his fingers and toes, and his ears sting. The cold has seeped into the deepest parts of his body and he's sure he'll never heat up again. It's obvious that Mick and Des aren't going to make it back to St Dismas and would be sleeping rough tonight, despite the ever-falling temperature. Maybe alcohol and practice make you immune to the freezing cold, but the strong ale isn't helping Jude. He plans to stay with the pair until they return to the hostel and, if they don't make it, sleep rough with them. But he now realises that, as soon as his money finally runs out, things are likely to turn really ugly. He calculates that, if it came to a fight, he, a fit guy in his early 30s who went boxing training, could take the two out-of-shape alcoholics. But that is hardly the point. And he was bloody freezing. Why not call it a night? He has more than enough for a heart-wrenching article of the plight of the homeless in the city. *The Reporter's* readers will get a first-hand account of the life of Southampton's rough sleepers: a story of bitter cold and cold bitterness.

'Bugger it,' Jude decides, 'I'm going home to the warmth of the pub, I might even have a nice hot bath to defrost.' For the first time, Jude realises that Mick and Des don't have his choice. They could have gone back to St Dismas but the money for another drink had taken out that option.. For an alcoholic, there isn't a real choice. 'I can at least give them my emergency fiver,' Jude thinks and takes off his right shoe to retrieve the cash, 'they can have another beer to keep the cold out.'

Shoe replaced, he hurries along the pathway, in the direction of the supermarket, through the middle of Hoglands Park. The cold permeates every inch of Jude's body on the moonless night as he heads towards the dim glow of the solitary streetlight, standing above the meeting point of the major paths right in the middle of the park. Hearing the muffled noise of a violent coming together - a football being kicked hard, or a boxing glove hitting a punchbag - he stops abruptly. The next noise is unmistakable, a groan uttered in pain. Without being sure why, Jude ducks behind one of the park's huge oaks, just a foot off the concrete pathway. He peeps out slowly and can just make out, maybe 50 yards away and under the glow of the streetlamp, Des on the ground, holding his stomach. Mick is standing apart and three big men, well-dressed in thick overcoats against the cold, stand around the prone figure. The words, 'OK, Brian, that's enough,' float to Jude on the still-night air. Standing next to Des must be Brian, who draws his right leg back as it to kick the alcoholic, aims but stops his foot inches away from Des' head, and laughs. The man who'd told Brian to stop must be the group's leader. He takes a step towards Mick, opens his wallet, pulls out a note and drops it on to the floor. Mick immediately darts for the money and scoops it into his coat pocket. The group's leader nods and, without saying a word, the three men head along the path and the tree Jude is hiding behind. The reporter jerks his head back behind the oak and presses his nose hard against its bark, hoping the wide tree will offer protection.

Jude feels his pounding heart race into overdrive. He thinks through his options: 'Run, but I've had a few beers and these are three fit-looking blokes; fight, ridiculous, see option one; or stay where I am and edge round the tree as they go past, hoping they don't see or hear me.' He decides on the final option. But suddenly, he can't move. His thoughts have frozen him to the spot, his body paralysed by fear. 'Three big men, one called Brian, what are the chance of that, unless they're the Quirk boys?' he rationalises. 'And there's only one reason they're in Hoglands tonight.'

The steps get louder, closer, heading directly towards Jude's tree. He can hear the men's conversation. 'I fucking told you, we should have got here earlier, but, no, Brian's had to go and see someone. We should have been here as soon as it was dark.'

An older voice took over. 'So, do we believe those two, that the journalist has fucked off? Brian, you didn't learn any more by hitting him, did you? He was scared enough, he pissed himself. They're fucking alkies and winos, that's all. A drink, or money to buy one, would've got you further than a giving him a kicking.'

Jude hears a new voice, definitely younger than the previous two. 'I was just making sure he told us everything, wasn't I? You didn't need to give him any bloody money. Why bother, Bill?'

'Because they'll now go and buy more sherry or whatever they drink, get really pissed and forget all about seeing us, that's why.' The voices are so loud and the steps so close. Jude realises he's holding his breath, that, thank God, some form of involuntary survival mechanism kicks in and he's slowing and silently edging around the tree, keeping the oak's generous trunk between himself and the gang.

Brian speaks, directly level with Jude, and no more than a few feet away in the darkness. 'The reporter could be hiding, we should have a good look around the park, just in case. This'll be the ideal spot to "have a word" with him.'

The snap of a twig under Jude's foot sounds as loud as a gunshot in the still, freezing air. 'Fuck!' Jude thinks, realising he's as scared as he's ever been in his life.

'What was that?' Brian asks quickly, loudly.

There's a second noise, a click. Despite staring into the tree's trunk from an inch away, Jude's peripheral vision, from his left eye, registers a glowing light. 'One of the three must have flicked on a torch, at least it's not a gun being cocked,' he thinks.

'Brian, for fuck's sake, it's a squirrel. Or a hedgehog,' Bill says.

The torchlight flicks around. 'I'm going to have a look,' Brian says aggressively.

Despite not believing in God, Jude silently prays. 'Please don't look around the tree, please don't look round.' He stands stock still, so close to the tree its bark dents his nose. Despite imminent death from his lungs bursting, Jude continues to hold his breath. There's another click. This time it really does sounds like a pistol being cocked. 'My God, he does have a gun. If Brian takes two more steps and shines his torch...' Jude fights to control the panic gripping his mind and body and tries to work out his options. He does: there aren't any. Jude returns to his silent prayer. 'Just turn back and keep walking, Brian, just turn and join your brothers, please!'

Bill is confident and assertive. 'I believe the alkies. Brian, leave the squirrels alone. Let's fuck off to Bojangles, grab a drink and warm up. It's perishing out here. Come on!'

One more step and Brian will be able to see Jude in his torchlight. The reporter shuts his eyes, as if he's about to be executed. The noise of the dull steps on the park's frozen grass stops. Jude doesn't know if Brian is staring at him and pointing the gun at the back of his head, or has stopped to consider his big brother's instructions.

'Bollocks. OK, I'm coming,' Brian says reluctantly.

'A drop of Scotch will warm us up,' the middle brother, Ben says.

Three sets of footsteps head away from the oak tree and along the concrete path. 'At least if mum phones the club, we'll be there and she won't be suspicious.' Bill lowers his voice. 'Don't mention this to her, she won't be happy about us looking for the journalist. She says she's given him a final warning.'

Over an age, the conversation and footsteps fade to silence. The only noise in the dark park is the hoot of a distant owl. Jude continues to stand motionless, nose buried in the bark of the tree, not sure how long it will be before he is safe, the brothers out of ear and gunshot range. But he does, at last, allow himself to breathe again. He waits another full minute before slowly turning his head and looking in the direction the three thugs had taken. Satisfied he cannot see anything that's a threat, Jude decides now is the time to make his escape, in case the brothers change their plans and return. The reporter is freezing, especially in his crotch area. Jude looks down and sees why. The rough sleepers aren't the only ones who have pissed themselves.

Ahead, under the lonely streetlight, he can see that Des is, with Mick's help, now standing. The reporter realises if it wasn't for the two friends refusing to give him up to the Quirks, it would be Jude, not Des, recovering from a beating. Or not recovering…

Jude walks towards the solitary light. 'Des, Mick, are you alright? Should I call the police?'

Des drew himself up straight. 'You've got a lot to learn, laddie. We don't call the police; they're not interested in us. We're just a problem to the bizzies.'

'Let me at least get you an ambulance, get you checked over in hospital after that beating.'

Mick pulls a £20 note from his pocket and waves it as if it were a miniature flag. 'This is all the medicine Des here needs. Is that right, big man?'

Des forces a smile. 'That wasn't a beating, when I used to box... anyway, let's no' waste time here talking, there's drinking to be done.'

Jude raises his hand to stop them walking off. 'Thanks for not giving me up. I owe you both, big time. You didn't have to...'

Des answers the journalist's implied question. 'Those bastards asked if we'd seen anyone unusual: better dressed, younger than the normal crowd of drinkers in the park. I said maybe, but my memory didn't work well when it was dry and a drink might help lubricate it.'

Mick took over the explanation. 'They were twats. That's when the youngest one hit Des in the stomach, saying, "That's all the fucking lubrication your memory needs."

Des finishes the story. 'So, I said you'd been here and then fucked off. If he'd offered a fiver, we'd told him where you were, soon enough. The tight cunt. I don't like being threatened, never have.'

The two pals head off in the direction of the supermarket and Jude calls after them. 'The shop'll be shut by now.'

Des turns around. 'Aye, but Old Gupta lives above. If we bang the door hard enough, he'll look out the window and we'll waive the £20 note. He'll open up for that, make no mistake.'

CHAPTER 19

What's There to Celebrate?

The old Peugeot's door is frozen to its rubber gasket and refuses to open. Jude eventually frees the passenger door and clambers across to the driver's seat. The car's heater blows cold air around the Peugeot cabin without heating it, the wet crotch of Jude's trousers has frozen solid and, during the long drive home to *The Proud Stag,* the reporter reasons that he's suffering from mild hypothermia and information overload. He tries to examine and make sense of what happened in the park, but struggles to find his usual coherency and insight. He can only think that one of the Quirk boys must have been tipped off that he'd be in Hoglands tonight. Mentally, he lists who knew about his plans to spend the evening with the rough sleepers from St Dismas.

'There was the manager of the hostel, but he wouldn't have a clue about the Quirk connection. Rule him out. Jimmy, Sarah and Robin; no, they're my mates, work colleagues and journalists, for God's sake. Not them. That leaves only Del. He said he was going to ask the sergeant at Central nick to increase police patrols. The sergeant and any police officers he told can also be added to the list. One of the Quirk boys must have been given the nod from a police officer. And where were the police patrols? I didn't see any, more's the pity. Did Del actually tell the sergeant at Central? Then, Hoglands is a bloody big park, but it was certainly convenient for the Quirks that no officers were around.'

After a fitful night's sleep, Jude is bleary-eyed at work the next day and decides, for the moment, to keep quiet about his close shave with the Quirks. The writing of the article about the rough sleepers is almost complete when Jude, without meaning to, says 'Bollocks,' aloud.

'Did the cold last night induce Tourette's Syndrome?' Robert asks and smiles.

'No, well, possibly. I've just realised I haven't asked Des and Mick, the two guys I spent last night with, for their permission to use their names. It doesn't matter – I don't need to, legally, and they're never going to complain.'

'Why don't you, Jude, and ask if I can take their photo at the same time? I've not got a lot in the diary today.'

The reporter dials the number for St Dismas and asks the hostel manager if he knows where Des and Mick are likely to be. There's an uneasy silence down the phone line. 'Sorry, of course, Jude... Look, you don't know, do you.'

'Don't know what? I mean, what don't I know?'

'It's Des. A milkman found his body, all but frozen solid, early this morning. It was half hidden behind a skip near the park; it's one of the regular places our rough sleepers use if they don't get into to the hostel. It offers a little privacy from passers-by.'

'Hang on. Did you say Des is dead? He can't be, can he? It was less than 12 hours ago I was with him. Er, what caused the death?'

'There should be a post-mortem but, because it's a rough sleeper and post-mortems are expensive, they may find a reason not to bother. There were no major signs of violence. Poor Des, look, you saw for yourself, he wasn't in great shape, none of them are, not really. There were a lot of empty beer cans around the body. Guess he found some money from somewhere. You didn't buy him drink, did you? The temperature was below freezing last nights and Des was 62, which is pretty old for someone who's been drinking as hard and as long as Des has, er, had.'

'What, 62 is old, is it? And Mick, where's he?'

'Jude, you need to understand, everyone here is sad about

Des, but it's what happens. We do our best to get them off the booze, but, in truth, it's not easy.' The manager takes a breath to keep his emotions at bay. 'There's been no sight of Mick and I don't expect there will be, not anytime soon.'

'He didn't have anything to do with Des's death?'

'Very unlikely. Again, it's what happens. Mick, like all the rough sleepers, doesn't trust the police. He won't want to be around to answer any questions – he'll head off to Portsmouth or Bournemouth or Salisbury and lie low for a while, I suspect.'

During the call Jude feels all the air escape from his lungs. He thanks the manager and replaces the receiver, wondering if he's going to faint, he feels that dizzy. The reporter walks to the sink for a drink of water and tries to clear his head. Back at his desk, Jude grabs his typed story and tears it dramatically in half before throwing it in the bin. He threads two sheets of blank paper, as always, separated by sheet of carbon, into his old Imperial and starts typing furiously. His three colleagues exchange glances but say nothing.

When Jimmy sees the first draft of the story, he demands more: 'Every last bloody spit and cough.' The editor tells Sarah to start phoning the different authorities, local and national, who deal with the homeless and with alcoholics, and gets Robert to take photos of the site where the body was found, and of the outside of St Dismas, then to start trawling his library for pictures of the city's rough sleepers and then to check if the hostel has a photo of Des.

The resulting story, complete with Jimmy's headline of 'OUR CITY'S SHAME,' under the strapline 'sleeping rough, dying alone: the life of our homeless,' is the front-page splash, framed with a heavy black border, and runs to four pages inside. The editor adds a quote from Mahatma Gandhi, in bold 72-point type, that took up almost half of page three: *The true measure of any society can be found in how it treats its most vulnerable members.* Jude writes the story in the first person, describing Des's generosity, humour and fondness for a drink. How he shared a bitterly cold evening with a gregarious Scotsman just hours before his frozen body was found, alone and, prophetically, next to a rubbish skip. He tells how the charity, St Dismas, did its best on scarce resources to help, and how the manager had described Des as being 'pretty old, at 62' and how his death wasn't a surprise, 'it's what happens.' The journalist omits the fact that he'd bought Des strong beer, which may have contributed to his death. The report is brought to life by Robert's photos and given a sense of hopelessness from the quotes Sarah obtains from the local social services, the Health Service and the Home Office. All institutions express sadness at the loss of life, none accepts any responsibility or offers any real possibility for genuine change. It is difficult for any reader with a beating heart to get to the end of the article without feeling despair, outrage and deep sadness.

When Jimmy is finished setting out the story, he stands, rubs his neck and suggests an early exit to *The Osborne*. 'This week's *Reporter*'s a great paper; we should recognise our achievement in the traditional manner. The first round's on me,' he says as he limps towards the door.

Sarah grabs her huge satchel and Robert slings his camera bag over his shoulder, both pleased with this edition of the paper and to be knocking off work early. Jude doesn't move from his desk.

'Come on, star journalist,' Sarah chivvies, 'you're buying the second round to celebrate your success.'

'I've nothing to celebrate,' Jude murmurs. 'A man's dead. How's that a party?'

Jimmy is halfway out of the office door, stops, turns and, from his one good eye, looks laser-like at Jude. 'Lad, don't go getting confused. We're not celebrating his death, we're celebrating that, thanks to our team, the four of us here, the world will now *know* of his death.'

Jude understands Jimmy's argument, but petulantly refuses to accept it. 'What difference will it make? How will our story help the others who will be sleeping rough tonight?'

'Those quotes, from the different authorities, highlight the real cause of Des's death: indifference. If it wasn't for us, the people of this city wouldn't have a clue about Des or Mick or the other rough sleepers. Jude, you and me, Robert and Sarah, we've stopped them, our readers, if only for five minutes, from looking the other way. That's what we do. That's what you should be proud of. Now, grab your coat, because that's what we're going to drink to.'

CHAPTER 20

The Big One

Jude's story causes major ructions across Southampton. The city council makes lots of announcements and issues press releases, the Echo and both the BBC and its independent opposition, TVS, follow up on the story. But Jude realises no new money will be forthcoming – he knows that if it had been, the politicians would already have been crowing about it.

In the week following the story's publication, Jude shares a lunchtime sandwich, at *The Osborne,* with his editor. Jude is still unconvinced his story of Des's unmourned death will achieve anything and is feeling depressed. 'Jimmy, the article was pointless – it's changed nothing. It's like a gun firing blanks, lots of noise and smoke, but no lasting after effects.'

'Jude, don't be so bloody morose. Look, your analogy is close, but think of it as a starting pistol.' The editor adjusted his eyepatch minutely. 'Yes, it fires blanks. But it's started something, a race if you like, and we don't know where it will end, who will win it. We've started something. It's what the press should do, in a democracy.'

'But it's not changed anything.'

'It has, it's changed people's knowledge; they can never unknow what they know, can they? We've no way of knowing what, if anything, will result from the story. But if you want to make changes, well, get yourself elected to the council or become an MP. That's your choice.'

'Suppose,' Jude says forlornly, before smiling. 'I don't think being a councillor is for me. Having to sit through bloody council meetings to report on them can be boring enough, but to take part... Please, shoot me now!'

Back in the office, Jude is further buoyed by a tantalising phone call from his old pal, Inspector Phil Broski. 'I can't tell you much about it, except bring your photographer with you and be at Dock Gate 20 for 6am tomorrow. I told you a while ago we were working on a major operation, this is it; the big one.'

It's cold and blowing a healthy northerly November storm at 5.45 the next morning but Robert and Jude are kept warm by the expectation and excitement of a great story, whatever it may be. Jude introduces his photographer to the inspector. 'Thanks for coming, sorry I had to be all cloak and dagger yesterday, but this is something of a combined operation, so if any intel gets out, I want to be bloody sure it's not from our side. We're working with Special Branch on this, they've got a base here in the docks and we've got a good relationship with them, so we're happy they're here – the more bodies the better. We've been monitoring a container on the seas for over a month. It's on a vessel that's docked at more ports than a horny sailor, but it's now going to be unloaded at its final port, Southampton. Because we're the biggest dock in Britain for containers and passengers, policing for drugs coming into the port is a real issue.'

Robert is impressed with this sensible, calm inspector. 'So, are you expecting a big haul?'

'Fingers crossed, but we won't know for sure until the container is landed. If the intel is correct, this will be the largest ever seizure of drugs in the UK. Right lads, jump in my car and I'll give you the background as we head out to the quayside.'

As they drive through the huge, grey docks the inspector says the container is to be offloaded from *The Pride of the Seas* directly on to a waiting railway truck. 'It's scheduled to head up immediately to the huge Freightliner terminal in Dudley, between Birmingham and Wolverhampton, as part of a large consignment of containers. We'd planned to follow it, to its final destination and then see who collects it and follow them. But the plan changed last night, and now the container will be impounded as soon as it lands on to the railway truck at the port.' The Inspector shakes his head. 'Hampshire Police have got involved. Apparently, because the container will cross a number of different police forces' jurisdictions, no one wants to take responsibility for the safety of the drugs from Southampton to Dudley. So, we won't be finding out who the end client is, the Mr Big.'

Inspector Broski brings his Ford Granada to a halt some 10 yards from the train line that runs along the dockside.

His frustration is clear as he says, 'I do understand – if the drugs go missing, well, it'd be a massive embarrassment. But it *is* also a massive opportunity to find out more about the drug distribution network.' The Inspector lets out a sigh. 'At least we're still taking a huge volume of drugs off the street and causing economic pain to whoever's bringing these drugs into the country. Right, let's go. Oh, that's all off the record, Jude, OK?' Jude nods in agreement, never expecting to be able to report the internal workings of the police forces, but pleased to understand the big picture.

The container ship is massive and next to it, dockside, is crazy busy with men and machines scurrying around, hopelessly trying to find shelter from the growing storm. Two huge blue cranes monotonously lift containers from the stack on the vessel's deck and lower them, either on to more stacks on the quayside or directly onto the freight train's expectant trucks. The containers swing violently on their chains as the gale continues to grow in strength and it takes all the skill from the crane operators to guide their heavy, swinging and heeling loads to safety. Below, on the ground, they're guided the final few feet of their descent by the brawn of an army of dock workers pulling on dangling ropes.

Jude opens the Granada's door and hears the throaty growl of a V8 engine as a Rover SD1 skids impressively to a halt a few yards away, between the train track and dockside.

'Oh no, that's all I bloody need,' the inspector says, half under his breath. 'Smarties and his old mates from vice. Bloody great!'

Jude overhears the inspector. 'Smarties, do you mean Chief Inspector Michael Matthews? I thought it was only the city's working girls who called him that.'

'I think they used it first; how do you know him, Jude?' the inspector smiles.

'He runs the press office now, although I've never met him or even spoke to him.'

A tall impressive figure, hair heavily Brylcreemed in place, large moustache perfectly clipped, leaps from the Rover and shouts, over the wind, towards the Transport Police Inspector, 'Good to see you're here, this must be the Bronski Beat.' And laughs loudly.

Broski's face reddens. 'Chief Inspector, as I suspect you're aware, there's no N in my name, like there's not one in Smarties.'

Chief Inspector Matthews looks unimpressed. 'No matter, you're still a,' the chief inspector emphasises, *Smalltown Boy*. Right, what's happening. Everything under control, Inspector?'

'I think so, although I am rather surprised to see you and officers from vice here.'

The Chief Inspector pulls his sheepskin coat tightly around his tall body. 'As head of press relations, I think it's vital that I'm here, especially if this is to be the largest single haul of drugs ever landed, although I'm only here in an advisory role. And vice will be responsible for the safe storage of any drugs, given its expertise and the expected amount, once you've impounded them.'

'Sir, can we chat in private for a moment?' Broski asks. The two officers move away from the little group and talk animatedly before rejoining the journalists.

The chief inspector looks at Robert and Jude. 'Ah, the gentlemen of the press. Your names?'

'Jude Devlin, journalist on *The Reporter*,' Jude replies, almost shouting to he heard over the ever-growing gale, 'and this is our photographer, Robert Freeman-Adams.'

The chief inspector ignores the pair. 'Shame you couldn't get the major media involved, Bronski. Still, no worries, I've got TVS turning up in a couple of hours, that'll give us time to weigh and count the haul.'

Broski thinks it'll also allow Smarties time to find a nice dry spot inside, comb his hair and arrange to be interviewed against a backdrop of an artfully arranged drugs haul. His thoughts are interrupted by the loud clang of metal on metal, followed by a high-pitched screeching and a tremendous bang. The whole group look around to see a dirty blue container, directly above them, falling from the sky. The massive metal rectangle stops abruptly, then dances and bounces. It's now held by just one of the four chains that the crane lifted it from the ship with, and swings precariously like a mad, giant pendulum. The wind pushes the container, each time higher and higher, like a wild playground ride. The container clangs into *The Pride of the Seas'* hull and then crashes into it again and again, blown by the storm force winds. Everyone watching realises the container could break free at any second and come crashing on to the quayside where they stand.

Inspector Broski yells as loud as he can for everyone to move back from the under the swinging metal box. Some can't hear him in the fierce winds or are rooted in place by the intense drama. He physically pushes them away from the side of the dock. The container continues to swing wildly and chaotically in the ever-increasing storm, smashing into the vessel, ripping its metal plates and gouging a gash in the huge ship's side. The crane-driver slowly and sensibly moves the wildly swinging container as far away from the quayside and vessel as he can, out over the turbulent sea, but its wild gyrations still put the ship and quayside in jeopardy.

The group of five police officers and two journalists gather a safe 100 yards back from the quayside. All heads are pointed at the crazy dancing container and Inspector Broski listens to a message on his police walkie-talkie and nods. He shouts to be heard as he tells the group that his concerns are correct. 'That's the container we've been following.'

As he finishes shouting, the blue container's doors finally burst open and an unending supply of cardboard boxes arc out of its moving mouth, scattering into the seething Solent below. 'Oh fuck,' Chief Inspector Michael Matthews shouts, and, catches the eye of his senior Vice Squad colleague and nods towards his Rover. The most junior of the Vice Squad officers is ordered to risk his life by collecting the police vehicle, which, despite the crane driver's efforts, is still under the extreme end of the container's oscillating arc. The terrified officer sprints to the car, jumps in and leaves rubber on the dockside from the Rover's squealing tyres, before parking the vehicle next to his superiors. Seconds later the remaining chain fails and the container smashes down onto the docks, first hitting the spot where the Rover had just been parked, before clipping the edge of the flatbed train wagon waiting for it, and finally bouncing over the quay's unprotected edge and into the foaming sea below. Smarties shakes his head, jumps into the now waiting Rover and is quickly followed by the two Vice Squad officers, and the car speeds away from the dockside.

'Not quite the triumph Smarties was hoping for, then,' Jude says to the photographer as the pair watch brown boxes bounce in the turbulent Solent. 'Robert, for fuck's sake, where's your camera?' Robert has been transfixed by the action, shakes his head, grabs his camera bag and instantly starts shooting. The first boxes out of the container are already heading down the Solent. The boxes are pushed by gale-force winds and the ebbing tide: some become waterlogged and disappear under the grey waves, others bob and dance and head towards the Isle of Wight, battered by wave after wave. A police launch is standing by and does it best to round up the floating boxes but is defeated by a combination of extreme weather, tide and sensible safety concerns.

Inspector Broski walks over to Jude, puts his mouth to Jude's ear and shouts fiercely to be heard. 'What a cock-up and bloody unlucky it should be the exact container, the one we've been tracking, with the drugs inside, that got smashed. You saw me talking to Smarties privately. I told him I was postponing the operation until this storm blew itself out. But bloody Smarties overruled me, despite being here only in an "advisory role". He said, "We can't let the TV down." Then he can't get away quick enough, desperate not to be connected with this fucking farrago, in case it slows his next promotion.

'Sorry Jude, the shows over for today. I'll need to sort this mess out – I'll get someone to run you back to your car. Give me a call this afternoon and I'll let you know what's happening. OK?'

Jude and Robert thank the inspector, shake his hand and head back to *The Reporter* office.

CHAPTER 21

Half a Glass

Later that day Inspector Broski phones Jude to say the whole job has been taken out of his hands. 'Hampshire Police has claimed jurisdiction and will run the show from here on in. I reckon they're trying to keep a lid on Smarties' cock-up. Nothing is going to happen today, Hampshire has decided that the weather will remain too rough for divers, so efforts to recover the container and its contents will have to wait until tomorrow.'

Jude asks his Transport Police pal if he's disappointed. 'Not really, Jude. I've enough on my plate and this is going to take some sorting out. And let's not forget that a huge volume of drugs now won't find their way on to the streets. I prefer to believe the glass is half full, rather than half empty.'

He asks Jude to inform *The Reporter's* readers that any packages washed ashore should be immediately handed to the police. 'But the geniuses from the Vice Squad say there won't be anything washed ashore. They say the cardboard boxes will break up and the plastic bags inside will be torn open by the sea and the drugs will be washed away harmlessly. Regardless, Jude, I'll get a press release issued a little later.' The inspector laughs. 'And if any of your readers are fishermen, tell them not to eat their catch for a while.'

Over a coffee, Jude explains the latest development to his colleagues. Robert checks the weather out of the window and is surprised that the storm has passed and the sun is now shining weakly. 'Looks fine to me outside,' he says and turns on the office TV to check the weather forecast on Ceefax. 'The wind will continue to die down, according to the BBC. Don't see the problem for a dive.'

Jimmy laughs. 'And when did you, Robert, become qualified to judge when it was and wasn't safe to go SCUBA diving?'

Robert's eyes widen. 'When I gained my PADI Divemaster qualification, I suppose. I've been diving since I was about 12, on family holidays in the Caribbean at first, then the Keys. Bit warmer than diving here in the UK.'

Jude smiles from ear-to-ear. 'So, do you have any cameras, you know, that work under water?'

'Of course; it's the same camera,' Robert lifts his F1 Canon 35mm SLR from his bag. 'But it fits into a special watertight container and I've got really high-powered underwater lights. You need them if you're going to dive and take photos in British water.'

'So why don't we go and take some photos?' Jude asks.

Jimmy stops the conversation. 'No, lad, no. It's too dangerous and we'd be breaking all sorts of laws. I'm up for this story, but if anything happened, Alex would have us all sacked. You know I'm on thin ice already.'

Robert is not so easily dissuaded. 'Jimmy, I don't think we'd be breaking any laws. I'll have to enter the water outside of the Docks, so we're not trespassing, and swim to the container. Anyway, no one would know I was there. And, to be fair, I'm the only person qualified to judge if the conditions are safe.'

'This sounds dodgy to me,' the editor says, thinking that, just once, a quiet day in the office would be welcome. 'What happens if something goes wrong? You're injured or arrested?'

'What can go wrong? I'm experienced and wouldn't be doing anything illegal. And, if I time it right, just when the tide's turned and the water is flat, I could slip into the sea at Mayflower Park, swim underwater the mile of so down to *The Pride of the Seas* in the container port and take photos of whatever is there.

Then I'll be pushed back to the park on the ebb tide. It'll take, what, 40 minutes, an hour, tops.'

Jude nods in agreement. 'Jimmy, just imagine, if it does work... Robert could get a photo of a fortune in drugs, all scattered on the seabed in Southampton Docks. What an exclusive, the pics would go round the world.'

Jimmy is wavering. 'I don't know. It's still a risk.'

Jude goes for the kill. 'And, who knows, Robert might even be able to pick something up off the floor and bring it back; the drugs should be OK, they'll be wrapped in plastic to beat the sniffer dogs. What a headline that would give you, Jimmy, "*THE REPORTER FINDS POLICE'S MISSING DRUGS*" next to a photo of Robert in his diving gear.'

The editor scratches his eyepatch, obviously considering the plan. 'Robert, only if you're sure. Be bloody careful and if you think for one moment that someone may see you, just turn around and let's live to fight another day. OK?'

Robert smiles excitedly. 'Thanks Jimmy, this will work out, I know it. Right, I'm off home to collect my diving gear, the camera housing and lights. See you, Jude, at Mayflower Park in 90 minutes or so, the tide will be perfect then.'

Both photographer and reporter leave the office and, with Sarah out on an interview, Jimmy is alone and immediately regrets allowing himself to be talked into this unpredictable expedition. He grabs his battered old briefcase and decides to seek solace in the public bar of *The Osborne.*

At Mayflower Park the normal number of dog walkers, joggers and mums pushing prams is well down on usual; they'd made plans earlier in the day, when the storm was at its worst. Jude is pleased; there's less chance of having to answer silly questions from busybodies. Robert zips himself into his wet suit, pulls on his flippers, spits into his mask, checks the regulator of his diving kit, and pushes off from the corner of the park into the cold sea. Almost instantly he disappears from view, a few bubbles popping through the murky-grey water the only evidence that Robert still exists.

Robert knows he should have been attached to a buoy, to warn boats where he is...but that would have been a dead give-away. Instead, he's swimming at a lower depth than usual, away from sharp propellors and dangerous keels. The busy ferries to and from the Isle of Wight leave from further along the Solent, so Robert has one less concern. It's more than 15 minutes of hard swimming before Robert can, he believes, just make out the huge hulk of the underwater hull of *The Pride of the Seas* above him. It's dark-grey form emerges from the lighter greyness of the dirty Solent, still churned from the morning's storm. Robert smiles, lifts the bottom of his mask slightly and exhales through his nose to clear the sea water that's slowly seeped under its rubber gasket.

He spots a dull light, first one and then, straining his eyes, two, no, three more. The lights move around, two as low as him, some 50 feet down, near the seabed, the other two a little higher. The photographer realises they're divers, holding torches, or, most probably, wearing head torches that leave both hands free. 'So, the police have changed their plans. Interesting,' Robert thinks, and calculates that the nearest diver is more than 40 yards away. Given the murky sea conditions and that Robert's own torch is switched off and safely attached to his belt, he's confident that he's too far away to be seen by the police divers. Robert swims a little closer before treading water and quietly observing what is happening. The two lower divers are collecting items from the seabed and loading them into a large net – there must be a support vessel above, he figures, and thinks he can see the rigid orange hull and inflated sides of a diving RIB. The light from the second pair of divers' head torches occasionally illuminates the long, heavy chains they are manoeuvring into place. The black silhouette of one of the diver changes direction, his light shines down, on to the container, damaged and sitting awkwardly on one end on the seabed. The plan must be, Robert reasons, for the divers to attach the chains to the container and for it to be lifted out of the water and on to the quay.

Still treading water, the photographer ponders his options

and, despite Jimmy's advice, decides the swimming policemen are too busy concentrating on their own jobs to notice him. He silently swims a little closer, stopping some 25 yards from the hull of the *Pride of the Sea*. The divers work to attach the lifting chains, their headsets illuminating the container more consistently and clearly. Its gaping, open mouth pointing upwards reminds Robert of a shot he took in the spring, of a cuckoo chick in a nest demanding to be fed. Below, the lights of the two divers on the seabed pick out packages that they gather and drop into the weighted collecting net.

Robert realises his heart has been racing ever since he first spotted the underwater lights through the gloom, which means he'll be burning up his precious oxygen at a much faster rate than he'd anticipated. He checks the dial of his SPG to see how much gas is left in his tank and is shocked to find that he's used up 70 per cent of his supply already. 'Idiot,' he thinks, 'of course, swimming so deep and then getting stressed, no wonder I've used up so most of my air.' Robert consciously tries to slow his heart and breathing rate by taking long, slow breaths. Time is running out and, while the murky sea may offer him protection, it also means his photos will be poor quality and probably unusable. 'I'm too far away to use my photo lights or even a flash and, if I do, it'll alert the police divers I'm here. Definitely not a good idea – I don't fancy an underwater race against four full-time divers with, probably, full tanks of oxygen and help from their support boat.' Robert sees the chains are now attached and all four divers are in a row, level and with their backs to him. They are all studying the container as the slack slowly disappears from the chains hanging from above. The divers hold their position with the slow, funereal rhythm of their flippers.

'There's only one option left. Come on, it's now or never,' the photographer tells himself, dips his head, lifts his feet and slowly pushes forward, gently oscillating his flippers. He stops some 10 yards behind and slightly to the left of the divers, who are still in a line and concentrating on the container. Its lowest edge, resting on the seabed, slowly, very slowly, starts to lift.

Robert moves his legs to ascend very slightly. He wants to shoot down, getting the divers in the silhouette of their own head torches. If he's very lucky those same torches will help illuminate the container and the remaining drug packages strewn on the seabed. His heart is beating furiously, and he tries to slow his breathing to minimise the tell-tell bubbles escaping from the regulator in his mouth. Robert checks his flash is turned off and is thankful he's loaded Ilford 3200 ASA, the highest speed film he has, into his camera and had decided earlier on to use a 40mm lens, wide enough to capture the whole scene. He has time for one photograph only and prays the police divers don't turn around; they won't be able to miss him from 10 yards away. But he will need a long exposure, selects a 30th of a second and prays that, in the moving sea, he can hold the camera steady long enough so the photo isn't blurred. Click. He has his photograph but won't know if it's usable or not until he's back in the office and developed the film. The container suddenly drops back down, one of its chains has come free and swings slowly as the metal box hits the seabed, causing a plume of silt to engulf the divers and improving Robert's chances of a safe getaway.

He quickly glides away, using long powerful strokes of his legs and flippers, his hands by his side to streamline his resistance in the water. Only when he's confident that he's distant enough from the police divers not to be seen, he checks his SPG again. Only 15% of air left. Robert decides on 'the lesser of two evils,' and stays deep in the water as long as he can, even though the extra pressure means his air will run out more quickly. He'll have to surface closer to *The Pride of the Sea* and to the eyes of the police and dock workers than he would have wished, but he'd rather be spotted than be chopped into mince by a spinning propellor. Robert swims just above the seabed and follows the line along the base of the quayside. Here and there he spots large, sunken pieces of cardboard. Robert reasons they're likely to be from the damaged container. Ahead he spots a whole box resting on the seabed, all but undamaged. 'How didn't I see that on the way here?' he wonders, kicking down to it and easily pulling the sodden cardboard apart. The lowlight level means he can't see the boxes interior but Robert reaches inside, feels a packet, pulls it out and pushes it into his underwater onion bag, next to his camera. Nervously he lifts his SPG to view its dial. Bloody hell! He's almost out of air. Robert swims fluidly, trying to stay calm and rises to just below the water's surface, hoping that no vessel come close. He realises that he's got cold, that the 12-degree temperature of The Solent in November has travelled through his 5mm thick wetsuit and is contributing to his feeling of fatigue. Robert has to breathe harder to get the last of the remaining air from his tank. He has no option but to surface and, worryingly, estimates he's still a long way from Mayflower Park. But at least now the tide has ebbed and is starting to push him in the right direction. Robert breaks the surface and looks around. He turns and can still see *The Pride of the Seas*, but isn't surprised. 'It's so bloody big you can probably see it from the Soviet Space Station,' he laughs to himself. Robert spots that the damaged container is now fully out of the water, the sea pouring out of its open doors. But he can't make out any individuals on the docks, just people-like shapes. 'Well,' he thinks, 'if I can't see them, they can't see me.' He ducks back under the water and starts swimming smoothly, breathing through his snorkel and heading for the edge of the park. 'What a job,' he thinks. 'I must get Jude to take my photo wearing my wetsuit – it'll make a change for me to have a photo byline.'

CHAPTER 22

A Chorus Line

The pair drive back to the office and Robert immediately heads for his little darkroom. He quickly processes the film and exposes a sheet of photographic paper to the one negative it contains. The cold has eaten its way from the sea and deep into Robert's bones and he notices that the plastic tongs he holds shake as he prods the paper in the developing tray. From past experience, he knows it will be hours before he feels warm again.

This moment, in his cupboard-sized darkroom, waiting for an image to appear, is always the most dramatic. Will much of the white of the paper disappear miraculously under slabs of black and grey to make a photo? It always does, he knows, but that doesn't lessen the magic. The photographer worries that the print may not even be useable – it might be blurred because of the slow shutter speed and the murky sea. Robert realises he's holding his breath.

As he continues to prod the paper, he thinks, for the first time since stepping back on to dry land, of the risks he took, of the vital safety rules he broke during his dive. 'Rule one, never dive without a buddy. How could I, as a qualified instructor, break that rule? If I'd had a buddy, we could have shared oxygen. What I did today was wrong,' he tells himself. But all his thoughts of rules and safety are washed away by the image that is slowly forming in the tray. 'It's not good,' Robert thinks, 'it's bloody spectacular!' He lifts the print from the dev tank and drops into the stop tank, counts to 10, then lifts it with fresh tongs and drops it into the fix tank and counts to 30. He moves the photo and holds it under the running cold-water tap, to remove any remaining chemicals, and then dries it with a squeegee.

Jude is waiting outside Robert's cupboard – there's not enough room for two inside – and breaks into a huge smile when he's shown the print. The four police divers form a chorus line, suspended to the right of mid-photo, each head-mounted torch creating an almost religious silhouetting halo of light. The beams from those same torches dramatically illuminate the damaged and open-mouthed container. Four heavy chains, one attached to each corner, are about to lift it clear of the murky floor. At the bottom of the photo, not as clear as the container, but certainly identifiable, a large string onion bag is sat on the seabed, half full of cardboard boxes and cellophane packets of illegal drugs, with more packets still on the ground. On the left of the photo, in mid-distance, is a large, slightly blurred skate or ray swimming past, oblivious to the action around it and looking as if it's been added for comic effect.

'Robert, this is brilliant. In one photo you've told the whole story. I almost don't need to write any words.'

'It's funny, the first I knew of the skate was when I saw it appear in the print. Guess I wasn't looking for wildlife when I clicked the shutter.'

It's now late evening, only the two journalists and Old Jones, who's stayed to lock up the newspaper building as part of his new, unpaid security duties, remain. The caretaker joins the pair and admires the photo. 'That's a bit dull, was there some fog?' Old Jones asks.

'No, Jonesy, it's underwater; I took the photo in the docks, today.'

'Well, that would explain the skate, I suppose. Well done, lad, well done. Right, best you two head off home, my missus will be wondering what's happened to me.'

The pair collect their things and are about to drive out of *The Reporter's* car park when Old Jones appears from the front door and waves his broom towards them.

'Oi! You two, do you need this tonight?' the old man calls. He's holding the plastic packet that Robert had fished from the sodden cardboard box on the seabed. The photographer gets out of his car, shakes his head and walks towards the building. Old Jones has already torn open the plastic wrapping and is dipping his finger inside. 'What is it, sherbet, for the kids?' he asks and puts his white-stained finger into his mouth.

'No, don't... oh, bloody hell, Jonesy. I might have to take you to hospital, now.'

Old Jones spits into the dirt at the base of the solitary, leafless standard rose in the flower bed by the front door. 'That's bloody disgusting.'

'It's heroin. You shouldn't be taking it.'

'It bloody isn't.'

'It is, pure stuff, really strong and dangerous.'

Jude joins them, half smiling that the old caretaker has taken heroin, half concerned at what it may do to him. 'Bloody hell, Old Jones, what have you done. Let's get you inside and sit you down.' The reporter takes the old man's arm and tries to usher him back into the building.

Old Jones shakes his arm free. 'You idiots, what do you think I am, senile? Don't answer that! I know bloody talcum powder when I taste it. I was playing this game once with my wife, Chloe, after she got out of the bath. Well, enough about that, just to say I tasted talcum and it's bloody horrible. Give me sherbet any day of the week.'

Jude looks disbelieving but Robert licks his finger, pushes it into the white powder in the bag, and then tastes it. 'Ugh, he's right. It's talcum, I think.'

'Of course, I'm bloody right. Now, do you want this or can I give it to my Chloe, for after her bath?'

Jude grabs the bag. 'Sorry, Old Jones, we need it. Look, tell your Chloe is she does want some, there may be a lot of this turning up along The Solent over the next week or so.'

First thing next morning a high-level strategy meeting of *The Reporter's* editorial team is convened. Well, to be more exact, Jimmy, Sarah, Jude and Robert sit in the newsroom, drink instant coffee, eat biscuits and wonder what to do next.

Jimmy sums up the situation. 'From what you're saying, after a botched drugs raid a huge quantity of heroin falls into the Solent.'

Jude smiles awkwardly and nods. 'In a nutshell, kind of, that's it, Jimmy. But what do we do with what we know and the little of it we can prove?'

The editor continues. 'So, Hants police say the weather is too dangerous to send in divers to get the drugs but then, secretly do exactly that and lift the container off the seabed. They fish up, excuse the pun, all the drugs they can find without anyone knowing, but the drugs aren't drugs at all, they're talc, which looks like heroin. Is this just plain mad, or am I missing something important?'

Sarah's unimpressed. 'Look, the weather got better, so they changed their plans. That's how it seems to me. Of course, the police are going to want to collect the haul as soon as possible, that's obvious. And are we sure the package is talc? What proof do we have, other than Old Jones? I mean, shouldn't we get it tested first?' She takes a bite of a Jaffa Cake. 'Yum, these are good. Even if the packet we've got isn't heroin, it doesn't mean that the rest isn't. Er, that sounded complicated. I mean, how do we know the other packages aren't heroin? That's just one package. Isn't it possible that it got mixed up with something, by you, Robert? Or Old Jones?'

Robert feels his competence is being questioned. 'Sarah, I was there, no one else. I picked that package out of a cardboard box off the bottom of The Solent. I put it in my diving bag and brought it ashore. It only left my side for a few minutes and then Old Jones gave it back to me.' Robert picks up the bag in question and holds it up to the light. 'This is the same bloody bag, look there's tiny bits of seaweed on the outside.'

Sarah finishes the biscuit and reaches for another from the open packet. 'OK, fair enough. But look, what about whoever did the packing of the drugs, one of the lower paid members of the gang, probably? Couldn't they have done a quick swap, pocketed a bag of heroin and replaced it with the talc, to make a small fortune?'

Jimmy nods in agreement. 'It does sound possible. We need some more samples of the drugs. If needs be, I've an old mate who could get the samples tested for us; he's a journo on the News of the Screws. If the story goes big, we'd have to give him first refusal, that's all.'

The phone on Jude's desk rings and he answers, interrupting the discussion. Soon the whole team are straining to listen to the one-sided chat. It's a pensioner, an avid reader of *The Reporter*, who's phoned in to say his collie, Shep, bit into a cellophane-wrapped package washed up on Netley's shingle shore during their walk this morning. 'There was white powder inside. I had to put Shep on his lead, there were dozens of the packets dotted along the shingle, just above the tide line. Just wondered if you could get the council to clear them up? If I phone the bloody pen-pushers, they'll just think I'm a busybody wasting their time.'

Jude and Robert dash down to the beach, rendezvous with Shep and his owner, take photos and then call Del at Hampshire Police to warn him that some of the drugs have been washed ashore. It's not long before half a dozen police cars, blue lights flashing and sirens wailing, converge on Netley, on the east of the city, and start cordoning off the long shingle beach with blue and white plastic tape.

Back in the office, Robert is rooting around the bottom of his large camera bag. 'Jimmy, a present for you.' He digs out three packets collected from Netley and drops them on to the editor's desk.

Jimmy jiggles his dark eyepatch. 'That's either enough there for me to retire on or keep Old Jones wife happy after her next dozen baths. Right, I've got some phone calls to make and some favours to call in. But we've got our splash for this week's edition, *Shep the Sheepdog Rounds Up Drugs on Beach,* with the strapline, *Fortune in Class A Drugs from Raid Washed Ashore in Netley.* I'm going to use Robert's brilliant photo over two pages as the centre spread. Jude, I want 800, no, make that 1,000 words; we'll run it on the front and on to pages 3, 4 and 5.

'No mention of suspicions the powder isn't what the police believe it to be, we'll keep our powder dry, another great pun, for the time being. And no mention that it's a cock-up. Let's not piss the police off, not until we're sure. Let's just say the weather conditions were extreme but the decision to go ahead with the raid was made. And Sarah, can you do 150-word caption to go with Robert's photo. Right, what are we waiting for? Deadline is,' Jimmy looks at his watch, 'two hours away. Let's go!'

CHAPTER 23

Anonymous

The team are delighted with the week's paper: the coverage of the raid on the container wipes the floor with the rest of the city's media. The first *The Echo* and TV and radio stations know that drugs have been washed ashore on Netley's pebble beach is when they read about it in *The Reporter*. Jimmy tells Robert he should enter his brilliant underwater photo of the police divers collecting the drugs into the National Press Awards.

Jude has overcome his early concerns about being a journalist and is starting to enjoy his life: he feels he can handle the job and, now that his cousin is paying for 'protection', living at *The Proud Stag* with Gerry and his family has settled back on to an even keel. OK, his love life currently lives next door to non-existent, but he's working on that and spends much of Friday finding excuses to hang around outside of the advertising office, trying to accidentally bump into Danielle.

On his sixth trip to the loo that morning – each expedition allows him to hover in the corridor outside of the advertising department – Danielle eventually emerges from the swing door to the advertising office. 'Jude, I keep seeing you head to the loo; aren't you a bit young to be suffering with incontinence. Don't tell me, dodgy curry last night?' She smiles, and as Jude's face colours, her smile turns to a knowing grin.

'No, er, yeah, something like that. Look, Danielle, I'm glad I bumped into you. You're not free tomorrow afternoon, are you?'

'No, and nor are you; Saturday afternoon you're covering the Saints-Aston Villa game for the paper, aren't you?'

'Yeah, that's right. I wondered if you'd like to come to the game, into the press box.' Jude looks at his shoes, trying to sound nonchalant. 'But if you've got other plans, no worries.'

'I do, actually, but my old Dad hasn't. He's not seen Saints live for years, not since his stroke; too much pushing and shoving, and he struggles to get through the turnstiles. He's always been a massive fan. But if you could drive to the car park at The Dell and get him safely into the press box without using a turnstile... he'd be really, really chuffed. Thanks, Jude, that's so sweet of you.'

'Er, yeah, great, my pleasure, he'll be safe with me.' Jude tries to work out how his plan to impress Danielle has turned into babysitting her disabled dad.

'Great, let me know what time you want to pick him up on Saturday and I'll give you Dad's, that's Tom to you, address. Must dash, layout are waiting for these designs.' Danielle skips off in the direction of the Layout Department.

Jude collects the second post from reception and, wondering how he can get out of taking Tom to the game without upsetting Danielle, distractedly opens the dozen or so letters. There are two press releases that might yield a story, and Jude is about to bin the rest when he again looks at a poor-quality Xerox copy now sitting on top of the pile. There's no compliment slip, no explanatory letter or note with the copy, and the reporter, his mind elsewhere, hadn't thought an almost illegible A5 form sent anonymously in the post was worthy of his attention. But he looks more closely and can just make out the heading: Home Office Destruction Order Certificate. Jude holds it up to the light and then looks at it with a magnifying glass he borrows from Jimmy, but the image is too dim to really make out anything other than the large print of the heading.

Robert is walking past and laughs at the reporter. 'What's the problem, Sherlock, struggling with the hieroglyphics?'

Jude grins. 'This copy is so faint and the writing's tiny. Don't suppose you can do something to make it clearer in that dark-room of yours?'

'I might, I've got a film in the camera with a couple of frames on the end that I'm waiting to use before devving it. Give it here and I'll have a play.'

An hour later Robert walks back into the newsroom and gives Jude an A4-sized photo. 'I had to play with the exposure and contrast a bit and waste quite a few sheets of photographic paper, but you should be able to make sense of it now'

The image is twice the size of the original and, although not perfect, certainly readable under the magnifying glass. 'Thanks Robert, I owe you. It's probably just some nutter, but I ought to check.'

Jude may never find out whether the anonymous sender of the copy was 'some nutter' or not, but he soon realises he's been sent journalistic gold. The form is the official Home Office docu-ment authorising the destruction of the cannabis seized on the first police drugs raid he went on, not long after he joined *The Reporter.*

But Jude has worked out that there are two anomalies on the form. The quantity of cannabis authorised for destruction is listed as 150 blocks, each weighing a quarter kilo, a total of thirty-seven and a half kilos of cannabis. The next line on the form asks 'Are all the illegal drugs from this operation being des-troyed under this authorisation?' The 'Yes' box is clearly ticked.

Jude knows the police stated that 300 blocks were seized at the raid. Privately the police admitted, when faced with Robert's photos of the scene, there was much more that they kept back to ensure they could meet future drug seizure targets. So, the weight of drugs authorised for destruction may be as little as a quarter of the total confiscated.

Secondly, the senior officer whose name is clearly printed and who's signed the Destruction Order is Chief Inspector Michael Matthews, aka Smarties, formerly of the Vice Squad but now, and at the date on the form, running the force's press office. 'Why would the head of the press office get involved in sending drugs to be destroyed, unless there was something in it for him?' Jude wonders.

Straight after lunch the reporter talks his editor, who, for once, returns to the office after a single pint at *The Osborne*, through the document with Robert and Sarah listening in. Jude hopes Jimmy will see it's as damning of the police as he does. But the editor is sceptical. 'Jude, number one, how do we know it's genuine? Number two, if it is, there could be perfectly logical reasons for what's happened. But just say, for a moment, that the document is genuine and there's no explanation for Matthews signing it or that half the drugs, maybe more, disappearing, then what is our story? Even better – and this is always the real test to see if a story really is a story, not just kind of interesting – tell me what the headline for *The Reporter* will be?'

Jude thinks for a moment. 'I guess the headline is, 'POLICE DRUGS GO MISSING', and we only mention Smarties' involvement tangentially. But I reckon this is the tip of the iceberg. What if those drugs are finding their way on to the street? What if, somehow, the dealers are getting them from the police?

'That's a bit far-fetched,' Sarah says, smiling. 'This is Southampton, not bloody Miami, Jude.'

Jimmy nods. 'Jude, Sarah's got a point.'

'How else are the Quirks getting drugs to sell so cheaply? What else has happened to the huge pile of cannabis if it isn't being sold? Why would anyone, especially someone in the police, take such a risk unless there's something, a lot, in it for them?'

As usual when faced with a decision, Jimmy fiddles with his eyepatch. 'OK, Jude. Ask the police press office. For obvious reasons you better speak to Del, not Smarties, I mean Chief Inspector Matthews. Oh, you also mention the drugs from *The Pride of the Seas* – that last phone call was from my mate on the News of the World. He's got the analysis of the powder that we sent him by Red Star. The lab rushed it through – Old Jones' wife is right; all four samples are talcum powder. Ask Del about that at the same time, will you? My mate wasn't best pleased to waste his paper's money on analysing talc.'

Del is his normal upbeat, amusing self and writes down Jude's questions as if he was jotting down a shopping list or directions to a restaurant, and promises to call the reporter back 'asap'. Before hanging up, Del's voice takes on a serious tone. 'Jude, you've been OK, nothing out of the ordinary's happened?' The reporter reassures the policeman that, no, all has been fine. 'Good, keep it that way, remember that advice I gave you? Stick to it. You should know that Comrade Robert's photo, which, by the way, I thought was brilliant, really pissed off the boys from vice, as did your article. But I've told them, you're both doing the job you're paid to do, and doing it very well. Keep up the good work. Byee.'

The following day, Jude is pleased to have a break from drugs and dodgy policemen and is looking forward to watching Saints' play. When he first started covering his beloved football team for *The Reporter,* he'd found he couldn't enjoy a match; he was too busy making notes, desperately trying to be impartial and analyse what he was watching. Now, almost halfway through the season, he's relaxed a little and can appreciate the rare occasions when Saints play well.

Despite his best efforts, Jude has no option but to take Tom to the game and find him a space in the already cramped press box, having failed to come up with a plausible excuse that wasn't sure to end his nascent relationship with Danielle. But the reporter is surprised to find he enjoys Tom's company; despite being frailer than his years, he's bright and funny, although his slurred pronunciation is, at first, difficult to understand. Danielle's father certainly knows all there is to know about The Saints after following them, man and boy, for more than 50 years. But he manages to wear his knowledge lightly and doesn't get in the way of the reporter doing his job.

Back at work on Monday, Danielle seeks out Jude to thank him. 'Dad loved the match, he reckoned Saints' striker, Colin Clarke, is going to be special.'

'He's cost the club a record fee, £400,000, and looks worth

every penny.'

'Dad was thrilled that you managed to introduce him to the manager.'

'Chris Nicholl was happy to say hello after the press conference. He's a good guy, always helpful. And he was in a good mood after the win.'

'Dad remembers him when he was a player for Saints; meeting him meant a lot. That was kind of you, Jude, you didn't have to do that. Thanks.' Danielle gives Jude the most radiant smile he's ever received, except, perhaps, from his own Mum.

Jude feels himself blushing, and mutters something like 'no problem' before remembering an important phone call he needs to make, and scurries off back to the safety of the newsroom.

Still embarrassed and not quite understanding why, Jude takes a call. It's Del from the police press office. 'Is that *The Reporter's* specialist drugs and football correspondent? Good, well, hopefully, Jude, I've some answers for you. You're right, if was Chief Inspector Michael Matthews who signed the destruction form. Unusual, given he's based here at the Press Office in Winchester. But, on that day he was visiting the Vice Squad in Southampton, to discuss publicity concerning a new initiative they're planning. The squad's chief inspector wasn't around and, as the document has to be signed by an officer of that rank or above, he offered to help out. So, no great mystery there. Matthews said that if the box on the form was ticked, the box that indicates all drugs from the one operation are being destroyed, well, that must have been a clerical error. He said that another load had previously been destroyed. Sorry, there's no great story for you, Jude.'

'Thanks for checking, Del. Look, I don't want to be a pain, but did Chief Inspector Matthews sign another destruction form for the other lot of drugs from the same raid?'

'I thought you'd ask me that, so I checked with Matthews and he said, "No, that lot was nothing to do with him.'

'Del, have you seen the other form, authorising the destruction of the rest of the cannabis from the raid?'

'Ah ha, I also knew you'd ask me that, you fiendish hack, you. To be straight with you, that's why it's taken me until today to phone back. In all honesty, Jude, I've checked and re-checked and can find no documentary evidence of any other drug destruction in connection with the cannabis from the raid in question. When I asked vice directly, everyone vaguely remembered it going to the incinerator in Marchwood, but can't prove it.'

'Del, don't take this the wrong way, but are you telling me the police can't track 150 blocks of cannabis, each weighing a quarter of a kilo, that it had in its safe keeping?'

'Jude, on the record, I have a statement prepared for you. I thought you'd push me on this, so here goes, hope your shorthand pencil is sharp: "Hampshire Police are confident that all cannabis confiscated from drug dealers and users in the county has been destroyed safely and securely at Hampshire County Council's incinerating facilities. However, some of the paperwork audit trail in connection with one such destruction is currently untraceable. This in no way impacts the security or the safe storage of drugs seized within the county. A senior officer will be conducting an enquiry into the appropriateness of the audit trail and make recommendations for any future improvements that he feels are necessary."'

'And off the record, Del?'

'At best, it's sloppy paperwork, at worse it's a huge embarrassment to the force and there's more than a few red faces in vice right now, I can tell you.'

'Thanks, Del, sorry to put you in a difficult position with your colleagues. And thanks for being so straight with me.'

'No worries, got to go, B–'

'Del, before you disappear, I've just thought of one last question. Who's the senior officer who's going to conduct the enquiry?'

'On the record, it will be someone with the relevant experience and standing from within the force who has the trust of all the various divisions of the force. This is an internal matter and we will not be releasing either the name of that officer or the results of his enquiry.'

'Off the record?'

'I couldn't possibly comment, Jude, but I've a question for you: what's your favourite, multi-coloured, candy-coated chocolate sweets that are only sold in tubes? Byee!'

The reporter slowly puts the phone back onto its cradle, not sure he's actually heard what he's just actually heard. He slides down his chair and runs his hand through his blonde hair, unsure of his next step. 'Bloody hell,' Jude says to himself.

CHAPTER 24

The Marvin Effect

'DOPEY POLICE "LOSE" £130,000 OF DOPE,' the front page of *The Reporter* shouts. Jimmy's strapline hits home 'is seized cannabis ending up on city's streets?' The editor is confident, after grilling Jude, that the story is rock solid and even the conservative managing director, Alex, is happy for the story to run, with the proviso that 'it's on your head, Jimmy, if every fucking word isn't gospel.'

The fact that the police have lost almost 40 kilos of cannabis they've seized from drug dealers and should have been holding securely is shocking to the casual reader of *The Reporter.* But to those inside or connected to the force, the fact the enquiry into the loss is to be conducted by Chief Inspector Michael Matthews, an officer implicated in the drugs loss, highlights a more systemic problem.

Early on Friday, the day after publication, Jude's phone rang. It was his old Transport Police inspector pal, Phil Broski. 'Hi, Jude, haven't seen you down the gym lately... come early tonight, say 7pm, and I'll give you an interesting session.'

Jude thinks the call is slightly weird – he'd seen Phil at the gym earlier in the week. Then the penny drops. 'Great, be there at 7,' he replies. He'd have to tell Danielle he couldn't pick her up until 8 but, she'd be fine with the slight change of plan...he hoped. It was Danielle who'd suggested they 'have a bite out together' as a thank you for taking her dad to watch The Saints.

The next caller isn't so friendly. Chief Inspector Michael Matthews – Smarties – is considered by everyone Jude knows as 'ambitious, charming and slippery,' except massage parlour owner Queenie, who simply hates his guts. There is no charm on this call.

'What the fuck are you doing, Jude? Have you gone stark raving mad? How much compensation and legal fees can *The Reporter* afford to pay out? Do you want any help from this police force ever again? How big are your balls?'

Jude stutters and falls over his words, nervous and worrying that he's screwed up the story, and allows the Chief Inspector to continue bullying him.

'Well, Jude, for your sake I hope you know what you're doing. I never, ever phone up to complain about a story. But to suggest drugs held by Hampshire Police are finding their way back on to the street is a fucking outrage and hits at the heart of the integrity of our force. You've got one chance to redeem yourself, Jude – and this is it. You quote an unnamed source who says, and I'm reading back your article directly here, "I have concerns that the drugs missing from the police are fuelling the epidemic of cheap drugs on the city's streets. Cannabis is only half the story; it's a gateway drug, leading to heroin, which is responsible for the great majority of overdoses causing hospitalisations and the current spate of deaths in our city." Who is it, Jude? Who is your unnamed source accusing the police of killing people?'

Jude moves nervously in his chair, knowing the Chief Inspector is trying to intimidate him. He remembers, from last year, the lecture at journalism college on 'integrity' – how a journalist must never reveal their source, even if it means being in contempt of court and ending up in jail. 'Chief Inspector, you know I can't and won't reveal my source.'

'I bet it's some fucking do-gooding social worker, probably off their head on drugs themselves, who doesn't know which end to fart out of. Don't you listen to them, Jude. It's total bollocks. Any more stories like this and I'll personally see the fucking *Reporter* is shut down and I'll have you done for libel. Do you understand, Jude? You'd better fucking understand, for your own sake.'

Smarties slams down his phone. Despite being sat safely in his own office, Jude finds he's shaking a little, and wonders how sensible it is to have made an enemy of not only a very senior police officer, but also the one who runs the press office. Before he can come to a conclusion, his phone rings again. This time the voice is female, frail and very old. After Jude introduces himself, the upper-class accent announces 'Young man, I've a complaint, my copy of *The Reporter* has not been delivered this week.'

'That's not a problem,' replies Jude absent-mindedly, 'I'll fill in a form and get a copy posted out to you.'

'That's no good to my *Tibbles* is it, what am I going to use to line his litter tray tonight?'

Jude all but collapses with laughter. The call is the antidote to Smarties' bullying he desperately needs, and as a thank you, he promises to drop a copy of the paper through the old lady's letterbox himself.

That evening, at the gym, in the quiet period when the after-work boxers have gone home and the serious evening workout brigade have yet to arrive, Phil asks Jude to go into his office. 'Have a look in the bottom of my old gym bag, under my desk. There's a file in there you'll find interesting. It's for your eyes and your eyes alone. Have a look, I'll make sure you're not disturbed, and make whatever notes you need. When you're done, put the file back where you found it. It contains all the forms completed when drugs are seized or confiscated, and a copy of all the Home Office drug destruction orders. Compare the two and you'll have a list of all the drugs held by the police that do not have a full paperwork trail.'

'You mean, drugs that have gone missing.'

'No, Jude, I mean drugs that do not have a full paperwork trail. What has happened to them, if they've gone missing or not, is a matter of speculation that, I, as a police officer, cannot make. That's for your readers to decide.'

'Thanks, Phil, I really appreciate this. How long have you known about drugs "disappearing" from the custody of the police?'

'I've had my suspicions for a while – there was a rumour that was the real reason Smarties got shunted sideways from the Vice Squad to the Press Office. But the container fiasco and then reading your story at home, last night, well, I couldn't sleep and went into work at 5am this morning to trawl through all the records I could access. Jude, what's been happening is shocking and taints the whole force. Well done for exposing it, keep it up. Now, get working and, when you've finished, get changed into your boxing gear and go and get a sweat on in the gym.'

'Sorry, Phil, I've got a date.'

'She'll have to wait, you can't come in here and go out straight away without doing a workout and having a shower; it'll look suspicious. You can make a call from my office, if necessary, to explain.'

So, Jude spent the next hour ploughing through the paperwork, becoming in turn surprised, amazed and finally totally bewildered. Shaking his head, he carefully replaces the file at the bottom of Phil's battered gym bag, covering it with a smelly singlet and trainers, and heads to the changing room, his bulging notebook safely in his jacket pocket. He knows he can do nothing about the story until he's back at work on Monday, so he focuses on skipping, punching the bag and shadow boxing until the sweat flows in small streams from his body. In the shower, he thinks of Danielle and smiles.

It's gone 9pm when he pulls up outside her flat. Jude is greeted by Ben E. King's *Stand by Me* playing on the stereo and a beautiful looking Danielle, who, instead of being annoyed, kisses the reporter on the cheek. 'I figured you might be later than you said when you called, so I decided to cook in, hope that's OK? It won't compare with the restaurant, just a steak, salad and a bottle of Cote du Rhone; what I could pick up at the corner shop.'

Jude is delighted, not only with his surprisingly warm welcome, but to have the chance to put the relationship on a proper footing, 'That's if Danielle sees this as a "relationship,"' Jude wonders.

'Great, sorry, I would have bought flowers or some After Eights or something. I was at the gym, it's in connection with the drugs story. I just can't believe the police are involved. But every week recently something happens and you can see everything is pointing back to our very own police force. Oh, sorry, you didn't suggest a night out to hear me banging on about drugs.'

Danielle cocks her head and smiles. 'No, it's interesting, more interesting than trying to get someone to increase their order from a one-column ad to a quarter of a page.'

Jude follows Danielle into the kitchen, where she starts preparing dinner. Jude pours himself a glass of the wine and tops up Danielle's glass, admiring the way she hadn't waited for him to arrive before having a drink. 'What did you decide about taking the sales rep's job? When we last had a chance to chat, you seemed really, I don't know, conflicted.'

'Well, Jude, I took your advice. You said, "These opportunities don't come round often." So, if I hate the job, then it's all your fault.' Danielle laughs openly and without inhibition.

'Very unladylike and very sexy,' Jude thinks. 'Let's toast your success,' he says, raising his glass, and 'chinking' it with Danielle's.

The two savour the red wine and then Danielle looks serious. 'But this isn't a career move. Or maybe it is. I'm going to work really, really hard and try to earn as much commission as I can. It might take a year or it might take two, but I'll save every penny to be able to put myself through college.'

'Wow, impressive. What will you study? Is this a career change?'

'I'm going to become a journalist – you took a year out and retrained, so it can't be that hard!' Danielle roars with laughter again, exposing her long throat, and then puts her hand over her mouth. 'Seriously, when I put my mind to something, well, I stick at it.'

'Congratulations. Of course, you can do it. And you're right, if I can be a journalist...'

'I've checked it out, there are grants available. It won't be easy, but it's possible.' Danielle looks down into her glass, her long, dark hair falls either side of her face, obscuring all but her chin. 'Look, I told you I'd broken up with someone. We lived together, actually, for a few years, never quiet making that trip down the aisle, thank God. But it's only since I left him that I realise how much he'd held me back, tried to control me, really. OK, he was happy that I paid half the bills, but he didn't want me to be successful, certainly not more successful than he was. So, if I've seemed a little, I don't know, stand-offish, well, I'm kind of protecting myself. I've decided that I'm never going to be held back or controlled by any man.'

Danielle raises her face, her hair falls away, and she looks straight into Jude's eyes, into his soul. 'Is that something that you can cope with? Not every man can.'

'Yes, Danielle, it's your life to lead as you want, I get that. We've got a woman Prime Minister, for God's sake. And she's proved she's got more balls and determination than the rest of the Cabinet combined.'

Danielle's shoulders seem to relax and she smiles again. 'That's the right answer. Jude, you're passing my tests: taking Dad to the football, giving him a memorable day out, and now revealing yourself as a women's libber. As a reward, I'll cook those steaks. Or perhaps you should?' The pair laugh and Jude realises he hasn't only passed Danielle's test, they've both moved forward and there's a real chance of something special between them.

The evening is wonderful; Danielle lowers her protective guard and Jude feels both relaxed and excited in her company. After a great meal, and after washing and drying up, the pair sit, only slightly awkwardly, together on Danielle's settee. With Marvin Gaye's *Let's Get It On* playing, they, inevitably, start to kiss, more and more passionately. Jude pulls away. 'Er, look, I wasn't expecting this. Maybe hoping, but I'm not quite... prepared.'

Danielle smiles quizzically, her full eyebrows almost joining together; not quite sure what Jude means.

'I've not got, you know, any condoms or anything.'

Danielle smiles again. 'Don't worry; I never quite made the trip down the aisle, and I never quite stopped taking the pill,' and pulls Jude back towards her.

CHAPTER 25

Transparent

Perhaps it's the rubbish singing, perhaps it's the ear-to-ear grin, or the offer to make coffee for everyone in the office. But, come the following Monday, Jude's three editorial colleagues at *The Reporter* don't need their investigative skills to deduce that the reporter's cup of bonhomie is flowing over.

Jimmy tries to ignore Jude's ebullience, but finally snaps. 'What's wrong with you, lad? Anyone think you've got eight score draws on Saturday, a call from Michelle Pfeiffer asking for a date on Sunday, and this morning Rupert Murdoch has asked you to become editor of the Sunday Times.'

'Well, I'm sure you'll be delighted to know that I've had an exceptional weekend, thank you, Jimmy.'

'We know, you're as transparent as the double-glazed windows that takes up half the advertising space in our paper.'

'And, wait for this, I've got a great follow-up to our missing police drugs story that's even better than the original.'

Jude stands, thumbs through his notebook, collects the coffee from his desk and walks the few paces to his editor's. 'The drugs that went missing from the police's secure stores, well, it isn't the first time, not by a mile. I've seen records stretching back a decade and each and every year, drugs have gone walkabout. Not only cannabis, but Class A drugs as well. Our story last week about the dope, that's the highest value to go missing, but in total there's more than a million pounds of drugs that can't be accounted for.'

Jimmy whistles through his teeth. 'Bloody hell. This is dynamite. How sure are you?'

'Jimmy, I've seen the records with my own eyes, the police records. It became so common that, a few years ago, Hampshire Police even amended its forms, adding a column entitled "Discrepancies". That's where a very brief explanation is written of any difference between what they should have in their stores and what is actually sent for destruction. In that column I've seen written: "admin error; clerical error; previous over-estimate; spillage." All total bollocks.'

'Jude, this is good work. I need to see the reports but this is a huge story. It'll be the splash and–'

'Sorry, I can't let you, Jimmy.'

'And four pages inside... Hang on, what do you mean, "You can't let me?" I'm your bloody editor.'

'My source, he's nervous it'll get back to him. He said they're for my eyes only, I wasn't allowed to take photos or move them out of the building. You'll have to trust me.'

'Bloody hell, Jude. You want me to trust you? You've only been here 10 minutes; you've had your probationary period extended for misconduct and now you want me to run a story saying the police have been stealing drugs for a decade? All on your say-so, with no evidence for me to actually see?'

'But it's all true, I've seen it with my own eyes, the original documents from an unimpeachable informant. You know I can't break my word to my source. You've told me as much, in no uncertain terms.'

Jimmy loosens his tie. 'I can already feel the noose tightening around my neck. Look, even if I did back you, there's no way Alex is going to let the story through unless I can prove to him it's watertight. You know that, Jude.'

Journalist and editor look at each other, an English, more civilised, version of a Mexican stand-off – more a 'who blinks first' kind of thing. Robert, habitually polishing one of his camera lenses, breaks the deadlock.

'Why don't you just tell the police press office you've got the facts and see what they say? If they don't deny it, well, you've got your story, haven't you?'

Jimmy scratches his eyepatch. 'We'll make a journalist out of you yet, Robert. That's exactly what I was going to suggest.' No one believes the editor's face-saving comment, not even the editor.

Jude calls Del and relays his list of dates, substances, quantities and street values of illegal drugs that have gone missing from the 'safe keeping' of Hampshire Police, prior to their destruction. Late afternoon Del calls back, saying that he 'can't argue' with the facts, but that, once again, the force believes the 'anomalies' are a result of book-keeping errors rather than incompetence in storing the drugs safely. 'Jude, as the Americans say, the shit has really hit the fan. That's off the record, off course. Vice are going berserk, and people are running for cover. Make sure you keep your head down, don't even get pulled over for speeding or a faulty rear light on your car, not for a while. Good work, Jude. Byee.'

'POLICE LOSE £1MILLION OF DRUGS' shouts the next edition of *The Reporter,* under the strapline of 'deplorable: a decade of deceit.' Jimmy has given a Jude a front page photo byline and labelled the story '*Reporter* Exclusive' in red print.

Once again, the freesheet's front page has to be followed up by a jealous local media. Even The Times, Daily Mirror and Daily Mail run short versions of Jude's story. Jimmy's delighted. 'Look, even the nationals are following us.'

'They've all used my quotes, word for word. Do you reckon I should invoice the nationals for payment, Jimmy?' Jude asks.

'Best of luck with that. No, don't waste your time, son. But keep the cuttings, if you ever try for a job on Fleet Street, they'll stand you in good stead.'

Later that day, Jude takes a call from Queenie, the first time he's spoken to her since covering the arson attack on her massage parlour. 'Jude, slightly strange question, are you free, now?'

With the week's paper out on the street, Friday afternoons are normally quiet. 'Nothing I wouldn't drop for you Queenie.'

'Good, you know where I live, I'll put the tea on.'

Some 15 minutes later the reporter is sitting in the lounge of Queenie's smart, detached modern house, which is tucked away discreetly behind a tall, impenetrable hedge of Leylandii. Drinking tea from a china cup and saucer, he thinks, 'I could be in the mayor's parlour, not a madam's sitting room.' Queenie is her normal fun, unpretentious self, putting the reporter at ease and encouraging him to attack a plate of fig rolls.

'Jude, I'm not going to beat about the bush: this is pretty weird. I don't really know how it's come about, but it has. Look, it's the Quirks. They're no friends of mine, just the opposite since they burnt down *Queenie's Massage Palace*, even if I did end up making money out of that. But I can't ignore them. Debbs Quirk's driver, Raymond, well, he's been a client of the massage palace for years. Says he gets a stiff back because of all the sitting behind a wheel he does. Well, I've only ever known him get stiff in one place and it's not his back, but that's neither here nor there.'

Jude tries not to choke on the fig roll he's eating; as always Queenie is making him laugh.

'Debbs knows I know you – she must have read the story you wrote about the arson attack – and, through Raymond, has asked, well, told me, to say she wants to meet you.'

'What, the head of the city's top, well, only drug dealer, wants to meet me? Are you sure, Queenie?'

'Apparently, it's a "clear-the-air" meeting. She thinks you've got the wrong end of the stick about her and her family.'

'She's the only one who does.'

'As maybe. But Raymond says, by involving me, your safety is guaranteed. It all sounds like something out of *The Godfather* to me.'

'Long as she doesn't make me,' Jude tries his best Sicilian fake accent, 'an offer I can't refuse...'

Queenie grins. 'It's not funny, really, Jude. She's suggested a neutral venue, a pub or similar. Look, Jude, if I'm honest, I don't think it's a good idea. There's nothing in it for you – she's not going to tell you how the police hand over the drugs to her sons, is she? But, as I say, it wasn't really a request to me, more an instruction.'

'Hang on, as a journalist I've got the chance to meet and question Debbs Quirk?'

'I've got a feeling it won't be you asking the questions, Jude.'

'Look, I've got to go. And if you know where it is and when, well, I'm going to be safe, aren't I?'

'Thanks, Jude,' Queenie says flatly, shaking her head. 'If any-thing does happen to you, I'm the one who's going to have to tell the police about the Quirks setting up a meeting. Doesn't exactly put me in a good spot, does it?'

'Queenie, do you know when Debbs wants this meeting?'

'I'm not supposed to... but there are moments, during a spe-cial massage, when the masseuse has all the power, if you know what I mean.' Queenie grins seductively and finishes her tea. 'It's tomorrow night, 8pm at *The Ship Inn,* on the Old Redbridge Road. It'll be busy on a Saturday night, which is good for you, and there's a little room out the back, *The Focsle,* which you'll have to yourself.'

'Tell Raymond or whoever that I'm happy to meet.'

'OK. You need to go to *Bojangles,* the Quirks' club, for 7.30 tomorrow night. There'll be a bouncer, with a beard, on the door. Give him your name and he'll tell you where the meeting is and you'll have just enough time to drive to it. You *do* need to do that, Jude, otherwise the Quirks will know that I know where the meeting is really going to be.'

Queenie takes a deep breath. 'Are you sure you're doing the sensible thing? These aren't people to mess with. Jude, you know this.'

'Queenie, I don't see how I can miss this opportunity, not really.'

'I thought you'd say that. Look, I've been told to stress this point – you have to go alone...'

Driving home, the journalist formulates the basis of a plan.

Rightly or wrongly, he decides not to disturb Jimmy's weekend by telling his editor about the meeting. Jude does call Robert and Sarah; he's going to need their help.

CHAPTER 26

An Awkward Start

The next night at 7pm, an hour ahead of the planned meeting, Robert turns off the *Fairport Convention* cassette he's been listening to and parks a few streets away from *The Ship Inn.* He's wearing his warmest dark clothes and he stops only to gather his camera bag before quietly hiding in a large rhododendron bush in the front garden of a house directly across the road from the pub. The garden has no wall or hedge and Robert, protected by the substantial dark evergreen, is far enough away not to be seen. But, through his long lens, he has an excellent view of the entrance to *The Ship Inn.* He's pleased that a pair of coach lamps, one either side of the pub's large oak front door, will ensure a good view – and photo – of everyone coming and going.

Some 45 minutes later, Robert starts to worry he'll be unable to operate his camera's shutter; the feeling in his fingers has been stolen by the damp, cold air during his wait. Then a blonde woman, in her late 40s, arrives. She's wearing an elegant blue coat and is flanked by two big men, aged in their 20s and obviously brothers. Robert clicks away and gets good pictures, especially of the older brother, who, once his small group is safely inside, furtively turns and looks up and down the street and directly at the rhododendron bush hiding Robert, before closing the pub's front door.

The cold penetrates deep into the photographer's bones and

he wishes he hadn't agreed to remain hidden until the Quirks have left. But wait he does, knowing that when the Quirks leave the pub, they'll be looking straight down the barrel of his long lens.

Arriving at exactly 8pm, Jude makes a point of asking a helpful bartender where *The Focsle* bar is, and shares a joke about the temperature outside and brass monkeys. Now, if needed, the bartender should remember Jude arriving. The reporter walks into a dark and dingy room that smells of damp rugs and decades of stale beer and cigarettes. In the corner, holding a tall glass and flanked by a huge guy in his late 20s, is Debbs Quirk. She looks like a fairground fortune teller, eerily illuminated by a yellow and red table light, making her gold jewellery sparkle, and the slice of lime in her glass glow as if radioactive.

'Jude, how lovely to meet you at last. I'm Deborah Quirk, everyone calls me Debbs. This is my son,' she extends a long, painted red fingernail to her left, without taking her eyes off of Jude, 'Bill, the eldest.' The giant nods in Jude's direction. Debbs smiles confidently. 'Come and sit down at the table with me. There's a pint of lager for you; I believe that's what you drink.'

'What doesn't she know?' Jude wonders, and walks towards the small table. Debbs is vaguely familiar but Jude can't place her and, while trying to remember, trips in the gloom and stumbles down on all fours, dropping his notebook and getting into a tangle with an electric cable and its plug.

'Sorry, er, I'm a bit nervous,' he mumbles. Dusting himself off, Jude sits, placing his notepad and a gleaming mobile phone, a Motorola 8000X, on the table in front of him. Robert has borrowed it from an old school chum who is now, proudly, a 'yuppie' working in The City. Jude is banking on the Quirks' ignorance of mobile phones and their inability to realise that it's already connected on a call.

'Is that one of those mobile phones? It's the size of a house brick,' Bill says, picking it up, 'and almost weighs as much.'

'Please…' Jude reaches, prises the mobile from Bill's sausage fingers and places it gently back on the table, hoping the call hasn't been ended accidentally. 'It's really expensive. I hope you don't mind me bringing it, Debbs, it's my, er, insurance. If I don't phone in an hour from now, well, they'll know something is up.' It's a plausible story, Jude thinks, and it will stop them realising that Sarah is on the other end, listening and taking a shorthand note of the whole conversation; his real insurance.

'Why don't you take a drink of your lager and relax a little. You have nothing to fear here,' Debbs smiles naturally and, Jude hopes, sincerely. 'It's such a shame that you and my family have got off to, well, let's say, an awkward start. I'm a big supporter of the press and the Tory Government. I do have to say that I preferred *The Reporter* before it started covering all this nonsense about drugs. You know, holes in the road that needed repairing, fund-raising for children with cancer, those sorts of stories. Much more the staple diet of a free newspaper, don't you think, Jude?'

'Er, well, all stories have, em, merit, I suppose, Debbs,' the reporter's shaky voice betraying his nervousness.

'What I want to talk about, Jude, is how can we make things better between us; how can we resolve any differences? You've hinted in your stories at some, well, let's not beat about the bush, unpleasant things about my family. But I'm not vindictive, I always prefer to look forward, not backwards, don't I, Bill?'

'You certainly do, Mum,' Bill's giant head nods, 'always forwards.'

'So, Jude, what will it take to ensure there's no more silly drug stories in *The Reporter*?'

'Bloody hell,' Jude thinks, 'I'm being offered a bribe. I hope Sarah can hear everything clearly.'

He looks at the mobile phone, then the ground and, realising Debbs is waiting for a reply, directly at her. 'Debbs, I'm just a reporter, writing stories. I'm not after money.'

He doesn't know what to say next. Debbs doesn't speak, allowing the silence to engulf the gloomy room. Suddenly, inexplicably and without thinking, Jude blurts out, 'You buy the police's "missing" drugs and then you sell them on the street, don't you?'

The reporter's pulse is racing: he can feel his heart thumping and cold sweat on his forehead. 'Oh, fuck, how, why, did I say that?' Jude asks himself, knowing there can never be a sensible or logical answer. And knowing that he's now in real trouble. 'If Sarah hears me say the code word, *front page*, down the phone, she'll call 999 immediately, like we've agreed,' he thinks, desperately trying to reassure himself.

'Yes, Jude, that's what I, what my family, do, although we don't "sell them on the street," – we have people who do that, much less risky.' The matriarch takes a sip of her fluorescent drink, letting her confession seep in the reporter's consciousness, before raising an eyebrow and adding, 'I suspect that little admission surprises you?'

Jude is dumbstruck; of all the scenarios he imagined, listening to the infamous Debbs Quirk 'fess-up to buying drugs from the police and then re-selling them, well, that certainly wasn't one of them.

Debbs is totally engaged, capturing Jude in her attractive stare. 'It makes perfect business sense: it's an awful lot cheaper and less risky than bringing them in from abroad or dealing with the untrustworthy Scousers. So, we've been able to undercut the opposition, and, using other tactics as well, force them out of business. We're now building the market and will increase the price in due course, once sales are high enough and we've established a clear monopoly of supply. Any good business school teaches this strategy for selling washing powder or cornflakes. Why not recreational drugs?'

Jude can't believe his ears. Sarah must be thinking exactly the same, he reasons. 'You're really not denying it?' His heart is about to burst through his chest.

'No, just the opposite. And, may I,' Debbs takes a longer drink of the glowing gin and tonic, leaving a faint smudge of lipstick on its rim and adding to the sense of drama, 'congratulate you? I never thought anyone would uncover what we've been up to. Oh, and your estimate of a million pounds, in *The Reporter*? It's a little on the low side.'

Jude reasons that for Debbs to admit what she's just con-fessed, well, she can't let him walk out of the pub. He has one last card to play, and goes all in. 'Debbs, you can't touch me, you can't kill me, all this is being listened to. Sarah, the other reporter on the paper, has heard every word.' Jude nods towards the big 'brick' black mobile standing upright on the table, it's black rubber aerial pointing to the ceiling.

Debbs lifts the phone and, without ever taking her eyes from Jude, says in her most charming voice, 'Sarah, how are you?' She listens and then nods. 'Good. OK, you can go and enjoy the rest of your evening now with David, that handsome hunk of a man of yours. Give him my best. And I'll see you at swimming as usual, before breakfast on Monday? Good, the post-swim cocoas are on me. Bye.'

The reporter realises he's underestimated, among other things, the drug dealer's knowledge of mobile phones. But is she just pretending to know Sarah as some sort of double bluff? Jude is confused to the point of inaction. Debbs continues staring at the reporter. 'Sarah won't be sending in the cavalry anytime soon, Jude. She and I have, well, let's call it a friendship. But don't worry, you don't need the cavalry, the police or even the SAS. We have no intention of harming you. We want to help you. You're ambitious and obviously you're good, very good at this new car-eer of yours. You should be working on a national paper, far away from Southampton, in London. I have contacts, Jude, and so do my friends. I'll like you to become one of my friends, Jude.'

The reporter's head is now royally spinning. He doesn't know what to think anymore, everything has been thrown up in the air in the last few minutes and he doesn't trust himself to make any sense from anything. Sarah, his insurance policy, is best mates with Debbs Quirk? He's going to be killed by the drug dealers, then he isn't and now their leader wants to be his friend and get him a job in Fleet Street? As hard as he can he presses the nail of his right middle finger into the soft skin between his index finger and thumb. 'Ouch,' he says involuntarily aloud, and thinks, 'OK, this isn't a bad dream, this is real.'

There's a noisy commotion from outside, the door into their room bursts open and Robert is bundled inside by two large men, both as big as Bill.

'Mum, look what we found hiding in the rhododendrons,' the older of the pair says, pushing a bedraggled Robert towards the dim light that spills from the small table. The younger brother drops Robert's camera bag heavily on to the floor, making the photographer wince.

'Jude, I don't think you've met my other boys: that's Ben on the left; and Brian's on the right, he's the youngest.'

Suddenly seeing Brian, he places where he's seen Debbs before: at the hospital. She came out of the lift with a man, probably Bill, when he and Robert went to visit Roy Bruce, not long after Brian had smashed a pint glass in his face. Jude is beginning to make sense of his surreal situation, slowly tying together the disparate strings of thoughts in his mind. 'That was how she "fixed" Roy whilst he was in his hospital bed, with a combination of bribery and threats; carrot and stick. And that's what Debbs and her boys are offering me, he thought, carrot and stick. A job in Fleet Street is the carrot, but what's her 'stick?'

Jude sees Robert is shaking, unable to control his fear. Almost incoherently, the photographer starts to speak. 'I've been pissed on by a bloody great Alsatian. It must have drunk a gallon of water.' Jude looks at Robert's jacket and trousers, both ringing wet, despite the weather being dry and bitterly cold.

Brian laughs, 'I thought you stank of dog's piss, I just reckoned all photographers smelt like that.'

'Thank you, Brian,' his mother interrupts. 'Jude this is disappointing. I do believe you were politely asked to come alone.'

Brian opens the photographer's bag, takes out the Nikon, opens the camera's back and pulls out the roll of film, exposing it to the light. 'Looks like you got pissed on for nothing.'

Robert is fuming. 'You can't do that, it's my, well, *The Reporter's* legal property and–'

Debbs stops Robert simply by raising her painted right index fingernail to her lips. There's absolute silence in the room. 'Robert, your little girl, Elizabeth Jane, goes to a childminder in Warren Avenue two days a week. The childminder is very good and the arrangement allows your wife, Jules, to go back working, part-time, at the gynaecology unit at the General Hospital. She loves her job, I believe. Need I continue?'

Cold, wet and scared, Robert is already a defeated man. He slowly shakes his head, the warning clearly received and understood.

'And you've never been here tonight, have you?'

Robert again shakes his head.

'Good, Elizabeth Jane will be fine at the nursery and Jules can safely continue her excellent work at the hospital. You're free to go.'

Brian opens the door; Robert picks up his camera bag and walks slowly from the room, his soaking trousers sticking to his legs, making his strides large and pronounced. Jude tries to follow but Brian steps across the doorway immediately after Robert leaves. 'Not you, Jude,' and pushes him, hard, back across the room, towards the table.

'Sit down,' Ben's hand on the journalist's shoulder guides Jude forcibly back on to his chair. Ben and Bill stand just behind him, out of sight, but ominously close. Jude remembers his final insurance policy: Queenie. If he doesn't show up, she'll tell the police about the meeting.

Debbs finishes her drink, places the empty glass on the small table and looks at Jude. 'Oh, and don't think Queenie will help. Tonight, her lovely Mini will inexplicably combust on her driveway. First thing tomorrow a new, top-of-the-range model will be delivered to her door. I think she'll get the message quite clearly, don't you?'

Jude fights to stop his mind racing, to gain back control of this thoughts. Slowly the big picture comes into focus, and it's not pretty. 'OK,' he thinks, 'I'm totally screwed. Will they kill me here, or take me somewhere first? The New Forest, it's certainly close enough.' He pictures a dog walker, watching his Golden

Labrador paw at a shallow grave, discovering a part of his torso, no, a hand, it's fingers freshly gnawed by foxes.

'Jude' – the reporter is brought back to the present by the mention of his name – 'imagining your future?' Debbs leans towards the reporter. 'It doesn't have to be the way you think. You have a choice.'

Turning to look first at one and then the other of the burly brothers flanking him, the reporter laughs. 'Yeah, looks like I've got a choice.'

'Jude, you will realise there is always a choice.'

'So, I can choose: kill me here or in the Forest? Is that it.'

'Obviously that's an option, but a messy one. No, my offer still stands. Be a friend and you'll find your career away from Southampton advances very, very quickly. Almost meteorically.'

The room is silent and Jude realises Debbs understands the power of silence. But the pressure is too great and the reporter is first to talk. 'Or?'

Debbs smiles the same, sincere smile he first saw earlier that evening. 'I'm not in the habit of quoting The Bible, but this is from Job, I believe, and is particularly appropriate. "The Lord giveth and the Lord taketh away." Jude, you are going to have something very precious taken from you. The strange thing is, you don't even know that you have this most precious of objects. But, trust me, it's something you will treasure.'

Jude looks pained and confused.

'Don't bother trying to figure this out. Just do yourself a very large favour, don't write anything about drugs or my family until what I've told you actually occurs. It will be soon, I promise. Then you can make your choice.. We'll be in touch.' Debbs lowers her eyes; the meeting is over. Jude collects his notebook and mobile phone and leaves through the door that Brian, smiling, opens with great panache.

CHAPTER 27

More Feline than Serpent

On a Sunday morning at 6am there is no clatter of milk bottles, no whistles of cheery postmen nor little else to disturb the silence that engulfs the horse chestnut-lined avenue. That is, until Jude, who's slept very little, bangs the brass doorknocker of one of the street's pretty semi-detached houses.

It's early, but Jude reckons Sarah will be expecting his visit. Her partner, David, barefoot and wearing only striped pyjama bottoms, eventually opens the stripped-oak front door. 'OK, OK, where's the fire. Oh, it's you, Jude. Everything all right is it? Insomnia or guilt, it's usually one or the other. I normally go for a jog if I can't sleep.' David pulls on the grey dressing gown he's been holding and remains remarkably calm, his gentle Welsh tones, normally so soothing, just further irritate the already seething reporter.

'Where is she, that snake?'

'If you mean Sarah, she's asleep, well, was, probably awake now, with the banging. I've always thought of her as more feline than serpent.'

Jude tries to push past the amiable David, but is stopped by the boyfriend's surprising strength. 'Now, look, Jude, let's not be hasty.'

'It's OK, David.' Sarah's sleep-starved pixie face appears under her boyfriend's raised arm, 'let him in and make some tea, would you? I've got some explaining to do.'

'You bloody well do.' Jude spits out the words. David looks at Jude then Sarah, who gives a little nod, dismissing her boyfriend.

'Let's go into the lounge,' she says, leading the way, pulling her old tartan dressing gown around her tightly, realising she's not dressed for an argument, certainly not for asking for forgiveness and absolutely not for using her feminine charm.

Jude follows but refuses to sit. 'So, what's the fucking story, Miss it's "us journalists against management and the world?"'

'Jude, look, I understand, you've got every right to be angry.'

'Don't fucking tell me what rights I have or haven't got.'

'OK. Just let me explain, will you?'

'Sarah, it was help I needed last night, not an explanation now. You were my insurance, in the end my only fucking insurance. And just when I needed it...' Jude stops, embarrassed at the realisation that he's shouting.

David knocks the lounge door gently with his forehead before pushing it open with his backside, places a small tray of mugs of tea on the coffee table, mouths the words 'help yourself to sugar,' to Jude, and leaves the room quietly and quickly, as if hoping his presence hasn't really been noticed.

'Jude, I'm sorry, OK. But everything isn't as it seems.'

'What, you're an undercover cop, and Jimmy's really 007, I suppose?'

'Don't be a knob, Jude. I met Debbs over a year ago when she joined the early morning swimming club I go to. I hadn't a clue who she was, but as she was older, well, I showed her the ropes: where to change, how the hairdryers work, that kind of thing. She was nice: sincere and easy to talk to. I never even knew her surname. We'd have a coffee or hot chocolate after the swimming and a chat.'

'How cosy, swimming, hot chocolate and plotting together.'

'Just listen, then you can be as sarcastic as you like. At the time me and David were trying to buy this house.' Sarah looks up at the high ceiling and then out through the large bay windows facing on to the quiet avenue. 'But it was really out of our price range. Then Debbs loaned us five grand, telling me that she'd been left some money, that she had no use for it at the moment and for us to pay it back when we could, but no rush. And she knows lots of people, introduced me to some at her "little gatherings". They gave me stories, really solid, good stories. Debbs is my best contact.'

'And she didn't want anything in return,' Jude sneers.

'No, well, not at first. Then she suggested that "if I hear anything" to let her know. Anything from the police or anyone about drugs or gangs – she said it was "an interest of hers". I told her one or two snippets, nothing major. Six months ago, Debbs said I should "forget" the five grand I owed her. She said she'd been left some money that she didn't know what to do with and she'd decided she'd use it to help out a young, struggling couple – me and David. She asked us to sign a sheet of paper, just for her accountant's records. Jude, you know how little we earn as reporters. David works down the docks, in the office, so we're not exactly rolling in money. Then, without telling us she set up a standing order and pays £100 a month into my bank account. When I found out, I asked her a couple of time to stop giving us the money. She said she would, but it kept coming, every month. Eventually I stopped asking. I said to myself, "well, where's the harm?"'

'OK, a hundred quid a month is difficult to turn down. But, Sarah, that doesn't explain about last night, not really.' Jude's voice was less angry, less judgemental.

'Think about it, Jude, it kind of does. After your stories about drugs started to appear, well, maybe a couple of weeks ago, over the after-swimming hot chocolate, Debbs said that real friends help each other that she needed some help and asked me to tell her what you were up to.'

'A few weeks back, before I slept rough in the park with the homeless, did you tell her that was what I was planning?'

'No, the only time I've really talked about you was yesterday, Saturday. Debbs phoned me at home before your meeting, and asked what I knew. I said nothing, not really. That's when she said the "sheet of paper, just for her accountant's records" that we'd signed was actually the signature page for a legal charge against this house.'

'You believed her?'

'No, I told her she was being ridiculous. She said to go to the front door. I did, and on the mat was a letter.' Sarah walks over to sideboard and picks up an envelope, opens it and pulls out an official document and shows it to Jude. 'She wasn't being ridiculous, look, it's a charge over this property, stamped, registered and enforceable in law.'

'You didn't check it out before you signed?'

'There was only the one page, so no, I didn't bloody look a gift horse in the mouth, OK. I thought it was wiping off the five grand we owed, five grand we wouldn't be able to repay for years and years. Debbs said that if I couldn't repay the whole five grand within 48 hours, she'd go to court and have us kicked out of our home and the property sold. Given the state of the housing market, we'd end up homeless and probably owing money.'

'So...'

'So, I told her about Robert hiding in the bushes, the mobile phone you were taking to the meeting and how I was to take a shorthand note of everything.'

'You left me high and dry. Anything could have happened to me, and to Robert.'

'No! Nothing was ever going to happen to either of you, she promised. She said you wouldn't need a phone or any insurance. That she just wanted to talk to you, on your own, to explain.'

'Explain? Last night I thought your friend and her boys were going to kill me.'

'I'm sorry, but I couldn't imagine that Debbs could be a danger to anyone. Not the middle-aged woman I know who wears an all-in-one black swimming costume and pink swimming hat with daisies on.'

'Sarah, you're an experienced journalist, not a naïve 17-year-old. She might look like a genteel mum but her sons are all huge and look like they know how to handle themselves. They're all bouncers, for God's sake. And all the stories we've been writing about, the family's involvement in drugs.'

'What else could I have done, Jude? If she'd told Alex or Jimmy that I was taking money from her, I'd lose my job and we'd lose our home. You must see that.'

Jude rubs his forehead, ignores the tea that's going cold in its mug and stands to leave.

'You must understand, Jude, I had no choice.'

'As Debbs said last night, "There's always a choice," Sarah.' And Jude walks out of the house, slamming the front door behind him.

CHAPTER 28

A Missing Daughter

The Housemartins' acapella *Caravan of Love* playing loudly on the old Peugeot's stereo never fails to lift Jude's spirits, but there's a first time for everything. On this overcast Monday morning, the reporter's mood remains lower than the sub-zero outside temperature. He needs to collect something he'd left at *The Ship Inn* on Saturday night but is worried, maybe unreasonably, that someone may still be watching the pub. And he's no idea how he'll react to seeing Sarah at work. Jude understands the pressure Debbs has brought to bear and how clever the Quirk matriarch is at manipulating people, but can't find it within himself, at least not yet, to forgive Sarah for the way she's hung him out to dry and put both Robert and him in serious danger. In the office Jude is relieved to find that Sarah is out on a story, interviewing the city's "first female butcher" who's opening a shop in Shirley. He plans to find an excuse to visit *The Ship,* but Jimmy has other plans for the reporter.

'There's a police press conference, your mate Del phoned first thing to tell us. A youngster's gone missing. Starts in,' Jimmy looks at his watch, '30 minutes at Portswood nick. Take Robert with you; hopefully the child will still be missing come deadline on Thursday. If the girl is found, we might get a backgrounder out of it, "My Relief," or "Every Mum's Nightmare." One way or another, I'm sure you'll find an angle for a story, Jude. Just make sure you can contact mum, whatever happens.' Jude shakes his head and wonders if he'll ever become anaesthetised like Jimmy to the reality of what they do for a living. He hopes he will never hear himself say 'hopefully the child will still be missing come deadline'. In Robert's messy car, driving to the police station, photographer and reporter are silent, both not knowing what to say about Saturday night. In the end, Jude speaks. 'You haven't told Jimmy, then?'

'I thought it was your call. I think we should. If something happens and we haven't told him, well, we're just making a desperate situation worse.'

Jude nods. 'I know, but where do we start? After not telling him that we were going to meet with the Quirks, how can we now? Let's just see how things pan out.' Jude realises he can't stop explaining now and takes a deep breath. 'Sarah was in on it; she'd been pressurised by Debbs.'

Robert swerves the car, almost taking out a cyclist. 'What the...? Jude, really, that's not funny.'

'That's how they found you in the bushes, Sarah had told them. And they knew she was listening on the phone.'

'But Sarah is one of us. We could have been given a right thrashing. And Debbs threatened my daughter. I wouldn't let her out the house yesterday, not even in her pushchair with me pushing it.'

'Sarah didn't do it voluntarily. Debbs blackmailed Sarah. She gave her money to buy the house with Dave, but took a charge over it and then threatened to evict them if Sarah didn't reveal our plans to the Quirks.'

'Good God. How terrible for everyone, even Sarah.' Robert tries to think through the implications.

His thoughts are interrupted by Jude. 'After you went, Debbs was all mysterious, said she'd give me something precious, then take it away. That it would happen soon and not to write anything until it did.'

Robert shakes his head. 'Then I guess we'll find out soon enough.' He pulls into the car park at the back of the police station, narrowly missing one of the BBC TV staff pulling a camera stand from a large van. Robert tries to lighten the mood. 'Look at these bloody TV crews. It's bad enough carrying around my heavy camera bag all day, but all the kit these TV cameramen need, bugger that for a laugh.'

Jude and Robert are among the last to arrive and have to stand at the back of the press room; the TV crews have set up their cameras, while the radio stations have positioned their microphones on the table on the little stage at the front. A couple of journalists nod a quick 'hello' at Jude and Robert. Del steps on to the stage, stands in front of the table and gives Jude a smile and Comrade Robert a quick salute before speaking without a microphone.

'Thanks everyone for coming at such short notice to this speedily-arranged press conference. I'll quickly give you the background, then Inspector Terry Tarrant and the child's parents will come forward and chat. There'll be a short period for questions and, afterwards, I've got some photos of the missing girl, Catherine Dixon – that's Catherine with a C, not a K, to give out. Catherine is nine years old and a pupil at Aldermoor Primary School. Yesterday morning, Sunday, her parents, Sue and Richard, went to wake her from her bedroom of their home in Saxholm Dale, in the Bassett area of the city, but she wasn't there, although her bed had been slept in. A check of her friends and then a search of the area has been unsuccessful in finding Catherine. She's never gone missing before. She is a bright and able student and we would ask all media organisations to appeal for help from the good people of Southampton in finding her. Right, I'll go and ask Inspector Tarrant and Mr and Mrs Dixon to join us.'

As he goes, the journalists start chattering among themselves. They only stop when, a few minutes later, the inspector walks on to the stage, followed by the missing girl's parents, and they all sit on the three waiting chairs.

Jude's heart stops. He's sure it stops. His legs go weak and he starts to slowly crumble. Robert lets go of his camera and grabs his colleague under his arms. 'Jude, what's wrong, I'm missing the picture, come on.' Then Robert realises that something is really amiss. 'Jude, are you alright? You look like you've seen a ghost.'

Everyone else is concentrating on the stage and fail to notice Jude's near collapse. 'Not really. I feel dizzy, just give me a minute.'

The inspector gives more details of the police search but the photographers' cameras never leave Sue Dixon. She momentarily wipes her eye and all the photographer's flashes ping, illuminating the grey room and harshly lighting the distressed mum.

Every reporter is scribbling furiously, but Jude is using all his concentration just to remain upright. Layer upon layer, year upon year is being peeled away in his mind. His quick-witted brain wants to explode at each new conclusion it reaches, at each new bizarrely-shaped jigsaw piece that fits perfectly into his bizarrely-shaped history.

With Jude still reeling, Robert focusses on Sue. He thinks she is about 30 years old, dark-haired and gorgeous in a way that, his photographer's eye tells him, she's matured into. His camera lens loves her and he thinks he has never seen a more beautiful, sad sight. 'Perhaps Picasso's *Melancholy Woman*,' he thinks – he saw it at the Detroit Institute of Arts during a trip to the US with his parents – and continues to focus his lens solely on the young mum.

Sue pleads for 'the safe return of my little girl,' and answers questions. All the time Richard, her husband, is holding her hand. *The Echo* reporter, standing next to Jude, asks what Catherine was wearing. As Sue turns to answer, she recognises Jude and hesitates before looking away and putting a hanky to her eyes. All the cameras flash and whirl at once, stealing her grief and preserving it for eternity.

As suddenly as the press conference start, it's over. The inspector and parents disappear from the stage, Del hands out copies of a blown-up colour photo of a smiling nine-year-old

Catherine in school uniform and the reporters, photographers and cameramen all dash off to meet their deadlines. Under no such pressure, with *The Reporter* not due out for days, Robert enjoys the moment of calm. 'I've got some great shots.' He looks at Jude. 'You still look crap. Hang on, you haven't even opened your notebook.'

Jude is in a daze, transported past the 10 years that he'd been away from the city, to the time when he loved, and was due to marry, the woman who has just appeared in front of the press conference, Sue, Sue Wraith as she was. How he'd heartlessly all but left her standing at the altar because she'd refused to choose a life with him over one with her criminal family – Sue had found it impossible to cut the umbilical to her malign mother, Chantelle, a choice Jude could never understand or accept.

Movement in the police car park brings Jude back to the moment in the empty, soulless press room as he sees Sue, still wiping tears from her eyes, being tenderly helped into a car by husband Richard. The door is finally closed by an older woman, who can only be Chantelle, aged 10 years since Jude has last seen her.

'Sue,' Jude hopelessly calls and dashes out of the briefing room and towards the car park. But the older woman has now reached the external door of the police station and bars his path.

'Talk about a bad penny turning up.'

'Chantelle. I've got to talk to Sue.'

'No, no you don't. You had your chance to talk 10 years ago and look what happened then.' The tall, elegant and immaculately well-dressed woman doesn't have a hair out of place, but is obviously fighting to retain her poise. 'Don't you think my Sue has enough on her plate right now, without you dredging up the past? If you want to help, publish the appeal for Catherine. That's what's needed right now, the poor mite.'

'But Catherine, she's my daughter. She has to be. You never said... Sue... neither of you ever said a word.'

'You left a forwarding address, did you? No, nothing. You fucked off and never looked back.'

'I had no idea.' Jude feels tears forming in the corners of his eyes.

'And didn't care. Catherine is nothing to do with you. Not after the way you treated Sue. And me. She's got a father now, a daddy who cares for her. And who's to say she's yours, anyway?'

Jude's voice rises. 'She is, I know she is.'

'Don't be so bloody–'

'That's why she's been abducted, to get at me!'

Jude cannot recall Chantelle ever being lost for words. Until now. 'Wha, how...'

'It's to warn me off a story.' This grim truth escapes Jude's lips before it's fully formed from the mush that is currently his brain.

'It bloody better not be, Jude, for your own sake. I've still got some friends left in this city.'

'Catherine will be fine, I'm sure of that.' Jude hopes he sounds more convincing than he actually feels. 'If she's harmed, well, they no longer have any hold over me, do they?'

'They, Jude? Who are they?'

'The Quirks.'

Chantelle's right hand involuntarily cups her mouth. 'Oh, fuck,' she says quietly.

CHAPTER 29

A Quirk of Fate

'Jude, you are going to have something very precious taken from you. The strange thing is, you don't even know that you have this most precious of objects. But, trust me, it's something you will treasure.'

Debbs Quirk's words keep going round and round in Jude's head. Everything makes perfect sense. Everything is totally mad. And a little girl is missing, in danger, and she is, probably, certainly, Jude's daughter. How the hell can Debbs know about Catherine when he had no inkling? It doesn't add up.

Jude is jolted out of his own thoughts by Robert dropping a 10inch by 8inch black and white print on the reporter's desk. It shows a beautiful dark-haired woman, tears running down her cheeks, hands clutching a tissue, trying to hold herself together, and in the background, purposely slightly out of focus, the husband, equally distraught, trying to comfort his wife. Jude thinks it's the saddest photo he's ever seen. 'Genius or what?' Robert asks, showing the tact worthy of a Fleet Street photographer, 'if the girl is still missing come Thursday, we should use this across the whole of the front page.'

Jude wants to hit his friend, but manages to stay seated, telling himself that, if this missing little girl wasn't his daughter, he'd agree with Robert. There's no way the photographer has any inkling that Jude knows Sue or that he's the father of missing

Catherine. It takes all the reporter's self-control to remain silent. Not trusting words, Jude gives Robert a thumbs up and his best effort of a false smile. Jude retreats back into his own thoughts, trying to figure out how Debbs can have possibly known or worked out he had a daughter when he didn't even know he had a daughter. Or was it just chance? Had the girl just wondered off or been abducted by a local pervert? No, that was too much of a coincidence, surely?

'Jude, are you going to do any work today? We've only 10 pages to fill and two days to do it, so, you know, take your time, why don't you?' Jimmy's lunchtime beers had moved his mood, first to 'matey' on his personality scale, and now to 'tetchy.' Soon, no doubt, it'd edge towards to 'tetchy and thirsty' and he'd decide there was nothing worth doing in the office and head back to *The Osborne.*

Jude realises this is the moment to explain why he can't concentrate and why he hasn't written a word since attending the police press conference for the missing Catherine. He looks at Robert, who is staring back and, reading Jude's thoughts, nods vigorously. 'Now or never,' Jude thinks, and tries to find the right words to explain the disaster that he's created. He opens his mouth to speak. 'Jimmy, I need to—'

Sarah burst into the office. 'Bloody hell, Jimmy, did you send me to interview the city's first female butcher because I'm a bloody vegetarian. Is that your idea of a joke?' She slams a brown paper parcel, blood leaking through its wrapping, down on the editor's desk. 'Here, she insisted I take it, two pork chops and, apparently, "a nice piece of rump." I could take *The Reporter* to an industrial tribunal; this is bloody constructive dismissal.'

Jimmy stands up, drops the meat parcel into his brief case and heads for the door, saying, 'I don't need all this. But the steak will be appreciated.' And he disappears out of the office, no doubt to *The Osborne,* taking with him Jude's chance to confess.

Sarah turns to Robert. 'Mrs Sweeney Todd, or whatever her name is, the hag with the meat cleaver, could be available now if you're free to take her picture. You might even get a free burger as well.'

'I am, as it happens, Sarah. I had an author's book signing at a local junior school to photograph, but he's been arrested this morning for "touching up kids" so it's been cancelled. Still, he'll make a good story if it gets to court. Is it the butcher in Shirley High Street?' Sarah nods, Robert grabs his camera bag and heads out.

Sarah waits for the door to close behind the photographer. 'Jude, you know I'm sorry about Saturday, don't you? I didn't know what else to do.'

'I do. Debbs has the ability to make people do what she wants. But, for a journalist, a good one, you were bloody naïve, Sarah. Naïve and greedy. But it's done now. I had to tell Robert, but Jimmy doesn't know, so your job's safe.'

'Thanks, I appreciate that.' Sarah tries a smile which Jude assiduously ignores.

'Sarah, I can't trust you, not ever, because Debbs still has a hold over you, doesn't she? Don't bother answering. Look, to be honest, I've got worse things going on, right now.' Jude looks at his watch. 'And I've got an errand to run. You'll be OK holding the fort on your own?' He doesn't wait for an answer, scoops up his things and is gone.

In the corridor, Jude stops dead. He turns on his heels, opens the newsroom door and pokes his head inside. 'Sarah, just one question. Nobody, except my family and you, know about Sue and why I suddenly left Southampton 10 years ago. I told you everything about Sue, about leaving her on the day we were due to get married, about her criminal mum, Chantelle. You remember, don't you, it was at the opening of that wine bar, after Alex had ripped my head off and threatened to sack me.'

'I remember. It was when I told you to ignore Alex, the wanker, and that you'd be a good journalist.'

'You told Debbs, didn't you?'

Sarah could only stare back at Jude's head, silhouetted in the doorway, and slowly nods, her face expressionless.

Jude strides over to his desk, picks up Robert's photo of the crying mum and slams it down it in front of Sarah. The beautifully sad and tear-filled eyes stare back at the female reporter. 'That's Sue, the woman I left 10 years ago. The mum whose nine-year-old daughter, little Catherine, has gone missing.'

Sarah had heard the report of the missing girl on local radio as she drove back to the office from the butcher's shop.

'Sarah, thanks to you, my daughter, the daughter I didn't even know I had, has been abducted. Her life is in danger, a nine-year-old.'

'Jude,' Sarah gulped, 'I'm so sorry,' and the corner of her eyes glistened with tears.

'Until a second ago, that was the bit I couldn't figure out; how did Debbs know? Then, in the corridor, I suddenly remembered that I'd told you about Sue. And you told Debbs. And she must have checked everything and everyone and then worked it all out.'

Jude doesn't wait any longer but heads for his car, worried what he might say or do if he remains breathing the same air as his colleague. He drives out to the edge of the city, to the scene of Saturday night's disaster, *The Ship Inn.*

Fuelled by anger and the realisation that he needs to act, Jude speeds to the pub and brings his car to a skidding halt in its car park. But then he realises he's being hasty; that he has to be careful, for Catherine's and his own safety. He fights the urge to dash inside and, instead, parks at the side of the car park, where he has a good view of the entrance to the old inn. After 15 minutes, when he's sure he hasn't been followed and that no one is watching him or *The Ship Inn*, he quietly slips into the pub and heads for *The Focsle.*

Once inside the dark, dingy room, Jude locates and turns off the 13amp socket on the skirting board and pulls out the plug and lead. No one has noticed it since Saturday, when, at the start of his meeting with Debbs, he had pretended to trip, dropping his note book and allowing him to switch on the socket undetected. That action sent power to his Phillips cassette recorder, which he'd hidden earlier in the day, among the old, dusty books lining the room's shelves, its red 'record' and black 'play' piano keys already pressed down to the 'on' position. With the mains turned on, it should have started recording, he desperately hopes. Jude retrieves the recorder and microphone and leaves the pub quickly, deciding it would be sensible to listen to its cassette tape in the safety of his car, on the drive home, away from the pub.

Jude slots the cassette into his car's stereo and pushes play. The recording, although sometimes faint and occasionally muffled, transports Jude back to Saturday night and that little, musty room of stale beer, cigarettes and fear. He shakes himself, trying to dispel the panic that is creeping back into his soul. As he drives, he listens intently to the conversation, recalling every word up to the moment Debbs Quirk signalled for him to leave with a short nod of her heavily-lacquered hair. He listens to his own footsteps leaving the room, the door closing behind him and, after a few seconds, the sound of the brothers laughing lightly.

Then Debbs speaks. 'Well done, boys. That went as well as I expected. Let's hope this reporter is as bright as we think he is and understands that we mean what we say. Right, Bill, drop me home, will you? Brian, Ben, either of you need a lift? No, see you tomorrow at home, as arranged?' There's a short silence in the recording, probably as the sons nod their consent. 'Good, I'm doing lamb. Night, boys.'

Jude hears the clack of high hills and the door again close. Then there's another voice, probably Brian. 'Right, let's get down town.' A brother, probably Ben, replies. 'OK. Dad will be pleased with the outcome tonight.' The voice gets a little fainter. 'I've got a date and she's bringing her sister. You should come along.' The door bangs shut and, for the rest of the tape, there's silence.

Jude rewinds the cassette and listens to the last part of the recording again. 'OK. Dad will be pleased with the outcome tonight.' But there is no dad; it's common knowledge that Debbs brought up her sons single-handily. She all but boasts about it.

It's an interesting aside, and Jude congratulates himself

briefly on concealing the cassette in the pub ahead of time and planning a way to turn it on without being noticed. But Jude knows there's nothing he can do with the recording. Not now, not ever – unless he's prepared to further endanger his daughter's life. If anything does happen to her, the tape might just help. Somehow Jude feels bolstered, a little less nervous now that he has the cassette safely in his possession. But he also feels out of his depth, about a million miles out of his depth. 'Jimmy would know what to do,' he thinks. 'Why haven't I told him about what's been happening? He's experienced in this kind of stuff. I'm a rookie reporter who used to work as a salesman. I'm the amateur crashing around while Catherine is the one who's suffering…if she's still alive.'

Next morning, on the drive to work, Jude is only half paying attention to the familiar Hampshire accent of the Radio Solent newsreader coming from his speaker. It's an accent that, despite countless BBC coaching sessions, remains rooted in the heart of the county, ensuring its owner will never get a job in London.

The Peugeot radio is tuned permanently to Radio Solent, the local BBC station, which the journalist hates with a passion – its music and phone-in shows are targeted at listeners aged 50 plus – but it has the best local news coverage of any station, so he to listen to it. The newsreader drones on, 'The search for the missing nine-year-old Southampton girl, Catherine Dixon, was called off yesterday evening when she was found safe, well but hungry inside a large rubbish bin less than a mile from her home in the Chilworth area of the city. Police believe she may have climbed inside while playing and been unable to get out.'

Jude has to pull over and stop the car. He leans his arms and head onto the steering wheel and sobs and sobs. The tears aren't just for the safe return of Catherine to her family, they're also for the nine missing years of having a daughter and not knowing it. They're for the guilt of putting her in harm's way. They're for being a selfish bastard.

It's an eternity before Jude feels he is safe to drive without a veil of tears and self-reproach. Thankfully, the traffic has now increased and he has no choice but to drive slowly among the commuters.

Sat at his desk, he phones Del for the full story. Apparently, the driver of a commercial rubbish removal company was about to tip the bin into the back of his huge wagon when he thought he heard a noise from inside the two-metre tall galvanised-metal dustbin. He checked it out and found Catherine. 'It was odd, because two groups had already searched the area, including the bins, during the day and found nothing. Catherine must have been asleep, inside and covered over, when they looked,' Del says.

'Has she explained how she got into the bin?' Jude asks.

'Last night she wasn't making a lot of sense and the family just fed her and put her to bed. To be honest, they're just delighted she's home: safe and unharmed. We reckon she must have wandered off.'

'What was she wearing, her nightclothes?'

'Yeah, but she had her parka jacket and thick trousers on as well, so she must have planned to go out. It's a story with a happy ending, for once. And the police want to thank the hundreds of volunteers who turned out to help with the search. Write something like that, Jude, you know the sort of thing.'

'Del, what company did the driver work for?'

'Let me check… why do you ask?'

'Ah, well, um, look, this isn't a huge story for *The Reporter* any longer but if I could track down the driver, he might become the hero who saved her life. If he'd just emptied the bin into his truck, who knows, she may have been crushed by the van's compactor?'

'Good idea – here it is, Quirk Brothers Waste Removal. And I've got your headline, Jude: 'QUIRK OF FATE SAVES GIRL'S LIFE!" Byee.

CHAPTER 30

It's Confession Time

Through some unspoken pact, Sarah and Jude are rarely in *The Reporter* newsroom together, taking it in turn to find stories to cover out of the office. Today, come knocking off time, Sarah is out on a feature with Robert, and Jimmy limps over to Jude's desk. 'I don't know what's got into you, or Sarah come to that, but you and I are going to *The Osborne*, I'm going to buy you a pint and you're going to explain... everything.'

'That's kind of you, Jimmy, but I've got a job on tonight.'

'No, you haven't, I've checked the diary. This office is too small for squabbles or cliques, so, no excuses, grab your bag and let's go. It's confession time, let's get this, whatever it is, out in the open and try to sort it.'

Over two hours and four pints, Jude unburdens himself and tells his editor the whole story: the reasons he dumped Sue 10 years ago; the attacks on *The Proud Stag*, Sarah's involvement with the Quirks; the meeting on Saturday with Debbs and her sons; and the abduction of Catherine, who he now knows is his daughter. Jimmy, being the experienced journalist he is, knows when to nod, when to prod and when to keep quiet. And he lubricates the conversation by ensuring his reporter's glass is never empty, and never stops listening intently. At the end of the story, Jude takes the cassette player out of his bag and plays Jimmy the secretly-recorded tape of his meeting with the Quirks.

When it's obvious Jude has finished recounting all the facts and summing up his predicament, Jimmy lets out a thin whistle. 'Bloody hell, lad, for a relatively new, trainee reporter, you've got yourself in deep. Look, you should have told me all about this stuff earlier – you know that already, so I won't waste time going over it or with bollockings. More importantly, what do you see as your options, now?'

'I'm not sure I have any, Jimmy. If I don't co-operate with the Quirks, well, we've seen what they can do, taking Catherine from her bed without anyone knowing, pretending she ran off. I can't risk something like that happening again, can I?'

'No, you can't.'

'But I can't just let this go, either. It's a huge story. The Quirks are taking drugs from nightclubbers and buying them from the police, then getting the city's youngsters hooked by selling them cheap.'

'And don't forget the big increase in deaths by overdose in the city, which, from what you say, can be laid squarely at the feet of the Quirks.'

'Jimmy, I'm out of my depth and I know it. I can't just blunder on any more.'

'If you continue looking into the Quirks and they find out, well, they know where you are most vulnerable, where to apply the pressure. And it's your family, Catherine in particular. Are you really prepared for that?'

'I can't ignore this story. If I do, what happens? Who do the Quirks control next? Isn't it our job, as journalists, do get to the truth? Regardless of cost.'

'It has to be your decision, Jude. One thing I have learned is that when you're trying to break a big story, well, there's a time to kick down the front door, and a time to slip in unnoticed around the back. This is a time, if you're sure you want to continue with the investigation, to walk on tiptoe round to the back door and open it very quietly.'

'OK. What do you suggest we do next?'

'I'm glad you said "we." But there aren't many options.'

'There must be something?'

'I've got one idea – on the tape, that line about, "Dad being pleased," or whatever it was. You said Debbs brought up the boys single-handedly. But they're obviously in contact with their dad. It was mentioned when Debbs had left the room, so perhaps she doesn't know. It might be worth trying to get the boys' birth certificates. Find out who they're talking about; who the dad is. But it's a longshot. No one will know you're looking for the certificates and, if we find them, who knows where that may lead?'

Jude realises he's over the drink-drive limit and keeps the car under the speed limit driving home, so not to be stopped for speeding and then breathalysed. It gives him chance to think about the decision he's taken to carry on, however discreetly, with investigating the Quirks. Has he the right to put his own daughter, Catherine, in harm's way? The girl he's done nothing for, except fathered. What right does he have to put her at risk? But yet...

The next day, at Southampton Register Office, Jude pays £9, at £3 each for three long form birth certificates, and gives the registrar the Quirk boys' names and approximate ages. She takes the money, completes the forms and says she'll do her best, but without the exact date and location of the confinement, she can't promise to find the birth certificates. 'It's not a common name in the city, more popular on the Isle of Wight, I believe, but come back tomorrow at the same time and we'll see what I've come up with.'

Next day Jude collects two certificates, for the middle and younger brothers, Ben and Brian. It's a dead-end: under the heading 'Father' the form has been left blank. There's no trace of a certificate for the eldest brother; the registrar apologies and returns £3. 'I'm sorry, Jude, but there's no mention of a William or Bill. He wasn't born in Southampton, I've checked two years either side of the date you've given me, so I'm pretty sure of that.'

Jude is itching to know how his newly-discovered daughter is recovering after her ordeal. As soon as he's back into the office he grabs the local telephone directory and finds there are five listings for R Dixon, and starts dialling. On his fifth call the un-mistakable sharp, business tones of Chantelle, Sue's Mum, echo down the phone line. There are no pleasantries. 'What do you want, Jude. I think you've caused enough trouble, don't you?'

'Chantelle, I just wanted to make sure Catherine and Sue are OK. That's all I'm phoning for.'

'Yes, they're both fine, no thanks to you. That's why I'm here with them, to make sure they stay that way. Catherine is back to her normal happy self and Sue is OK, but won't let Catherine out of her sight.'

'What did happen, do you know?'

'What's it got to do with you? Looking for a better story, are we?'

'Chantelle, you know me better than that. This is my daughter we're talking about.

'That's just where you're wrong, Jude. I've told you; Catherine has a mummy and a daddy. You are not her parent. You gave up that right.

Jude has no answer, no argument that will shatter Chantelle's hard-as-glass heart. He sniffs back a tear. 'I know. I do. But just tell me what happened, please?'

'She's fine now, thank God. Look, not a word of this is for publication, OK?

'No, of course not, Chantelle.'

'Well, the police think she just wandered off. But I'm not so sure. Catherine's never been a sleepwalker. She's a sensible girl; I can't imagine she would have put clothes on over her nighty, she'd have got dressed properly. She can't remember what happened, how she got into the bin, which was too high for her to climb into without steps or help. But I know she's told me everything; I know when people lie to me.'

'How did Catherine seem, in herself?

'She was drowsy for the evening she came home and the next day. Sue and I checked on her in the bath. She hadn't been touched in any way, thank God.'

'Thank God.'

'Jude, what did you mean, after the police appeal, when you said Catherine was abducted to warn you off a story. You mentioned the Quirks.'

'It's nothing, I was shaken, you know, seeing Sue after so long, realising I had a child, a daughter. And that she'd been abducted. I think I just let my imagination run away with me. Sorry.'

'Jude, you're lying.'

'Chantelle, it's probably nothing. I was just getting a bit, well, spooked, I guess. I've done some stories that point towards the Quirks and missing drugs from police custody. You used to know everyone who was anyone, honest or otherwise, what do you know about the Quirk family?'

'I've been unlucky enough to come up against Deborah Quirk, not that I circulate in the same kind or world that she does, not any more.'

'She was very unhappy about my stories and warned me off. She said I'd get a warning, that I'd lose something precious, something I didn't even know I had. Maybe I put two and two together and came up with five.'

'Jude, be careful. Ever since she came over from the Isle of Wight, I've had my eye on Ms Quirk. She reminds me of a younger me, which is high praise. You know the word is that she has some very senior contact in the police who ensures her protection? Her sons are all feared; the youngest, Brian, is a real tearaway, a thug. Watch out for him. His two brothers are more sensible, but Mum runs the show. If they know about Catherine, well, stay well away. Or you'll have me to deal with, as well as the Quirks. I've told you before, I may not still be in my old line of business... but I still have some friends in this city.'

When Jude arrives for work the next day, the office is empty except for Jimmy. Jude recounts the phone call to his editor. 'Well, Jude, that may explain the lack of birth certificate for Bill. Back in the day, it wasn't unusual for a woman to go home, wherever that would be, for the birth of their first child. Especially a single mum, looking and needing support. Unmarried mums were a social pariah then, and not much has changed now.'

'So, Bill could have been born on the Isle of Wight? That makes sense. I'll give the register office in Newport a call.

'Don't hold your breath, the island's a bit of a time warp – it works at its own pace, and that pace makes a snail look like Alain Prost. Oh, by the way, when you were out, there was a phone call from a Stephen Wouldn'tgivehissurname. I've a phone number for him somewhere, he said he'd only speak to you and asked if you'd call him tonight, after seven.'

'Probably another nutter.'

Jimmy is right about the Isle of Wight Register Office. Jude speaks to the loquacious registrar, 'call me Meg,' who is charming and says, in her strong island accent, that she's keen to help. 'I would love to be of assistance, my dear, but rules are rules. It'd be anarchy without them, and we don't want that on the Isle of Wight, now, do we? Of course not, the visitors come here for some peace and quiet, not revolution. They come to the island for a nice ice cream, a deckchair on the sand and good home cooking in a clean guest house. Not the smashing of the novelty shops' windows along the front at Ventnor or the rumble of tanks along Yarmouth Pier, do they? Just pop your request for the birth certificate in the post, along with a £3 postal order and a large, self-addressed envelope. And we'll be straight on to it. Of course, that's as soon as we can find a moment, which won't be easy, let me tell you, there's the bank holiday coming up. Rosemary, that's my assistant, not the sharpest needle in the sewing box, if you know what I mean, always takes a week's holiday then, well, it's only four days isn't it, not a full week? But I promise faithfully, we'll do our best. Must go, it's time for my tea break and I can't upset the union now, can I?'

Jude replaces the phone's handset, shaking his head. He starts addressing an envelope to the island's register office and wonders if he'll hear anything back this century, let alone next week.

CHAPTER 31

I Don't Have Long

That evening Jude rings Mr Wouldn'tgivehissurname and is surprised to find out that, far from being 'a nutter', Stephen Green is an articulate young accountant who is gay and dying of AIDS. Down the crackly phoneline Jude is astonished how calm Stephen is, as if he's come to terms with his fate. He wants to speak to Jude about an incident he saw first-hand; a glass being smashed into a young man's face at a nightclub. He saw and recognised the man who did the smashing, a dark-haired well-built bouncer. Stephen says he was so close to the attack that when he got home that night, he found shards of glass in his own hair. The name of the bouncer he saw? Brian Quirk.

Two nights later, Jude pushes through a beaded curtain that is the entrance to *Manna,* a post-hippy vegetarian café set in an old, dilapidated building in the Portswood area of the city. Across the room, a gaunt-looking shell of a man appears out of place in the café's interior of bright abstract paintings and heavy incense aroma.

Despite the unseasonal warmth, the old man is wrapped inside numerous layers of dark clothes and his own thoughts. Spotting Jude, he waves slowly.

'Stephen? Hi, Jude, from *The Reporter.* But you guessed that. How?' He tries to make these few words sound upbeat – he wouldn't have recognised this old husk as the home of the young accountant's voice he'd heard on the phone.

In person, Stephen's voice doesn't sound quite so bright or young. 'Well, the notebook you're holding was a clue, as was your photo byline in the paper a few weeks ago.' He smiles and his eyes sparkle.

Jude laughs and thinks that, although Stephen might be dying, he obviously has his wits about him, including a sense of humour.

'Hope you don't mind coming here, Jude, but I've switched to a vegetarian diet. I'm not sure if it makes any difference, but you never know.' During the next hour, and over two mugs of camomile tea, Stephen explains how he'd been in the nightclub on the evening when Roy Bruce had been glassed by Brian Quirk, who ran the bouncers there. How the evening was the club's weekly 'gay night' and that only gay men and lesbians attended, except for the 'odd straight person who either came with a friend to see the weirdos, or has walked in by mistake'.

Jude wants to know why Stephen hadn't come forward at the time of the attack. 'Jude, it's not as easy as that. I'd have had to admit to being gay. I work, when I'm well enough, for the government, at the Tax Office, as an accountant. They don't discriminate as such, but I'd never have got promotion and there would have been jokes behind my back; life would have been unbearable. I'd have had to move, probably to London or Brighton, and I like it here. I've got, well, had, a good life. The gay community in this city isn't big and is, pretty much, underground. Most of us know each other and look out for one another. When Roy dropped charges, refused to give evidence on his own behalf, well, why should I bother? If I'm honest, that's what I thought.'

Stephen tells the reporter he's been diagnosed with AIDS and has been given, at most, six months to live. He explains that he's already lost two close friends to the disease.

'Stephen, you know you are going to have to talk to the police? You're going to have to make a legal statement, have it witnessed, so it can be used in evidence, even if you're not well enough to go to court.'

'Let's not pretend, Jude. I won't be alive when... if, Brian Quirk stands trial. I understand that, which is why I called *The Reporter.* You've covered the story and it's obvious that you've tried to expose Brian. I'm not sure I trust the police. In the club, Brian would brag that he had friends and family in high places, that he was "untouchable".'

'Was that when he visited the club, to check on his bouncers, that you heard him boast?'

'Jude, it's more than that. Brian is pretty mixed up. I think he's gay, but he can't admit it to himself, let alone his family.' The reporter stops taking his shorthand note and looks quizzically at Stephen, like he doesn't understand. 'It's not as uncommon as you may think, Jude. Many men and, I don't know, probably women, struggle to accept their true selves. Society doesn't welcome gays, does it?' Stephen takes a deep breath and then another sip of his camomile green tea.

'A couple of times Brian had been at the club and, despite himself, fancied another man and would buy them a drink. He'd get off with them, take them somewhere and, you know, have fun. Immediately afterwards he was ashamed of what he'd done and would hit them. Not playing, really beat them. And then he'd give them a load of cash to keep quiet. Basically, he'd have sex with a man then loathe himself for it, and take his self-loathing out on the person he's just had sex with.'

'Is that what happened, with Roy Bruce?'

'No. I said, the gay community in this city is small. After the second time Brian hit someone, well, the word got out. Everyone knew to avoid Brian, unless you liked being beaten up. When Brian made a move on Roy, well, Roy said he wasn't interested. Brian got mad, called Roy some disgusting names. Everyone in the club heard. Brian shouted, "You arse-bending faggot, no one would fuck you." Roy just stood there, looked Brian up and down and calmly said, "Well, you just wanted to. You were desperate to fuck me a minute ago." That's when Brian lost it. His eyes bulged and he grabbed the nearest thing, an empty pint glass, and just rammed it into Roy's face as hard as he could.' Stephen starts to cough and grabs for his handkerchief; telling the story is exhausting him. When he takes the handkerchief away, Jude sees it is blood-stained.

Stephen takes a while to regain his composure and then takes another sip of tea. 'Jude, I don't want to die without talking about what I witnessed. I owe it to, well, I'm not sure, Roy, everyone, I suppose. But I don't want to be shunned by my family and my friends from work. I may not have long, but I do want to enjoy, as much as I can, my final days.'

'Don't your family and friends know?'

'What, that I'm gay or dying?'

Jude tries to smile as he answers. 'Well, both, I guess.'

'Only those friends in the gay community; none of my family, for sure. Maybe some people at work suspect, but no one has asked and I don't volunteer too much. Does that make me a hypocrite?'

'Stephen, it's your choice to behave in whatever way you wish.'

'They'll know for sure, when I die. It'll say so on the death certificate. But I'll be past caring then, won't I?'

Jude explains that he knows a policeman who can be trusted, Sergeant Del Simpson. He is sure that Del would agree to meet Stephen and take his statement, away from a police station, so no other officer would know. He'd work out a way to ensure it will be used to bring Brian Quirk to justice.

Jude wishes he could walk from *Manna* to Danielle's flat, where pizza and Chianti are on the menu, so he'd have the chance to think and clear his head. But it's too far to walk, so he climbs into his old Peugeot. On the way, he is so distracted by his conversation with Stephen that he almost hits a Vauxhall Astra. The Astra driver honks his horn and brings Jude back into the moment and forces him to concentrate on the road. But his mind cannot stop turning over the conversation with Stephen. Jude knows he's just spent an hour with one of the nicest, most principled people he's ever met, a person who is strong enough to accept who he is, but who still wants to try to do the right thing. Jude is humbled and wonders, if the roles were reversed, whether he would be so much at ease with himself, and his fate.

CHAPTER 32

I Want to Make a Statement

Jude spends the night, as he's been doing more and more regularly, at Danielle's. It isn't just the sexual attraction, which is strong enough, but the pair are genuinely comfortable in each other's company: relaxed, happy and respectful. Neither speaks about the future, content to let it take care of itself. But, after spending time with Stephen, Jude feels unsettled. He'd told Danielle, over the homemade pizza, about his meeting with the brave, dying man, and she understood why Jude had been so impressed. Perhaps it was the bottle of Chianti, but the reporter did wonder aloud how he'd react if he knew his life was soon to be taken away. From there it was a short step to Danielle saying how she thought that, really, how little everyone controlled their own destinies, despite fooling themselves that they were 'masters of their own ship.' Jude agreed, saying there was no better reason to 'try and live in the moment.' Danielle nods her assent, grabs Jude's loosened tie and leads him to her bed.

Next day at work, Jude has a spring in his step, and considers how lucky he is. 'I've a wonderful girlfriend – wow, how did that happen? That's the first time I've called Danielle that – and there's now a real chance of landing Brian Quirk,' he thinks as he climbs the stairs to newsroom. But he knows he'll have to be careful so that he doesn't put Catherine, the daughter he was yet to meet, at risk.

It's mid-morning when Sarah and Robert leave the office to cover the unveiling of a new painting at the council-owned art gallery, and Jude can discuss his meeting with the man his editor knows as Stephen Wouldn'tgivehissurname.

Jimmy says, 'So, from what you've said, it sounds to me, lad, that the problem is how not to give the Quirks any opportunity to even guess you're involved. If Brian is charged, let alone found guilty of glassing Roy Bruce, well, Debbs isn't going to be happy. We've seen the lengths she'll go to, to protect her son. If she thinks for one moment that you've had a hand in helping Stephen make a statement, she's going to come after you or your daughter.'

'Jimmy, you're right. I know you are. So, I have to walk away from this story. Brian Quirk will be free to do whatever he wants to whoever he wants to do it to.'

'Jude, we're not the police. We're journalists. Never forget that.'

'Maybe that's the way forward, Jimmy? Get the police interested, really interested. They don't want Brian Quirk free on the streets. They want to see him go down.'

'Of course they do, Jude. But the trick will be finding a way of getting the police to take action while you and the paper stay out of it. That's how to protect Stephen and your daughter. Then, when Brian appears in court, we can report what happens. Debbs would have to accept that, court reporting is what newspapers do, for God's sake.'

Jude nods. 'OK, I'll call Del. No, better than that, I'll nip up to Winchester and meet him somewhere outside of his office for a coffee. And we don't mention this to Robert. And we really, really don't mention it to bloody Sarah.'

'OK. Just, you know, be careful, Jude. One slip and it would be something you'd regret for the rest of your life, which, given the circumstances, might not be very long.'

Jude smiles, then, realising the implications of his editor's comments, frowns. He calls Del and the pair arrange to meet at *The Wykeham Arms*, which is far enough away from police HQ and has secluded booths in its bar.

Over his pint of lager, Jude tells Del about the new witness. Del, sipping from a vodka and tonic, quickly understands the implications. 'This is great news, Jude. We all knew that the Quirks got to Roy Bruce, but he denied it, so there was nothing we could do. This Stephen Green, is he reliable? I know it's wrong, but the courts, especially juries, don't give as much credence to homosexuals.'

'Del, he's an accountant at the Tax Office, for God's sake, he couldn't be any more respectable and boring if he tried, could he?'

'Fair point. There's one small issue, the statement should be taken by someone more senior than me, if it's to be really credible. I'll be there, but two signatures of witnesses, one a senior officer, would give the statement more impact, especially if Stephen isn't, sadly, around to give his evidence.'

'That's a problem, Del. I've said to Stephen that I can vouch for you, but anyone else…'

'I can vouch for Smarties, Chief Inspector Michael Matthews. He's more than senior enough, he's sound and I trust him not to go telling everyone in the police canteen.'

'Del… are you, you know, sure. Two people, one was a working girl, the other, from Transport Police, have both told me they've had trouble with Smarties.'

'I know he's ambitious and he does rub some people up the wrong way, but I work with him every day. Trust me, he's sound.'

'I don't know, I've not exactly got on well with him, either, Del. He threatened me after the "missing police cannabis story" and tried to find out who my source was.'

'He was protecting Hampshire Police's reputation, or trying to – that's supposed to be the job of the press office, after all. Look, he's got experience of running vice, so he'll make sure Stephen doesn't miss out anything important in his statement. And, as he and I are in the same office, there's no chance of "leakage."'

'But at the docks, when the drugs were dropped into the

Solent, he upset people and then legged it when the seizure was botched,' Jude argues.

'I've said that he's not everyone's cup of tea, Jude. But Smarties is no mug and the only reason he was at the docks was to ensure the force got maximum positive publicity from the raid. I'd have "legged it", as you put it, given the way things turned out. Trust me, Smarties is ideal and ticks the boxes: he's senior enough, has the right experience and, between him and me, we can ensure no one else knows about Stephen's statement.'

Jude thinks long and hard before responding. 'OK, if you're sure about Smarties, then Smarties it is. Just one other thing, don't tell anyone else, certainly not Sarah at our place, about this. And no one, not even Smarties, your boss or not, must know I'm involved.' Jude puts down his pint and looks Del squarely in the eye. 'Promise me Del; other people's safety relies on no one ever knowing that I'm anywhere near this.'

'Of course, Jude. I'll tell Smarties that Stephen saw my name against a police quote in the story you wrote about the glassing, and called me. Will that work for you?' Jude nods. 'Good, you tell Stephen that, after he read *The Reporter* article, he phoned me at the police press office, so we've all got the same story.'

Del finishes his vodka and says he'll check a suitable time with his boss and get back to Jude to make the arrangements to take Stephen's statement. He picks up his coat, smiles goodbye to Jude and leaves the old pub. Jude decides to allow five minutes before following the policeman, to ensure no one spots them together, and slowly finishes his lager, thinking through his plan. 'God, I'm getting paranoid. Now four people will know about Stephen: me, Jimmy, Del and, soon, Smarties. Actually, make that five, I told Danielle. Oh well, she's the least of my worries. I just need to get this meeting and the statement made sooner than later. I'm no doctor, but Stephen really isn't well,' Jude thinks and, leaving the dregs of his lager in the glass, heads for his car.

Back at work, Jude doesn't have to wait long before Del calls. 'Right, Jude, can you talk? Good, tomorrow night, will that work for Stephen, say 7pm at *The Old Farmhouse* in Northam?'

'That's great, I'll check, but I'm sure it will be fine.'

'Me and Smarties, er, Chief Inspector Michael Matthews, will be in two separate cars, me in my lovely blue Jaguar XJ-SC, and the chief inspector will be in his dirty brown Ford Granada. It's better we have two vehicles; one can check if the other is being followed. We'll be in the car park outside the pub bang on 7. Tell Stephen to approach either car and tap on a window. We'll have checked the pub out first, to make sure there are no "faces" inside. If he gets a thumbs up, tell Stephen to go into the pub. If there's someone inside who we don't fancy, we'll give a thumbs down and he should get into the passenger seat of that car and we'll find somewhere else to take the statement.'

'All sounds a bit cloak and dagger, Del. But no worries, I'll remember. If we can't go into the pub he'll get into the passenger seat, I'll jump in the back. I'll pick Stephen up and drive him.'

'Whoa! Jude, are you crazy? You can't be anywhere near the pub or even Northam. If I was you, I'd be outside of the city somewhere and be seen to be wherever you are, as an alibi.'

'But Stephen's not well enough to drive. And I don't want to miss out on hearing the statement being made.'

'He'll have to get a bus or a taxi. Jude, as you said, there are other people's safety at stake here, your daughter for one. Look, don't tell anyone about the meeting, not where or when it is, nothing. That's the only way you can be sure it'll remain secret. What do they say in the Navy? "Loose lips cost ships.".'

Reluctantly, Jude accepts the wisdom of Del's advice, replaces the receiver and calls Stephen to pass on the details of the meeting.

CHAPTER 33

No Show

Two days later, walking into *The Reporter* newsroom, Jude is anxious to hear how the meeting between Stephen and the two police officers went. But first, with no one else yet in the office, he has to silence a phone ringing off its cradle.

'Jude? Well, that was a waste of my time, wasn't it? Your brilliant contact didn't show, did he. What happened?'

'Sm–, Chief Inspector Matthews, sorry, er, good morning to you. What do you mean, didn't show?'

'Jude, you're paid, not very well, I suspect, as a reporter to use the English language. I believe that "didn't show" can only have the one meaning. *Didn't*, the opposite to did, and *show*, meaning to turn up or be present.'

The sarcasm dripped from the policeman's voice. 'So, to answer your question, it means, where the fuck was this Stephen, if he even exists?'

'Now, that's not fair, Chief Inspector. He does exist and he knows things that he could only know if he was present at the nightclub when the glassing happened. He found fragments of the pint glass in his hair later that night, that's how close he was.'

'Well, he wasn't anywhere near *The Old Farmhouse* last night, that's for sure. I waited an hour in the car park. Next time you've got a top witness, make sure he doesn't bottle it.' The line clicks dead. Something isn't right, Jude feels, but can't figure what it is.

His head is reeling from the unexpected bollocking from Smarties.

Throughout the morning Jude calls Stephen's number but the phone just rings and rings. He worries that the accountant's health has taken a turn for the worse but calls to the local hospitals prove negative. Come lunchtime, Jude is at his wit's end. With only Jimmy in the office to overhear, he calls Del at the police press office.

'Del, I need a favour. From phone numbers, you can get people's addresses, can't you? You've access to data bases to carry out a reverse search, don't you? It's Stephen; he's not answering his phone and I don't know where he lives, although it's probably somewhere in the Portswood area.'

'Good lunchtime to you too, Jude. He didn't turn up last night, Smarties was more than a little pissed off about wasting his evening. Apparently, he'd planned to take his missus to the pictures to see *Personal Services,* he said it would remind him of his time in vice. I suspect he thought it might get his other half in the mood...'

'No wonder he wasn't happy. Did you both just twiddle your thumbs, wasting an hour?'

'Well, he wasted an hour. I got there just after 8pm and Smarties was about to drive away, he was really pissed off.'

Jude thinks this sounds strange. 'Why weren't you there, Del?'

'Ah, on the way *The Old Farmhouse* there was a Code Zero call on the police radio. Sorry, that's an officer under attack emergency alert. It was in Fareham and I wasn't a million miles away so I turned around. If you hear a Code Zero you have to attend, it's the unwritten rule of being a copper, even if you're off duty. It was all a bit of a waste of time, really. When I got there the incident was all over, bit of a storm in a teacup, but some idiot jobsworth inspector insisted I stay and make a statement. By the time I got to the pub car park, well, Smarties had had enough and was about to leg it. We said "hello and goodbye" and that was that.'

Jude's head finally clears and he realises what's been bothering him. 'Hang on, how did Smarties know I put Stephen in contact with you? Del, you said, you promised me, you wouldn't tell anyone, including your boss.'

'I didn't tell him, honestly, Jude. I said that Stephen must have read my name in your article about the glassing and had contacted me. He must have figured it out; it wouldn't be very difficult for a chief inspector to work out the truth; it's what they've spent their whole life doing, and most of them are pretty good at it. And you're the only person, other than the police, who's ever been interested in this story. Truth be told, I'm not a very good liar, which isn't really the required trait for working in the press office, is it? Now Smarties has got me down as lying to him, which is all I need... Right, tell me about that favour you wanted.'

Jude thought for a moment about what Del had just said, but couldn't really make full sense of the situation. He pressed on. 'Del, it's Stephen's address. I've got his phone number, but he's not in the phone book and he's never told me where he lived and I never asked. I should have done.'

'Well, normally it would be illegal to give you this info, but as he is a potential witness to a serious incident and, as there is concern about his whereabouts and health, I might be able to help. I'll see what I can find out and call back.'

'Thanks, Del, you a star.'

By the time Jude had made himself and Jimmy a cup of coffee the phone on his desk was ringing. 'Jude, it's Del.'

'That's bloody quick, well done Hampshire Police.'

'I don't think you're going to thank me, Jude. I don't think you're going to need Stephen's address, either. I've just been reading the overnight logs and a body's been found at Northam Station. It looks like a man fitting the description of Stephen committed suicide on the tracks of the old station sometime last night. You know it hasn't been a working station for decades, so the body was only seen early this morning. Sorry, Jude.'

'How do you know it's Stephen?' Jude realised he was gripping the phone with all his might. He forced himself to relax his fingers and to breathe deeply.

'We don't, I'm just giving you a heads up. But he's dark-haired, average height, in his late 20s but looks much older and clearly suffering from a serious disease that has caused, according to the police doctor called to the scene, "significant atrophy". I've phoned the doctor and asked if this was consistent with AIDS. He told me he was "no AIDS expert" but believes it could be. And Northam train station is no distance from *The Old Farmhouse.* We're trying to contact relatives for a formal identification.'

'If I can help, Del?'

'I did wonder, but as you only know Stephen by what he's told you – I'm guessing you never saw any formal proof of identity – you can't formally identify him. But thanks, Jude. I'll keep in touch.'

CHAPTER 34

Piss or Get Off the Pot

Eventually the body, or what is left of it after being run over by the Waterloo to Weymouth express and then being left overnight to the mercy of the local foxes, is confirmed as Stephen by his dental records. The authorities have little doubt that, with his quality of life rapidly deteriorating and the inevitability of death from 'an AIDS related disease,' the young accountant took his own life. But without a suicide note or any other evidence of Stephen's intent, the inquest will, when it considers the cause of his death, be almost certain to record an open verdict.

'Why would Stephen have taken his own life before seeing Smarties and giving him a statement? He was eager, no, desperate to see Brian Quirk brought to justice. It just doesn't make sense to me,' says Jude as he places two mugs of tea and a packet of chocolate bourbons down on his editor's desk, happy he could talk openly with Sarah and Robert again out of the newsroom.

Jimmy thinks for a moment. 'Have you spoken to you mate at Transport Police, asked if they are happy with the suicide, if there's anything unusual?'

'Inspector Broski? Yeah, I've called but he wasn't in his office so I've left a message on his answerphone.'

'Jude, are you really sure you don't want to let this go? You know the risk you're taking by still chewing on this particular bone.'

'Look, if Stephen didn't commit suicide, well, the Quirks would be behind whatever happened to him. Which means that, somehow, they knew he was planning to talk to the police. If we let this go, well, who's next? There must be a way to make them back off.'

Jimmy dipped the chocolate bourbon into his tea for too long, and a waterlogged chunk fell into his *I'm A Daily Mirror Reader* mug. 'Bollocks,' he mutters, scalding his fingers in a failed attempt to fish the biscuit out. 'There is, but it's a high-risk strategy and the outcome is unpredictable, a bit like dunking this bloody biscuit.'

'Tell me more, Jimmy.'

'"Piss or get off the pot." It's what Richard Nixon said to Eisenhower, when he was running for President in '52. Eisenhower couldn't decide whether or not to drop Nixon as his running mate for Vice President from the Republican ticket. Nixon had been accused of accepting dodgy funds and told the future president to "Piss or get off the pot," to go all-in and back him, or sack him and move on. Poker players still use the expression and, Jude, that's what you've got to do... either forget all about the Quirks or raise the stakes. Going all in would mean getting the story out there, getting the police really interested and investigating. If the Quirks are centre stage with the spotlight shining on them, well, it'll be too dangerous for the family to move against anyone. If they know they're being seriously watched and investigated, you've raised the stakes.'

Jude whistled. 'That is high-risk. And the risk isn't just mine, is it?'

'No, but the choice is, you've got to decide. The bright decision is to walk away, right now. But if you can't do that, well, you choose. It's piss or get off the pot time, Jude.'

The reporter knew, deep inside, that he didn't have a choice. This was what he did, why he had wanted to become a journalist in the first place – to expose what needed exposing, to right wrongs. It was who he was. OK, he was still only a trainee, in the job less than a year, but if you were good enough, you were experienced enough, he told himself. He would minimise any risk, especially to others. Of course, he would…

'So, I've got to get the police interested, really, really interested, but stay out of it. No one who is remotely connected with the Quirks must be able to even guess that I'm involved? That's what you're suggesting, Jimmy, isn't it?'

'If you intend to carry on investigating the Quirks, which you obviously are, it seems to me that you have to make the police desperate to land the family, that it becomes the force's number one priority. But without anyone else knowing you've helped the police.'

'And how will I manage that?'

'Jude, that's your problem. But you have to get someone at a very senior level committed to the cause of landing the Quirks. Del's a great contact, but this is way above his pay grade and level of influence. Best of luck and be bloody careful. Now, in case you hadn't noticed, it's only two days to deadline and we've got a paper to fill.'

That night, at Danielle's, Jude cooked spaghetti bolognaise and thought about how he would make the Quirks public enemy number one. He knows as much about the family as anyone who isn't working for them. Once again, he goes over all the facts. First, the Quirks had moved against the city's other major drug dealers, all but handing them over to a grateful police force. Then they'd moved against smaller dealers, like his distant cousin, Kevin, who was certainly set up. Then the pub landlords, like his cousin, Gerry, were being forced to pay for protection. Even *Queenie's Massage Palace* was torched when she refused to pay 'insurance' to the Quirks. There was evidence, Debbs even admitted it on the tape, that the family were buying confiscated drugs from the police, and Brian had boasted about protection from people 'in high places' inside the force.

The one thing he isn't sure about is Stephen's suicide. No way would Stephen have taken his own life, it just doesn't add up, Jude thinks. Not if you'd met him. No way would he'd jump in front of a train, certainly not before giving a statement to Smarties. No way. Someone in the police must have told the Quirks. I could give evidence that Stephen Green had told me how he'd seen Brian Quirk smash a glass into Roy Bruce's face after he'd turned down his sexual advances. That would be risky, but I could–

'Jude! What are you doing? The spaghetti!' Danielle shouts, bringing the reporter back to the moment. He inhales the smell of burning pasta, coming from a pan just a few feet away.

'Oh, bugger, er, sorry. Ouch!' Jude grabs the saucepan's handle and instantly feels a searing pain in his hand and drops it back on the stove. He snatches a tea towel and wraps it around the handle before picking it up again. The pot is placed in the sink and filled with water from the cold tap.

'No matter, there's loads more spaghetti in the cupboard,' says Danielle. 'You better put your hand under the tap as well, that's going to sting. I said you didn't need to cook, I'd do it.'

Danielle finds a new saucepan and fills it with hot water from the kettle. As soon as it boils, she carefully slides a small bunch of long spaghetti into the bubbling water, waiting for each strand to become soft and bend around the pot before immersing the bunch completely and adding the next. 'What were you dreaming of?'

The ice-cold water from the tap is easing the pain in Jude's right hand. He feels embarrassed; it's the first time he's cooking for them both and he's failed at even making a passable spag bol. He realises he must look a total knob to his new girlfriend. 'I'm sorry about the dinner.'

'It doesn't matter, 12 minutes and this spaghetti will be ready. Mind you, it might take a little longer to get rid of the smell of cremated pasta.' Danielle smiles. How many other women would take an incident like this in their stride, he wonders? 'Seriously, Jude, what were you thinking about, other than cooking me a lovely meal?'

'It's the Quirks… again. I've decided, with Jimmy's blessing, to up the stakes. I'm sure they're behind Stephen's death; there's no way he'd have killed himself, not before giving a statement.

Someone in the police must have told the family, warned them about what he was going to say and that it would put Brian behind bars.'

'Jude, you said before these are dangerous people. It is wise to take them on, especially after what happened to Catherine? You said that was a warning.'

'That's the whole point. By raising the stakes, getting the police to focus on the Quirks, it will prevent them being able to hurt anyone else, to make any more moves. At least, that's the plan.'

'Sounds dangerous to me. Do you have enough evidence to force the police to investigate the family?'

'That's what I was considering, for the 50th time today. And the answer is, well, no, not really. I'd just realised that I don't have enough hard evidence for the police when you raised the spaghetti alarm. I think it looks pretty unlikely that I'll get enough hard evidence. It needs the resources, money and experience of a major police force. But if I don't have enough evidence for the force, I might have enough for one very senior officer, and, ultimately, he has the power to us those resources, the force's money and experience.'

'I'm not sure I understand, Jude?'

'Chief Inspector Michael Matthews, Smarties as we call him, was headed for the top but got moved sideways from Vice to the Press Office after some unproven rumours – he might even have been set up by the Quirks, who knows? I know he's still ambitious but he needs a big success to get his career back on track. If he doesn't, well, he'll end his career handing out press releases to reporters like me, rather than chatting to the Home Secretary or being invited to tea at The Palace, like Chief Constables do. I just need to convince him that the Quirks are his ticket back to the big time.'

Danielle drains the pasta in a colander, melts a knob of butter in the saucepan and returned the spaghetti to the pan, gently twirling it around as she did so. 'Right, given you've only got one hand, I'll serve up and then, while we eat, you can tell me how you're going to convince Smarties.'

Jude's 'plan' was far from fully hatched, more a rough idea. But as he spoke, through mouthfuls of Danielle's excellent pasta and his very average bolognaise sauce, he fleshes out the idea into a workable strategy. 'I'm just going to tell him all I know – he's spent a couple of years heading up vice, so he'll understand the details – and tell him that landing the Quirks is how he can be considered a serious officer again. And, as a bonus, I'll tell him that I might even be able to throw in the name of the Quirk father, who's involved up to his neck, but for some reason has always remained secret.'

Danielle nods but looks concerned. 'Jude, when we're faced with convincing an advertiser to place an order with us, we're trained to see the transaction from the customer's point of view and ask "what's in it for them?" So, tell me, "What's in it for Smarties?" Why should he buy this from you?'

'Good question. It's his route to getting his career back on track. I'll guarantee him that, when *The Reporter* has finished covering the story, Smarties will be seen as a cross between Bergerac, Kojac and Inspector Morse. I'll call him tomorrow and arrange to meet away from his or our office. But don't tell anyone, Danielle; the fewer people that know, the safer everyone will be.'

CHAPTER 35

Real Motivation?

Smarties and Jude agree to meet in the car park of *The Old Farm-house,* the same location the Chief Inspector had been due to meet Stephen a few days earlier. Smarties had been insistent that no one, not even Jude's editor, should know about their meeting. 'If someone is getting this information to the Quirks, they must either have contacts at *The Reporter,* or, God forbid, in the police. Either way, let's just keep this just between ourselves for the time being. OK, Jude?'

The reporter realises that Smarties is no fool; Jude hasn't considered the possibility, after ensuring Sarah was kept in the dark, that anyone else at *The Reporter* could be on the Quirks' payroll. The pub is a good place for a lunchtime meeting – quiet enough to be unlikely to bump into someone either of them knows, but with enough passing trade to make it unlikely they'd be remembered by the pub staff. Jude pulls into the car park and sees Smarties sitting in his Granada. The driver's window of the big Ford slides down, the chief inspector shakes his head and indicates for the reporter to follow him. Smarties drives the Granada out of the car park and soon pulls to a halt on the overgrown weeds that were once the cobbled drive into the long-disused Northam Railway Station. Jude brings his aging Peugeot to a stop and thinks it odd to be going to the site where Stephen Green had just died.

The Chief Inspector walks over to the Peugeot and opens the driver's door. 'Sorry about that, Jude, I saw a face I knew go into *The Old Farmhouse*; I can't take the risk. We can chat inside the old station, there'll be no one here to see us. Follow me, there's a gap in the fence – I found it when I came to look at where poor Stephen Green's body was found a couple of days ago. Look, sorry I was a bit sharp on the phone the other day. I thought I'd been stood up and, well, I had no idea of Stephen's fragile mental state.'

Jude nods. 'Forget it, Chief Inspector, I'd have reacted the same.

'Jude, call me Michael, no need to be formal.'

'OK, Michael. It's funny, Stephen didn't seem fragile. I'd spent time with him and he seemed calm, resigned to his fate. That was what I can't make sense of, he was really keen to make his statement about seeing Brian Quirk glass Roy Bruce in the club.'

'When you've covered as many suicides as I have, you stop being surprised. Ask any experienced police officer who's had to interview the last friend or relative to speak to someone who's committed suicide. Do you know what that friend or relative almost always says?'

Jude shakes his head at the chief inspector's question.

'It's "they seemed so normal: relaxed and calm." And they are, often, because they've decided and settled on a course of action. No more doubts or prevarication. They've decided to take their own life and then they go through with it calmly and peacefully. That is the difference from an attempted suicide and a suicide. The first is a cry for help. The second is a decision.'

Smarties pulls back some rusty wire fencing, nods, and Jude scrambles through. Smarties follow and carefully pulls the fencing back in place. They clamber up on to the desolate station platform, overgrown with weeds and broken glass, disturbing the pigeons as they go. 'How quickly nature reclaims,' Jude thinks as the pair walk along Platform 1.

'Let's go into the waiting room.' Jude doesn't hear the Chief Inspectors, the words drowned out by an express train hammering past at full speed. Hit hard by the 120-mph train's slipstream, Jude stumbles towards the track. Smarties grabs at the reporter, firmly holding his arm. 'Be careful, Jude, you only fall in front of a train like that once,' he smiles.

'Thanks, I owe you, Smart, er, Michael.'

'You can use Smarties, if you prefer, it's OK.'

'You know about your nickname? The word was you didn't.'

'You'll learn, Jude, that sometimes, most of the time in fact, it's better to let others think you know less than you actually do.' He holds open the waiting room door which, surprisingly, still swings noiselessly on its hinges. 'There we go, why don't you sit there, under the window, so you'll have some light to make notes?'

Jude blows some of the dust from the wooden bench and creates a mild sandstorm in the old grey and green waiting room. Smarties picks up a yellowing newspaper from the floor, shakes it before placing it on the bench and against the wall, to protect his designer suit from the dirt, and sits opposite Jude.

Jude draws a deep breath and begins, 'I've a lot to tell you Michael. Much of it, if not all, you'll already know. Basically, the criminal family, the Quirks, headed by mum Debbs, is taking over, or have already taken over, this city's crime scene. They started with nightclub bouncers, moved into drugs and now also run protection rackets throughout the whole area.'

The Chief Inspector nods and listens attentively for the next 20 minutes, asking sensible questions about how a piece of information can be confirmed or who else witnessed an incident. Jude concludes by saying that, with the resources of the police, all of what he says can be proved. 'But it seems to me that there can be no doubt that the Quirks are protected by a senior ranking police officer or officers in the force. That has to be the only reason they have avoided prosecution up until now. You're senior enough, as a Chief Inspector, to land the Quirks. If you do that *The Reporter* and the other media will make you a hero, I promise that. And Hampshire Police will have to recognise your achievement. Who knows where your career could then lead?'

Smarties lets out a deep breath. 'That's quite a story, Jude. If I'm honest, I've had my suspicions about the Quirks for years but I was never, when I ran vice, allowed to investigate them. There was always a lame excuse or dodgy reason given by "those above". But the police force is a structured and regimented service: you have to obey orders, however illogical or stupid they may seem.' He smiles at Jude. 'It's not like, well, journalism, where a rogue trainee reporter can bring in the scoop of the year, then gets to choose whatever job he fancies in Fleet Street.' The chief inspector scratches his head. 'As you say, landing the Quirks, will be a major operation and secrecy will be paramount. The family seem to know everything you've been up to, and it does look like there's a spy in one of our camps. I've told no one of our meeting. For an operation against the Quirks to have any chance of success I need to be assured that you've done the same? That no one in your office, not even your editor, Jimmy Graves, knows we're meeting now, today. Is that the case?'

Jude thinks for a moment and decides to discount Danielle, as she doesn't work in the newsroom, and looks the chief inspector in the eye. 'Michael, you have my word, no one knows I'm here or even meeting you at all. No one.'

Old Jones shuffles into the newsroom at *The Reporter.* 'Here you go, Sarah, not much afternoon post today. You'll have to make up the letters again for our *Readers' Views* page. Don't suppose there's any coffee going, is there?'

'Cheeky. Sit down and I'll put the kettle on.' Sarah takes the half a dozen envelopes and skims through them. Her eyes light up when she notices the postmark on one and immediately starts to open it. 'This is from the island, addressed to Jude in his own handwriting. I bet it's what he's waiting for, from the Isle of Wight registrar.'

'Don't open that,' Jimmy shouts, getting out of his chair. 'That's Jude's private post.'

'Too late,' Sarah smiles and pulls a copy of a birth certificate from inside the envelope and reads it. 'Oh, fuck me,' she gasps and sits down in Jude's chair, the nearest to her.

'There's no need for language like that, young lady. I'd put you over my knee if you were my daughter,' Old Jones says, then realises he may have just talked himself out of a coffee.

'What is it?' Jimmy has now limped as quickly as he can and takes the certificate from a glazed Sarah.

She slowly shakes her head. 'It's only Smarties. Fuck me, Chief Inspector Michael Matthews, is only Bill Quirk's dad.'

Jimmy studies the birth certificate. 'Fuck me indeed. Look, he wasn't a high-ranking officer then, his occupation on the form is given as "police sergeant."' The editor thinks for a moment, then looks concerned. 'Sarah, Robert, do either of you know where Jude is? I mean, right now?'

Sarah is still a little stunned but answers. 'Jimmy, you're the bloody editor, not us. If anyone should know...'

The Chief Inspector stands up, drawing himself to his full, imposing six-foot two-inch height. 'I've got to say you make a compelling argument, Jude, but what you're suggesting could, by the way, just as easily end my career as advance it. OK, I've been sidelined, moved into the Press Office, which was run by a plain Inspector before they put me there. But it could be worse and, down the line, I do get a very generous pension.' He's interrupted by the noise of a speeding Waterloo-bound express charging through the rickety station, and checks his watch. 'Every 30 minutes...' he says distractedly, before looking back down at Jude, who's still sitting on the waiting room bench. 'Just tell me, before I commit to doing what you wish, why didn't you back off when you had the chance? Why don't you back off now? They've kidnapped your daughter, a clear threat that they'll do something more serious next time, maybe even kill her or you. What is it, Jude? Do you believe what you said, by raising the stakes, getting us, the police, to watch their every move, they will stop moving, that we will nullify their threat? Or is it your lust for glory, the ambition of seeing your name on the exclusive story that exposes a city's major crime family and uncovers high-level police corruption? Which is it, Jude, what's your real motivation?' The Chief Inspector looms over the sitting reporter.

'I've asked myself that, late at night. But what does that matter to you? What does it matter if you can bring to justice the family that is terrorising the city, fuelling its drugs trade and is responsible for God knows how many deaths? I'm giving you the chance to re-establish your career by bringing in the Quirks: Mum, Ben, Bill and Brian. And, for a bonus, perhaps even the dad. I hope to know his name within the next few days, and he's certainly involved.'

Smarties looks surprised. 'A Daddy Quirk. That is a concern.' He nods, a quick, little nod at first. He then follows it with two, long exaggerated nods and stares past Jude.

The reporter hears the window behind him opening but, before he can look around, there's a 'swoosh' through the air and a muffled 'splat' sound, like a joint of fresh meat being thrown onto a butcher's slab, as a short truncheon hits Jude squarely on the back of the head. The cosh, along with the arm holding it, disappear back through the window. Smarties quickly steps forward and catches Jude's slumping body as it falls towards the ground.

CHAPTER 36

Won't Be Able to Find His Head

Danielle walks breezily into the newsroom, clutching a sandwich wrapped in Cellophane, an apple, a tin of Fanta and a bag of Smith crisps. Somehow, she also manages to hold out a packet of Smarties. In response to the editorial team's quizzical looks, she feels compelled to speak. 'Oh, I thought Jude was working in the office, sorry. I was going to give him the sweets, silly me.'

Jimmy looks perplexed but Sarah jumps up from Jude's chair and her voice has an unusually urgent tone. 'Danielle, can I ask, why were you giving those Smarties to Jude? It's important.'

'I'd just bought my lunch at the shop across the road and I saw them. That's all.'

Sarah raises her voice. 'Danielle, this is serious. Why Smarties?'

Old Jones, always the champion of the underdog, stands up, broom in hand. 'Now, look, Sarah, don't bully Danielle here. There's no need for that.'

Sarah's words are clipped and quick. 'There bloody well is. Don't you get it? Jude could be at risk, serious risk.' She walks over to Danielle, stands a foot from her and stares up, directly into her eyes. 'One last time, why did you buy the Smarties for Jude? What has he told you?'

'He told me it was... not for repeating, not to anyone.'

Jimmy catches on the possible significance of the sweets and limps over to the two women. 'Danielle, you might know some-thing vital. Don't worry about not telling, what has Jude told you about his plans?'

'He said it would be safer if I didn't tell anyone what he was doing.'

'Look, we think, really think, that Jude could be in danger. From what's in your hand, he was going to meet Smarties, wasn't he?'

'If you already know, well, Jude just said that he was going to call Smarties today and arrange to meet him, that's why I bought him these. I thought they'd give him a smile. That's all.'

Sarah shakes her head. 'Where did he say they were going to meet?'

'It was nowhere definite, it just had to be away from the office and not at any police station. I'm not sure I should be tell-ing y–'

'Come on Danielle, what else did he say?' Sarah cuts across the paper's newest sales rep. 'There must have been some pillow talk?'

Jimmy looks askance, unaware of the relationship between his reporter and Danielle, but says nothing. Old Jones points his broom at Sarah and is about to speak.

Sarah fixes him with a stare. 'Shut up, Old Jones, this is ser-ious. Well, Danielle?'

'Jude said that he'd get Smarties to investigate by promising it would get his career back on track; he was going to promise the Chief Inspector great publicity, that he'd make him look like a "cross between Bergerac, Kojac and, er, yes, that was it, Inspector Morse."'

Sarah nods, her tone is more conciliatory. 'Nothing else? Did Jude mention anything about a dad?'

'Yes, yes he did, let me think.' Danielle closes her eyes for a moment. 'He said, as a bonus, he'd tell Smarties that he expected to have the name of the Quirk boys' father very soon. He said the father was involved "up to his neck, but for some reason has al-ways remained secret."'

'Holy fuck!' Sarah shouts and grabs the phone on Jude's desk and starts dialling.

Jimmy shakes his head. 'Sarah, let's think a moment, don't be hasty.'

Sarah holds up her hand, indicating for Jimmy to keep his distance. 'I've thought too much. Now I'm going to act.'

Danielle has no idea what was happening. 'Can you explain, please. Why is everyone looking so worried? What's going on? Where's Jude, right now?'

Sarah puts a hand over the telephone's mouthpiece. 'That's what we're trying to find out. After what you've said, we think he may be meeting Smarties, the man who *is* the father of the Quirks. It must be Smarties who's the senior police officer protecting the family all these years, the man who's helped them take over this city.' She stops talking, puts her fingers to her lips for silence and then speaks into the telephone handset. 'Del, thank God you're in the office.'

'Sarah, lovely to hear from you, much more charming than that callow youth colleague of yours. How is he, by the way?'

'That's why I'm phoning. Jude's supposed to be meeting your boss, Smarties, but we don't know where and I've got to get an urgent message to him. It's important, Del.'

'What, dry cleaning needs collecting, or did he write that Mr and Mrs Job's daughter's name was Blow instead of Blaire in the report of her wedding?'

Sarah thinks Del has the capacity to be the most annoying man on the planet. 'Jude could be in danger, Del, serious shit. Do you know where he's meeting Smarties?'

'No, I didn't even know they were meeting. Let me check the diary. Hang on. No, nothing in there, nothing written down, which is strange as Smarties is the officer on call. If I hear of anything, I'll let you know. Bye.'

Sarah puts the phone back in its cradle and turns to face everyone. 'Well, we're bolloxed, aren't we?'

Old Jones raises his hand, like he was back in school, 60 years ago. 'I might be able to help. Jude got into his car about, I dunno, an hour or so ago. I asked if he was off somewhere nice and he just laughed. Said something about going to an ancient farm to talk about a family of rats.'

'Robert, follow me,' Sarah calls, grabs the Quirk birth certificate from the desk and heads for the door. 'And bring a photo of Jude with you.'

'Sarah, where are you going? I'm the bloody editor, I tell people what to do.'

'Jimmy, isn't it obvious?' Sarah stops in the doorway. "An ancient farm, to talk about a family of rats?" He meant 'The Old Farmhouse, where Smarties and Del were going to meet Stephen. "The family of rats" are the Quirks. Let's go, Robert.' The photographer grabs his camera bag, snatches a black and white print from his desk and runs to catch up with Sarah.

'That makes sense. Just call me when you get there, find a phone box and tell me what's happening.' Jimmy shouts but is unsure if Sarah has heard him through the now-closed newsroom door.

Tucking the little cosh into an inside pocket of his padded jacket, Brian Quirk joins his father, who nods towards Jude's feet. Together the pair lift the journalist's prone body through the swing door of the waiting room. 'I better get rid of the cosh, Dad, your lot will tie it up with the dent in his head.'

'Trust me son, once the Waterloo train has gone through, they won't be able to find his head. Now, less talking and more carrying. I want him on the track in the shadow over there, under the bridge,' arms full, the chief inspector points with his head, 'where it's so dark, even if the driver does see him, he won't have time to stop.'

'But if the train is stopping at the station, Dad, it'll be going slow enough to stop, won't it?'

'Brian, no train has stopped here for the last 20 years, that's why I chose it... God give me strength.'

Slowly, the pair carry Jude down the narrow concrete steps from the platform to the track. They place the body lengthways

along and on top of the rail furthest away from the electric con-
ductor, aware they'll be electrocuted if Jude touches the live rail
while they're holding him.

'Dad, shouldn't we tie him to the track? What if he comes
round, you know, and moves? Escapes?'

'He's not coming round anytime soon, not the way you hit
him, trust me. We can't tie him down – it won't look like suicide
then, will it? It'll be murder, plain and simple.' The Chief Inspector shakes his head, and, for the briefest of moments, wonders if Brian is really his son.

'Dad, I've never, you know… before.'

'There's no choice, Brian. He was going to do for us, if we
didn't do for him first. Sticking his nose in, crusading against the
family. We couldn't let that continue, could we?'

'But killing him. That's a life sentence.'

'Only if we get caught. And,' the policeman looks at his
watch, 'we won't if we get a move on. The Waterloo train is due
in five, no four minutes. Come on, let's get out of here.'

Sarah's car skids to a halt outside the front of *The Old Farmhouse*. There are no other cars in the car park. 'Not a good sign,'
she says, more to herself that the photographer. Inside the pub
Robert shows the photo of Jude to the landlord and the few,
early drinkers. All deny seeing the reporter or anyone fitting
the description of the tall, dark-haired and moustachioed chief
inspector.

Back in the car park, Robert looks forlorn. 'We're back to
square one. Jude's been lied to, or we've got it wrong.'

'No, we haven't got it wrong, Jude was definitely heading
here. I just know it.'

An elderly, white-haired gent, overweight but ramrod
straight and immaculately dressed in blazer, cravat and white
shirt, walks purposely out from the pub and heads towards
the reporter and photographer. 'Excuse me young lady, I've just
heard that you're looking for two people. I was in the gents when
you came asking.' Robert pulls Jude's photograph back out of his

camera bag, to show the portly gentleman. 'I didn't actually see anyone, not to recognise them, but a car came into the car park just after I pulled in. It was an old red Peugeot, a convertible, you don't see many of those these days.'

'That's Jude's car,' Sarah says excitedly.

'Well,' the former army officer continues, 'it drove in, its engine sounded a little rough, and stopped near a dark Ford Granada, I suppose they spoke to each other, the two drivers, then the Granada drove out of the car park, followed by the Peugeot.'

'Which way did they go?' Sarah asks.

'East, towards the scrap dealer and the old station.'

'That's it,' Sarah exclaims and dashes to her car, leaving Robert to thank the old gentlemen, who looks as if he hoped for an explanation of what was happening, and a longer conversation to fill his empty day.

Robert has to jump into the car as Sarah starts to pull away. 'That's fucking it,' she says. Bloody Northam Station. Where Stephen's body was found.' She floors the car's accelerator.

Robert can only whistle as he fights the car's movement, wrestling to do up his seat belt. Robert breathes in deeply to try to make the locked seatbelt fit, fails and has to remove the instamatic camera, his faithful Olympus Trip, from his jacket pocket, before the belt finally surrenders and clicks into place.

Along the track from Northam Station walks Transport Police Inspector Phil Broski, looking for, well, he doesn't know exactly what, but looking for something. Listening to Jude's message on the office answerphone has made the Inspector's antenna twitch. He reread the paperwork and instinctively feels the death doesn't fit the pattern of a normal track suicide – God knows he'd investigated enough of those in his career. Now Stephen Green's death doesn't sit well, regardless of the young man having been given only months to live. Even at night, a train driver sees a suicide jump from a platform, caught in his engine's headlights. That's what traumatises a driver, not the death, but seeing the person jump and not being able to do anything.

The experienced driver of the train that killed Stephen Green didn't see any one jump. It's possible the driver may have looked away for a split second, to light a cigarette or find a sandwich in his bag, but unlikely. Good drivers don't take their eyes from the tracks ahead for long, and certainly not whilst speeding through stations, even disused ones. The only other explanation was that Stephen hadn't jumped but had laid down on the tracks waiting for the train, and in all his years in the Transport Police, Broski had never known a suicide do that unless they were heavily under the influence of drink or drugs. The autopsy report had found traces of neither in Stephen. If, as Jude had said, Stephen was due to make a statement to the police which would have implicated one of the Quirks, but never arrived for the meeting, Broski was certainly going to take a proper look for himself. It was, he felt, the least he could do for poor lad.

In the distance, under the shadow of the bridge, Inspector Broski's attention is caught by two men walking quickly along the track and getting up on to the platform. What are they doing, this station is out of bounds to the public? he asks himself and presses the button to bring his police radio to life and raise the alarm, but is greeted with a crescendo of static. 'Bloody hopeless,' he says and starts to run in the direction of the two men. He realises they'll be long gone and has no chance of catching them, but runs towards them anyway. As he gets closer to the station, Broski spots a dark object on the track, under the bridge that connects the disused station's platforms.

By now the two trespassers have disappeared from sight and will be making good their getaway, the inspector reasons. His attention turns to the dark object, an animal, a deer or badger, he wonders and, without thinking, checks his watch. 'The Waterloo driver won't appreciate hitting that in a couple of minutes,' he thinks and jogs towards it, intending to pull the dead animal from the track.

As he gets closer, the truth dawns on the transport policeman. 'Bloody hell, it's a body,' and he sprints towards it. He bends down and turns the head of the body to check for breathing. 'Oh my God. It's Jude.'

Unsure if the reporter is breathing or not, Broski feels for a pulse. It's faint, but Jude is definitely alive and the experienced officer lets out a small sigh of relief. Already, Broski can hear the Weymouth to Waterloo express, the tracks are vibrating, and he knows the train is thundering towards him. He wraps his arms around Jude's body to lift it – Broski is in good shape for a man of his age but can't raise the 13 stone of dead weight lying across the train rail. He looks up and can now see the green and yellow of the front of the express. It's getting larger and closer by the second. He lets go of Jude, stands and grabs Jude's left arm and left leg and pulls for all he's worth. Finally, Jude's body moves, slowly bumping over the sharp stone chippings. The journalist's heads is the last part of him to leave the rail, tumbling with a soft thud on to the gravel. 'Sorry, son,' the policeman says aloud, 'but if I don't get you off these rails...' Broski slips on the oily and piss-stained stones and falls backwards, landing on his ass and only stopping against the base of the station platform. Jude's body comes to rest, just about off the track and the inspector, winded and bruised, sits on the filthy gravel and sighs with relief.

'Thank God,' he says aloud, above the increasing roar of the high-speed train that is now so close Broski can see the outline of the driver in the cab. Suddenly Jude's arm flops, his hand comes to rest across the nearest rail. With the train yards away, Broski doesn't have time to try and stand, but makes one last, desperate pull from where he sits, tugging at Jude's left leg for all he's worth.

To the inspector it seems infinitely slow, but Jude's palm and then fingers slide from the rail as, with a deafening roar, the train hurtles over the heads of Jude and Broski. The inspector leans back against the wall, looks up at the sky through the gap between the station's roof and the speeding train, its echoing crescendo buffeting his head as hard as any punches he's endured. He closes his eyes, involuntarily shaking at the realisation that his friend, Jude, had come so close to death.

CHAPTER 37

Just Money

Sarah races towards the abandoned station and spots a dark Ford Granada, tyres squealing, speed out of the station drive and head in their direction. 'Robert, the car.'

With reflexes worthy of a Fleet Street tabloid photographer, Robert raises his Olympus Trip and clicks.

'Well, ace photographer, did you get the photo?' Sue demands.

'Unlikely, and if I did, the way you're bouncing us around, it will be really blurry and most likely unusable. What was the registration of the car?'

'I dunno, I was too busy driving. But it was a dark Ford Granada, like the one the old gent said Jude followed out of the pub's car park. So, we must be in the right–' the thunder of a train passing drowns out the rest of Sarah's sentence as she turns her car into the driveway to the disused station. The reporter shouts over the noise from the express. 'Thank God, look, Jude's Peugeot, over there.' She stops the car next to the convertible and, eventually, they find the spot where the fence has been cut open. Together they roll the fence back, scramble on to the deserted station and start calling Jude's name as they hurry along the decrepit platform.

'Over here.' The unusually weak voice of Inspector Broski echoes back to them. Reporter and photographer peer over the station's edge, down towards where they think the voice has come from. There are two figures: an older man, wearing the uniform of a British Transport Police Inspector, sitting and resting against the concrete base of the platform. Next to him, lying on his back, dishevelled, bloodied and unconscious, is Jude's gangly form.

The Inspector sees the pair above him, gives a half-hearted wave, and to calm their obvious concern, says, 'Don't worry, he's alive.'

Sarah and Robert climb down the eight steep steps and Broski tries his radio to summon help, but can only raise a crackle of static. Sarah dashes back to her car and drives off, intent of finding a working phone box and calling for an ambulance.

Whilst she's away Jude starts to regain consciousness. His eyes move slowly from Inspector Broski to Robert and back again. He tries to talk and Broski puts his right index finger to his own lips to indicate for Jude to remain quiet. 'You're safe, now, Jude. There's time enough for explanations.'

Jude's looks changes to one of panic. 'Window opening, then,' he starts to move his hand towards the back of his head, but it falls back to his side.

Robert's photographer's eye sees scans Jude and see how poorly he looks; the hair matted with blood, the cuts and scratches to his face and hands, how pail his skin is. He raises his hand to indicate for Jude to stay still, 'The ambulance will be here soon, Sarah's gone to phone for one.'

The reporter lifts his head just a little. 'Please, someone… tell me what's happened.'

Broski understands Jude's need to know and, in a calm voice, tells the reporter an edited account of what he'd seen. 'I was down here after listening to your message, looking to see if anything was out of order, and I saw two men run off. Then I saw you, lying on the track. I just managed to pull you away from the rail as the Waterloo express went through.'

Jude immediately understands the implications of Broski's

information and, overcome, passes out again.

Sarah is worried that Jude appears not to have regained consciousness but tries to lighten the mood with a cheery 'the ambulance is on its way.' Hearing Sarah's voice, Jude's eyes open and, very slowly, he tries to stand but Broski insists the reporter stays still, 'at least until the ambulance arrives.' Jude rubs his head and Sarah fusses, trying to gently brush the detritus and blood from his jacket. Jude half smiles and asks her to stop before insisting on standing up, claiming he's 'feeling fine.' Painfully, deliberately and somewhat reluctantly aided on either side by an arm from Robert and Broski, Jude stands. The three shuffle slowly together along the track to the steps up to the platform. With great effort and concentration, Jude climbs the steps before sitting on the nearest platform bench.

He tells everyone a short version of what has happened, finishing with, 'And then I must have been hit on the head through the window. Who it was, well, I've no idea.' There's a huge sense of both relief and a realisation of how, so easily, things could have turned out tragically different. After a moment of thought, everyone has a million different questions. 'Look, thanks everyone,' Jude says as loudly as he can manage, quietening the excited group, 'but we've got to get back to work, there's so much to do.'

'Now, Jude, you may think you're tough, but, in the ring, well, I've seen what being knocked out can do to someone.' Broski smiles at his friend. 'Hang on, just wait and at least let the ambulance team check you over, make sure you're not concussed or worse.'

Jude slowly shakes his head in disagreement and stands, but is so unsteady on his feet, is forced to sit down again, realising he has little choice but to accept the police officer's advice.

'What car was Smarties driving, a dark-coloured Granada?' Sarah asks.

'Yeah, that's right, how did you know?'

'We saw him drive out. Robert fucked the photo up.'

Robert starts to protest but decides it's not worth it and Jude

243

tentatively stands again, this time managing to stay upright.

'Jude, we know why he's tried to kill you,' Sarah explains. 'The birth certificate arrived from the Isle of Wight in today's post. It's Smarties who is named as the father of Bill, the eldest Quirk boy.'

Jude realises he has to sit back down before he falls, and lowers himself. He scratches at his jaw. 'Well, I didn't see that coming. Jesus. I mean... Well, it explains just about everything, doesn't it? How the Quirks have been protected. Smarties was head of vice until recently, for Christ's sake.'

The two-tone whine of a siren growing in volume announces the arrival of the ambulance. The driver, an old hand, examines Jude and cleans his wounds while simultaneously stopping his assistant from fussing. As there's no obvious serious damage, he realises there's little point in trying to stop the reporter returning to work. 'I'd strongly recommend you go for an X-ray, if not now, later. But I promise you one thing, you're going to have one hell of a headache either tonight or tomorrow morning.'

Inspector Broski says he'll be in touch to take statements, as what has happened is under his jurisdiction, being on Railway Property. 'Jude, you know we'll get Smarties for this. You have my word. And no one, and I mean no one, will be able to stop me. I'll track him down, it shouldn't be too hard, and we'll arrest him today. I promise.'

Jude smiles and nods. Sarah takes Jude's car keys from his hand. 'Right, into my passenger seat, Jude, you're in no fit state to drive and you've got one hell of a story to write.' She hands the keys to Robert. 'You drive Jude's car, see you back at the office.'

On the drive back, Jude's head is still a fog, but he starts to realise that Sarah has made her choice between him and the Quirks and, he suspects, is trying to atone for her previous deception. 'What you've done, today, for me, well, you didn't need to. Sarah, why did you?'

'I'm sorry, Jude, truly bloody sorry. I've explained why I did what I did and I've had time to think. When they took little Catherine, your daughter... Before that, part of me had felt that,

I dunno, the Quirks were some sort of Robin Hood outfit. I mean, which of us hasn't smoked a joint, when we were at uni. or something? So, how can I criticise if they sell drugs without being a hypocrite? But threatening you and Robert was wrong, really wrong. But kidnapping a young girl.'

Jude looks quizzically at Sarah, scepticism in his eyes. 'Today, by deciding to help me take on the Quirks, you've put yourself in their firing line. You know that, don't you?'

'Doesn't every journalist, like every politician, start off as a bit on an idealist? No one knows this but me and Dave are trying to start a family. Taking Catherine, well, it reconnected me to that idealistic young journalist I once was. It reminded me of what is really right and what is wrong.'

'But you owe them money, Sarah, a lot of money.'

'Jude, I do, but it is just money, isn't it?'

The gulf between them, ripped open by Sarah's betrayal, narrows with every mile the two journalists drive together and, eventually, they start to plot their next moves. Instead of going back to the office, they stop at a phone box and arrange to meet Del at a café in Eastleigh, halfway between them and Police HQ at Winchester.

Sarah shows Del the birth certificate and, after a long briefing, the journalists are reassured, have agreed on a plan and head back to *The Reporter*.

CHAPTER 38

We've Been Talking...

Jimmy is delighted to see his two reporters walk into the news-room side-by-side, although he soon realises Sarah is supporting Jude, who looks like he's been in a fight and come second. 'Thank God they've finally kissed and made up,' the editor thinks before realising the real severity of Jude injuries and spots the dried blood staining the reporter's shirt and jacket.

Concerned, Jimmy gets up from behind his desk but Robert dashes in from his tiny studio and unwittingly positions himself so the back of his darkroom overall blocks off the editor, and waves a black and white print. 'You two, look at this. Not only do I have the number plate of the Granada, but you can clearly make out that it's Smarties who's driving *and* who the passenger is.'

Sarah grabs the 10 x 8inch print from the photographer and looks at it closely. 'Robert, I could kiss you. This is the final proof. It puts Smarties at the scene, it's independent verification of everything that Jude has said. Who's the passenger?'

Jude grabs the photo from Sarah and studies it closely. 'Fuck me,' he says, and shakes his head. 'We've got Brian as well. That's him, 100 per cent, sat next to Smarties in the passenger seat. It must have been him who hit me.'

Robert is grinning from ear to ear. 'As soon as the print came out of the dev tray, I knew it was bloody Brian Quirk. Just to be sure I've checked with the shot I took of him going into Southampton Magistrates Court – there's no doubt at all. I was surprised the photo is sharp, to be honest; bouncing along as Sarah drove like she's James Hunt. Bloody Olympus Trips, you can't beat them. Cost a fraction of my Nikon.'

Jimmy tries to regain his authority in the newsroom. 'Right, Jude, tell me every last little detail about what happened – Robert's given me the broad outline – then we'll work out what to do next.'

Jude's legs suddenly feel shaky, as if they're about to give way. He eases himself into his chair, realising just how weak he feels and how the effect of the earlier adrenalin surge must be starting to ease. 'Jimmy, look, we've been talking…'

Sarah butts in. 'Jimmy, you should sit down and pour yourself a vodka from the bottle you think no one knows about in your bottom draw. A double. And then listen to Jude while I make everyone a coffee; it's going to be a long day.'

The editor's first reaction is to thump his desk and demand 'who the bloody hell is running this paper?' But, to his great credit, Jimmy resists this old-school approach, sits down but ignores Sarah advice about the vodka, thinking 'I'm not a bloody alcoholic.' Jimmy looks serious and says, without a hint of emotion, 'Go on then, I'm all ears.'

Jude takes a deep breath. 'Jimmy, we all believe this story must be told now, not tomorrow, certainly not in three days' time when we're due to come out. And it must be told by us, by *The Reporter*. If we are brave and tell the full story now, there can be no time for cover-ups, no chance for Smarties to tap up his police mates and change the story or destroy evidence. Soon, in the next day or two, every other news organisation will hear about what's happened today. So, we've agreed, haven't we Sarah… Robert?' The reporter looks enquiringly at his two colleagues. Sarah nods enthusiastically, Robert less so. 'We've agreed that we're going to bring out a special edition. Today. There, I've said it.'

'What?' Jimmy now does as Sarah suggests, takes out his badly hidden half bottle of Smirnoff, pulls a good slug into an almost clean cup and takes a sip. 'What?' he repeats before downing the remaining vodka in one, and then refilling his cup. 'A special edition, for a free newspaper. It's never been done before, not ever, not to my knowledge.'

Jude nods. 'If you're not up for this, Jimmy, well I, we, understand your circumstances, you've got a mortgage and family and you really need this job. Look, just go home on the sick now, and blame your diabetes. We will, somehow or other, get this paper out today and tell the story of the Quirks. I'm going to ask, no, tell the advertising team to start selling like they've never sold before. I'll guarantee them that every word of the special edition of *The Reporter* will be read and read again; it will be studied from cover to cover. And I'll get distribution to start phoning around, getting the kids and the pensioners ready to start delivering this evening.'

The editor finishes his vodka and pours himself another. 'You're serious about this, aren't you?'

Sarah nods as she dishes out the mugs of steaming Nescafe. 'You better believe it, Jimmy.'

'And one last thing,' Jude thumps his right fist into his left palm, 'no one is going to tell fucking Alex. No one, or he'll pull the plug. OK, Jimmy, are you in or out?'

Jimmy screws the top back on his half bottle of vodka and replaces it in his desk draw. 'Well, I think you're all mad. But I can't go home and let you ruin the story of the decade with crap headlines, a piss-poor layout and loads of spelling mistakes, can I? I'm in... God help me.' And he empties the last of the vodka from his mug.

There's a small, embarrassed cheer from the news team.

Jimmy stands. 'But Jude, you start writing, that's what's needed now. I'll square it with sales and distribution. I'll also have a word with Ted, the printer's shop steward. He owes me, and, to get this special edition out today, he's going to have to defy his own management and his union, the NGA. Even you, Jude, wouldn't take them on. Now, get writing!'

The team get down to work to produce the first and only

special edition of *The Reporter.* Over the next four hours the team are mad-busy phoning, typing, printing photos, checking, shouting, swearing, subbing, re-writing, more swearing, banging phones and begging favours. The bins overflow with rejected versions of stories, tempers are frayed and Old Jones is barring unauthorised entry into the newsroom with his broom.

Finally, Jimmy shouts. 'That's it! Stop, we've got to go with this now, or we'll miss any chance of getting it delivered today. Well done, we've put together a whole, if slightly thin, edition of *The Reporter* in world record time.'

There are more embarrassed cheers but then Jude panics, remembering the vital, missing link. 'But we haven't got the quote from Hampshire Police yet. Without them confirming, we're on dodgy ground. We need their confirmation or we could be sued, couldn't we, Jimmy?'

Sarah remains calm. 'Del phoned, Jude, but I couldn't interrupt you. He's promised something,' she looks at her wristwatch, 'in the next 30 minutes. "Girl guides' honour," he said.'

Jude stands, feeling more exhausted than he's felt in his life. 'That'll be too late. Without the police confirmation, we'll look amateur and are taking a massive risk. I'm always up for a gamble, but if this goes wrong, we could close the paper, bankrupt *The Reporter.*'

'Yes, we could,' Jimmy smiles. 'Let's just keep our fingers crossed Del is really on our side and comes through. I've left a Fudge Box on the front page, where we can add, on the stone, up to a 200 word Stop Press for the police's quotes right up until the very last minute. Sarah, that's what you asked Del for, in the police statement, 200 words?' She nods her agreement. 'So, he's got a maximum of 40 minutes in which he can get back to us. Let's keep the faith. Right, I'm off to sweet-talk and bribe the printers. Wish me luck.' He limps out of the office and down the two flights of stairs to the print room.

Robert opens the fridge where he keeps his film stock, chemicals and, unbeknown to the rest of the newsroom, a discreetly hidden, emergency supply of Stella Artois. A bottle opener from his keyring lifts the tops from three bottles and he hands them round. 'Well, this time tomorrow, we will be the toast of the media world, or just toasted, unemployed and unemployable.'

'Thanks for reminding me,' Sarah says. 'I'm already unofficially bankrupt and homeless, or will be the minute Debbs sues me to get her money back.'

Jude has almost finished his lager. 'Even she wouldn't have the balls to do that, it would only add proof of her guilt, that she entrapped you.'

Sarah shrugs, 'Oh, well, we'll see. We've pushed the little snowball down from the top of the mountain and we know it's going to cause a fucking massive avalanche, don't we? The question is, who's that avalanche going to destroy? Us or them?'

The journalists are well into their second round of Stella when Jude's phone rings, making him jump. But it's not, as expected, Del. It's Jimmy, phoning from the print room in the bowels of the building, asking Jude to join him straight away. Jude is immediately worried, and tries to imagine what disaster could have befallen his story. Jimmy adds, 'Ask Robert to join us and tell him to bring his camera.' Reporter and photographer hurry down the first flight of stairs and then push open the big, metal soundproof door to the cavernous basement, where the huge printing press dominates the double-height room. They step on to the landing and jog down the steep blue metal stairs to the print room floor.

Jimmy is standing next to the short, chubby and ruddy form of Ted, the chief printer and also the father of the NGA printers' union chapel, a dichotomy that could only exist in the surreal world of newspapers. Ted's bald head is framed by two huge mutton chop whiskers that reach down to the top of his brown warehouse coat. Jimmy hands Jude the proof sheet of the front page. The headline shouts in huge black letters, 'CORRUPT POLICE CHIEF & NO.1 CRIME FAMILY ARRESTED'. Above, in smaller, white letters against a red background, 'attempt to kill '*the Reporter's*' journalist, and, underneath the main headline, is the block heading that all media people strive for: EXCLUSIVE.

The relationship between printers and journalists is rarely cordial, normally fractious, and it was no different at *The Reporter*. But Jimmy and Ted grin at each other like proud godfathers at a christening. In front of them stand half a dozen typesetters, printers and compositors, all smiling. Ted clears his throat, as if he was about to make a speech at the TUC conference. 'Well, Jude, me and the brothers have had a vote and I'm delighted to say the result is unanimous. We're inviting you to press the button to start the presses rolling. It's in recognition of what you've been through to get this story. You'll be the first non-NGA member ever to have started these presses, and,' he laughs, 'the last, unless the management want a major strike on its hands.'

'Wow,' Jude says, realising just what an honour this is - and a major breach of union rules. 'Hang on, we still haven't got the statement from Hants Police, confirmation the arrests have been made. Can't we wait, just another five minutes?'

Jimmy shakes his head. 'If the presses don't start turning now, we won't be able to distribute the paper today. It's now or never, Jude, press that big red button.'

Jude is concerned, but realises he has no choice if the special edition is to be seen in the city today, and lifts his right hand and extends his index finger. 'Here goes.'

CHAPTER 39

Stark Raving Bonkers

'Don't you press bloody anything, Jude. Not you, not anyone. Or it'll be the last thing you ever do in The Press; your journalism career will be finished!'

A reedy voice shouts and echoes around the aircraft hangar-sized printing hall. Everyone lifts their heads skywards, to the metal landing at the top of the double-height stairs. They see their managing director, his red-framed glasses slipped down his sweating nose and sitting precariously above his lips. 'One paper leaves this building and you're all sacked. I fucking mean it, union or not.'

'Alex, this is real journalism,' Jude calls back, his voice a plea, 'a special edition–'

The managing director leans over the landing banister and shouts as he literally looms over everyone in the room. 'Journalism? Don't make me laugh – I'm not sure there's anyone in this printing hall, other than me, who could even spell the word. Special edition, for a free paper? Are you all stark raving bonkers? Did you get something from one of those police drug raids you've been on, Jude, and slip it into the building's water supply? I can't think of another reason.'

Alex walks briskly down the stairs, and no one dares defy his orders. But Jude whispers to Robert, 'Have your camera ready, do what I tell you and don't argue. We're as good as sacked already, there's nothing to lose.'

At the bottom of the steps, Alex has to stop for breath, giving Jude his chance. The reporter asks, 'Ready, Robert?' and quickly moves to stand next to Alex, He holds up the printer's proof of the frontpage in front of the managing director and nods to his photographer colleague. Robert's clicks his shutter; the flash fires and Alex and Jude are momentarily blinded.

Jude speaks before Alex has the chance. 'Right, Alex, you're always telling us what a great journalist you were. This is your chance to prove it. Either this special edition goes out tonight or the photo Robert has just taken is wired to our industry magazine, *The Press Gazette*. And then it'll go to every publishing group in the country. You have to run this special edition. Otherwise, you'll be the newspaper man who refused to sign *The Beatles*. No, worse, you'll be the man who had *The Beatles* and sacked them!'

Light laughter comes from some of the watching printers. Jimmy tries to pour oil on troubled waters. 'Alex, we've sold enough advertising to more than cover our costs.'

'You're all bloody crazy,' Alex says, his red glasses pushed back and again bouncing on his nose. 'Have the police confirmed the headline, that they're arrested the family and the police officer?'

Jude knows he can't lie; this is too important. 'They're about to, they've promis–'

'Fucking amateurs,' Alex shouts, spraying spittle. 'I bloody knew it; you're just playing at being journalists. That's it, scrap the paper. Now.'

Jude, Robert and Jimmy quickly exchange glances, knowing they're beaten, their gamble has failed and, for different reasons, that they will all struggle to ever find another job in journalism.

Defeated, no one wants to be the first to move, despite everyone knowing they will have to carry out Alex's orders. The creak of rusty hinges breaks the oppressive silence and all eyes again lift towards the metal door at the top of the tall iron stairs. Sarah's elfin head appears around the door. 'Jimmy, I've got the

Stop Press 200 words from the police press office. Is it too late?'

Alex is looking at Sarah and, at first, shakes his head and sighs heavily. But then he laughs. 'Stop Press! Bugger me, we are playing at being a newspaper, aren't we?' The huge printing hall is silent.

'Sorry, everyone, is this not a good time?' Sarah asks, realising the answer before the words have left her mouth, and feeling 10 years old again, embarrassed and lonely.

'No, Sarah, this is a great time.' Alex states flatly, looking around the hall and back at Sarah. 'Come on, share, why don't you, your pearls of wisdom that can only add to the stupidity of this project, this, so called, special edition?'

Sarah looks unsure, down at her notebook and then at everyone below. She is desperate not to make matters worse and wishes she knew what has already gone on in the print room.

'Come on Sarah, don't be shy. Spill the beans,' Alex demands, with all but menace.

Sarah looks at Jimmy, who nods that she should read the words that had been destined for the paper's Stop Press, and takes a deep breath. 'Hampshire Police can confirm that a mother and her three adult sons have been arrested in connection with the theft of evidence from police custody; with the supply of Class A drugs; with bribing police officers in the course of their duties; and with the kidnapping of a minor. A senior Hampshire Police officer has been arrested in connection with aiding and abetting the theft of evidence from police custody, associating with known criminals, obtaining pecuniary advantage from illegal activities, attempted murder and the murder of Stephen Green. One of the three adult sons mentioned above is also being questioned in connection with attempted murder. The investigation into the attempted murder and the murder of Stephen Green is a joint operation with the British Transport Police Force.'

Sarah wets her lips before continuing. 'Hampshire Police would like to put on record its thanks and appreciation to *The Reporter* and its staff for their dogged investigation into these matters.

'We expect more victims of the family to come forward in connection with blackmail, protection payments and related matters as our inquiry progresses. We promise all victims that they will be treated by Hampshire Police with the utmost sensitivity and respect. We expect to work closely with our colleagues in HM Revenue and Customs as our investigation broadens and deepens.'

Jude whistles and then almost shouts, 'Good old Del!' He turns to face his managing editor. 'Playing at journalism, are we, Alex? That statement confirms everything that's in our special edition of *The Reporter.* There's only one person who should be sacked, Alex, and I'm looking at him.'

The managing editor stumbles over his reply and is cut off by Jimmy. 'Sarah, get yourself down here, and read that police statement over to a typesetter and hurry up about it. Ted, how long will it take to set that and be ready to print?'

'Five minutes, tops.'

'Brilliant. Will it still be OK for Jude to press the start button?'

The father of the chapel's face breaks into a smile. 'We're relying on him.'

Alex tries to slink out of the print hall, but first has to wait for Sarah to come down the double flight of stairs. Finally, he starts his ascent, one heavy footstep following another, his leather soles clanging against metal tread after metal tread. Resolutely, Alex only looks ahead, knowing everyone's eyes are on him. After what seems like an eternity, he reaches the landing and opens the heavy door into the reception area. Without a backward glance he tries not to hear the cheers echoing around the print hall as he closes the metal door. Alex heads for the exit, relieved to be escaping *The Reporter.*

The special edition is delivered, somewhat later and a little less smoothly than usual, to every household across the city and miles around. It becomes the most read edition in the paper's history and weeks later tyre-fitters and double-glazing companies are still enjoying the benefit from the advertisements they were convinced to place so hurriedly.

All the city's media immediately follow the story, as do national daily papers. They, in turn, are trailed by national BBC and ITV and the major news agencies, including Reuters and the Press Association.

The Reporter's readers are encouraged to phone in with details of any dealings they've had with the Quirks and the court refuses bail to Chief Inspector Michael Matthews and all four members of the crime family, accepting the prosecution's claim of 'demonstrable risk' to existing and potential witnesses from the defendants. This only inspires more people to come forward and helps the police build a case that, by the day, gets stronger.

CHAPTER 40

Solid Gold Doorstop

Over the coming weeks and months of the investigation, Jude is given the inside track by officers leading the inquiry, who are both proud and embarrassed to be removing such a senior but corrupt policeman from their midst. With their help, Jude and *The Reporter* break story after story in connection with the case. Some can only be published if Smarties and his family are found guilty; if they appear in the paper before the trial is completed there is a risk a jury could be prejudiced and *The Reporter* would be in contempt of court and its journalists face the threat of fines or a prison sentence. Other officers from vice are subsequently charged with a range of offences involving drugs and theft, whilst a greater number of police officers quietly resign.

With Smarties locked up, the Quirks' secret family history unravels. It isn't long before Smarties is confirmed as the father of all three boys. An ambitious constable, Smarties had moved south from the Midlands, keen to earn his sergeant stripes, but his wife had stayed in Dudley, refusing to uproot her young family and lose the support of her mum. The new sergeant met Debbs and she became pregnant with Bill. By the time Smarties' wife found out about his affair and divorced her husband, the sergeant was an inspector. Debbs Quirk was already too notorious for an aspiring and ambitious policeman to be seen to be with, let alone marry. So, they carried on their relationship in great secrecy, going to immense lengths to conceal it. Ben was born and, a few years later, joined by Brian. When the boys were old enough to be trusted, they first met and, over a period of time, appreciated their dad and how he quietly worked in the background to help protect and enrich the whole family.

The police investigation into Smarties and the family is not as difficult as expected: the Chief Inspector had become over-confident and sloppy. Believing himself untouchable, he'd failed to take enough time or precautions to hide the huge profits the family had been raking in. The joint Hampshire and British Transport Police team track down most of the ill-gotten gains: the villa in Spain; the small estate in Ireland; properties in London's Soho rented to pimps; keys to a safe deposit box at a discreet City bank; and even a gold bar, painted grey and used as doorstop, in the Chief Inspector's flat. Jude's story about the gold bar went around the world; two national newspapers even used Jimmy's headline: BENT COPPER'S SOLID GOLD DOORSTOP.

Life, for a while, settles back on to an even keel in Southampton. The city's criminal underworld hibernates, and pubs like *The Proud Stag* no longer pay protection money. Gerry, the *Stag's* licensee, believes he's the happiest gardener/pub landlord in Hampshire when Milly tells him she is again pregnant.

The story of how Alex tried to kill *The Reporter's* special edition, inevitably, leaks out. The managing director takes sick leave and, once the date for Smarties' and the Quirks' trial is set, leaves the company, letting it be known that he's been 'head-hunted; it's a great promotion.' His former colleagues don't waste too much of their time trying to work out how running a smaller newspaper group, with less responsibility and half his previous salary is 'a great promotion'.

With the court case less than two months away, Jude is invited out to lunch by Del and they meet at the Wykeham Arms in Winchester. Dale is dressed, as always, immaculately but, Jude feels, has aged in the three months since they last met. 'New suit, Del; our fine force still paying you too much?'

'Cheeky sod,' but I am paying for lunch, well, our fine force is

– I've put in the diary that I'm meeting a contact. It's kind of true, I suppose. I hear congratulations are in order; you've been shortlisted for the Annual Press Awards.'

'Thanks, but I've no chance of winning – the prizes always go to the big city evening paid for papers. Still, should be a good evening out in London.'

'Jude, I've got some news. I went and visited Smarties on remand on the Isle of Wight.'

Jude almost drops his pint of lager, he's so shocked. 'But Del–'

'Hang on, look, it's pretty grim for him. He's kept in isolation 24-7 for his own safety; he under the same roof as a lot of people he put there. The only people he talks to are the wardens and half of those spit into his food before handing him a tray.'

'I know, but, well, he tried to kill me, for fuck's sake. He lied to you, all the time.'

'He did, I know that better than anyone. But we worked together and no one else is going to go and see him, are they? The only people who care about him now are all locked up, waiting for their own trial.'

'OK, OK, it's your choice.'

'Yes, Jude, it is. But I'm glad I did and so will you be when I tell you what Smarties told me. He said he's decided to plead guilty.'

'Wow, guilty, really?'

'Yep, guilty to everything. He says that way he can make it easier for Debbs and the three boys. He's going to say that paying police officers for drugs they'd confiscated was all his idea and none of the family knew about it. That will get them off the 'corrupting police officer' charges. And he's going to say that he forced Brian to help him knock you out and put you on the train track. As Smarties says, nothing can make it any worse for him, everyone hates a bent cop and he's sure they're going to make an example of him. Funnily enough, he was quite relaxed about it, as if he's already accepted his fate. He said, "The only way they're going to let me leave a prison is in a coffin."

'Wow, that's strong stuff, Del.'

'The funny thing is, I don't think Smarties was ever, not

really, interested in the money, not for himself. Because of the weird relationship he couldn't ever be a proper husband to Debbs or a good dad and the boys, so he tried to make up for it in other ways.'

'That's pretty deep, Del. Do you really believe it?'

'Jude, when I saw him in prison, he told me that all he ever wanted to do was to try and help his family. I don't think Smarties was bent before he met Debbs, I think it was her influence. I know that's no excuse, but if he had never met Debbs, well, he'd been a normal cop... if there is such a thing.'

'Do you think Smarties pleading guilty will help the rest of the family, when it all gets to court?'

'If I'm honest, Jude, no, I don't, not really. I think Smarties is being delusional. No one is going to believe Brian was coerced. Not for a minute, and I've heard, between you and me, that Brian is pleading guilty to attempted murder. Your attempted murder. Maybe, just maybe, if the CPS accept that no one else was involved in getting the drugs from the police, it will save a year or two on the others' sentences. But I doubt it. Smarties pleading guilty will help one person. You know who that is, don't you?'

Jude takes a long gulp of his lager but looks perplexed. 'Not a scooby, Del. Who?'

'You, of course. If Smarties and Brian plead guilty, you won't need to give evidence.'

'I might, for poor Roy Bruce. I can't see Brian pleading guilty to that. I've given a statement about what Roy told me.'

'Sad to say, your evidence is all hearsay and a good defence brief would tear it to shreds. The good news is we now have five or six witnesses who have given statements saying they were in the nightclub and saw Brian glass Roy. A couple have even said they overheard the conversation that led up to the attack. I suspect, when the Quirks defence team see the weight of evidence, they'll advise him to plead guilty to GBH, if the CPS accept it. If they don't, he'll be charged with GBH with intent, which would see him put away for a very long time. With the attempted murder charge, even if the judge rules the sentences should be served concurrently, the only chance he has on being a free man by the time he turns 40 is to plead guilty.'

'Del, that's brilliant. If I'm not going to give evidence, I can report on the trial.'

Back at the office, Jude brings everyone up to date with the latest developments. Jimmy scratches at his eyepatch. 'I've got more good news, I've been wondering when to tell you all, and this is as good as time as any. Last night I worked out that, so far, we've been paid just over four grand by the national newspapers and TV for our stories and photos.' Jimmy waits for dramatic effect before continuing, 'And we're owed about as much again for stuff the national have used that they haven't paid us for yet.'

Sarah stops dishing out cups of coffee to calculate how much her one quarter will be worth. 'Bloody hell, that's brilliant. And with if we earn that much again during the trial, I might be able to pay off the loan from bloody Debbs Quirk and get the charge removed from our deeds,' Sarah says.

'We won't earn much, if anything, from the trial; the nationals will all send their own reporters down to cover it – it'll be that big.' Jimmy fiddles with his eyepatch. 'I've been thinking about the charge on your home, Sarah. Have you ever mentioned it to the police?'

'No, why would I? I mean, I not proud of it and I did sign the papers; it was my own freewheel, she didn't have a gun to my head or anything.'

Jimmy nods. 'No, she didn't, but you didn't really know what you were signing, did you? I wouldn't talk to the police, not straight away. But I would phone, not write, to Debbs' solicitor. Speak to the monkey, not the organ-grinder at the solicitors and say you expect it was a misunderstanding on Debbs part that she got you to sign. And suggest that the police might disagree, they may not think it was a misunderstanding. They may think it was blackmail.'

Sarah is thoughtful as she puts the editor's steaming mug of coffee down on his desk. 'Which, to be honest, was how she used the gift, which became a loan. To blackmail me.'

Jimmy reaches over from his chair and picks up the mug. 'It's worth a shot – why would she take the chance of having a black-mail charge added to the case against her. Who knows, it could add another year or two to her sentence.'

'Jimmy, you're a bloody genius,' Sarah kisses on the top of her editor's head.

Just one cloud hangs over Jude. Even thinking about it renders him all but paralysed. He still hasn't met his own daughter, Catherine. Up to now he's told himself he's too busy, too in demand to contact her. But he knows the real reason why he hasn't phoned her mother – he's scared his daughter won't want to meet him. And even if she does agree to a meeting, she'll be upset or disappointed in him. Jude knows he's responsible for putting her in harm's way once, and is desperate not to cause her any more disruption or pain.

Maybe it's Milly being pregnant or maybe it's the realisation that Smarties had to watch clandestinely as his own family grew up, but Jude eventually summons up a strong enough mixture of hope and fear to finally call Sue. It's Chantelle who picks up the phone, as if she's been keeping a vigil next to the receiver, waiting for it to ring, so desperate is she to protect her daughter and granddaughter.

Chantelle listens to Jude and when she replies she doesn't pull any punches. 'I knew that you, the bad penny, would turn up again; that you couldn't keep away and that this day, this phone call would come. And the answer, Jude, is no. Sue and I have talked about this at length. Catherine has a dad, OK, he may not be her biological father, but he's a great dad in every other way and they love each other.'

'But Chantelle, she has a right to know me. You must see that.'

'For how long, Jude? How long before you bugger off to London to work on a national newspaper. After your success here, I'm sure there will be offers and don't tell me you've lost your ambition. I know that's what you want, to be at the centre of things. Then what for Catherine? A visit once every six months, forgetting birthdays and letting her down?'

'That's not what I want,' he pleads. But Jude knows Chantelle is right, and the passion to argue drains from him, the doubt in his own voice obvious. 'What about Catherine? It should be her choice, not yours, not Sue's.'

The pause down the line from Chantelle is just long enough for the inhalation of a deep breath. 'Jude, when Catherine is 18 years old, which, remember, is not for another eight years, we'll tell her that Richard is not her biological father. Then she can decide if she wants to meet her real dad or not. But, if you make any trouble in the meantime, we will deny you, deny whatever claims you make. You have no proof and who will Catherine believe? A strange journalist who turns up claiming to be her dad, or the family who have cherished her all her life? That's the deal, Jude, take it or leave it. Be calm and stay away. If you do that, we will give Catherine the chance, if she wants it, to meet you.'

'I don't have a choice, do I, Chantelle?'

'Jude, there is always a choice.'

Reluctantly, Jude accepts the one realistic option open to him and agrees to Chantelle's rules.

He is not allowed long to dwell on his disappointment. Jimmy, Sarah, Jude and Robert attend the swanky dinner in the London Hilton on Park Lane for the annual press prize giving after the *The Reporter*, Jude and Robert are all separately shortlisted for awards. The four journalists make the most of the free wine on their table and the party heats up when Robert, for his underwater photo of the police divers, is placed second in the Regional News Photo of the Year category. Jude is named the Regional Reporter of the Year and, almost at the end of the evening, the celebrations go into overdrive when *The Reporter* is named Regional Newspaper of the Year, the first time the award has been presented to a freesheet. Jimmy is called onto the stage to make a short speech and, although his voice is a little alcohol-slurred and he fiddles constantly with his eyepatch, he gets a standing ovation by ending with, 'Out in the provinces, in the sticks, us little freesheets might not have much of a budget, we may be starved of resources by senior management who can see us journalists as a pain in the arse. But most of us still have a passion for the job and a commitment to unearth the truth and tell it the world. So, I accept this award on behalf on *The Reporter*, on behalf of my small but perfectly formed team of brilliant journalists, and on behalf of all passionate, pain in the arse reporters, photographers and editors, wherever you may be working!'

No one can remember much of the rest of the drunken evening, although Jude recalls being approached by two national newspaper editors who both, he thinks, suggested that, if he moves to London he should 'give my secretary a call'.

Two days before the trial is due to start Sarah also receives something she is delighted to accept. It's a new copy of the deeds to her and Dave's home with a covering letter, marked private and confidential, from Debbs' solicitor explaining that, as a goodwill gesture, he has been instructed to remove the charge in favour of Deborah Quirk from the deeds and that there is 'no charge or encumbrance neither now nor in the future' to either her or Dave. Jimmy's idea of a phone call to the solicitor has paid off handsomely.

Jude is disappointed to be told by a CPS solicitor that he can't report on the court case during the trial and can't even go into court to hear what is happening. 'It's really unlikely, but, just in case you are needed to give evidence – stranger things have happened.'

The great majority of charges are admitted to and others are dropped before the trial starts – the CPS decide that even if any of the accused are found guilty of those charges, the length of sentences the judge is likely to award are unlikely to be materially affected. There are no charges in connection with the abduction of Catherine; no one will own up to knowing anything about snatching little girl from her bed, nor for the murder of Stephen Green; with no new evidence his death remains, officially, 'an open verdict'. Eventually, and after toing and froing between the CPS, the defence and the judge, the only charges that go to trial are connected with the handling of money. Within a week the prosecution proves to the jury's satisfaction there is an audit path for 'funds in excess of £1.7 million pounds, salted away over several years'. All the Quirks and Smarties have benefitted from the funds. After the jury return a verdict of guilty on all the defendants, the judge says he will pass sentence on these and the charges the accused have pleaded guilty to, the following week. This announcement was the first time the jury had heard in court that there were other charges the five faced.

CHAPTER 41

What Is Justice?

It's with trepidation that Jude takes a seat on the wooden press bench of Court Number One at Winchester Crown Court. Now that Smarties and all the Quirks have been found guilty, he is allowed to watch and report on the sentencing. It's the final destination of a path Jude unwittingly set out on when he joined *The Reporter*, one that has changed so much of his life. With his reporter's note book open on the shallow shelf in front of him and his pen ready poised above it, he tries to tell himself that this is just another story to report on.

But when the four accused are led into the dock, Jude knows it is anything but 'just another story'. His breathing becomes faster and shallow and his right hand holding his pen is clammy. Brian Quirk spots the reporter first, stares, then, without taking his eyes from Jude, nudges the shoulder of each of his brothers, who are standing either side. The three hard men all stare at the reporter, no doubt wishing him dead. Debs, checking on what her sons are looking at, sees Jude and gives him a look that, in Old Testament days, would have turned him into a pillar of salt. Jude is unnerved, despite logically knowing he's safe, sat on the press bench. Then Smarties looks over towards Jude. Instead of staring or baring his teeth, he does the opposite. Smarties smiles, warmly and openly, towards Jude, like someone spotting an old friend across the room at a party they didn't want to attend. What Smarties does next causes Jude to drop his pen to the floor and everyone stare at the reporter as the noise of biro hitting marble tile echoes around the silent courtroom.

Smarties winks, slowly and deliberately across the courtroom at Jude.

The reporter feels overwhelmed and grips the brass rail in front of him, believing he's about to faint. He registers little of what follows, except the sentences the judge hands down: life for both Smarties and Brian, 12 years for both Ben and Bill. He hears the courtroom collectively gasp when Debbs is given a sentence of 14 years, and the Judge describe her as 'the spider at the centre of this huge tangled and criminal web'.

Thankfully, as he leaves the courtroom, Jude is grabbed by Sarah. 'Bloody hell,' she says, 'you look like you're the one who's been given the life sentence. Come on, I'll drive you back to the office, we'll tell Robert on the way out – he's outside, waiting to try and take photos of the Quirks when they're driving off inside the police van. Don't know why photographers bother, it never works, not with the van's blacked-out windows.'

Half an hour later all the news team are in *The Reporter* office and there's an air of anti-climax in the air. Robert puts down the lens he's been habitually polishing. 'Look, this is crazy. We should be planning a celebratory dinner somewhere flash, somewhere upmarket, not moping around like we're at a wake with the body in an open coffin on Jude's desk.'

Jimmy stands and adjusts his eyepatch. 'I don't say this very often, but Robert's right. We've won, justice has been served and now we are going to celebrate our success, something the English aren't very good at. But not with a dinner, but in the traditional way. Pack up whatever you're doing and we're off to *The Osborne*, right now. We've got loads of time, two days, to write the story of the trial. And all the background stuff is already written and laid out ready for the presses.'

Sarah jumps up from her desk. 'That is a great idea, Jimmy. Why don't I see if Del can join us?'

'Do that, Sarah, and while you're at it, ask Danielle if she can skive off for a couple of hours – she was part of all this – and Old Jones, he's always up for a free pint or two. Right, the first round is on me. No, the whole session is on *The Reporter,* and our taxis home will be as well, the paper can afford it after the advertising we've been getting. And who is going to sack any of us now Alex is gone and we've been crowned Regional Newspaper of the Year?'

At the pub Sarah organises a tab with Jackie, *The Osborne's* long-suffering barmaid, and, liberally lubricated by lager, the mood of the journalist soon lifts. Except for the dark cloud that hovers somewhere above Jude's head. 'Come on lad, you've hardly touched your pint; everyone else has almost finished their second,' Jimmy instructs as he returns from the loo. 'Spill the beans, what's eating you?'

Jude shakes his head and, against his better judgement, starts to try and explain. 'It's what you said in the office, Jimmy, that "justice has been served". But has it? What is justice for Stephen and his family, for Catherine and her mum? What about all those drug overdose inquests we've covered, all the kids who died because of the Quirks and Smarties. What is justice for them and their families?'

Jimmy doesn't rush to answer; he knows there is no real answer. He lets out a long stream of air through his pursed lips, takes a protracted draft of his lager and then starts laughing. 'Look, sorry, I'm not making light of what's happened. I was trying to express what I really think, because this is serious. And I remembered a quote, a lifetime ago, from Sunday school, probably from the book of James. I'm not sure of the exact words, but it means "God is the only judge."'

'So what, Jimmy? How does that help the grieving families?'

'Jude, it doesn't. And I'm no great Christian, so it doesn't help me particularly. But it does remind me that we're all imperfect, just doing the best we can. And if you hadn't been so determined, no, obstinate and bloody bull-headed, there's every chance that Smarties and his secret family would still be at large, hurting people in so many ways. So, well done, we've improved the lives of many people, most of whom we will never meet. Now, how many men and women can say that? So, pick up your beer and drink it down and I'll get us some more in.'

Jude gives a half smile and raises his glass to Jimmy, realising that his old editor's answer was far from perfect, but did, kind of, make some sense in a mad world. His thoughts are interrupted by the pub's big front door swinging violently open and crashing against a chair. 'Er, they should put a spring on that,' the mildly camp voice of Del announces loudly as he flounces into the room. 'And I present to you, your very own, all the way from Southampton seafront, the lovely Danielle. Now this party can really get started.' The sales rep lives up to her billing – she's obviously slipped home and changed – and dances into the room before seamlessly pirouetting across the floor, a blaze of golden tassels and red bellowing skirt, and elegantly falls into Jude's lap.

Everyone, except the stunned Jude, applauds the routine. Sarah sorts out another round of drinks. Del helps but his years on the force has turned him, even when off duty, into an observer of human behaviour. 'Antibiotics, is it Sarah?'

'No... what do you mean?'

'I've been in pubs, bars and restaurants with you, I dunno how many times. And you've never, ever, not been worse for wear when we've left. So, how many months? I'm guessing four?'

Without thinking, Sarah nods and her face takes on a smile and red hue. Del claps his hands and grins as widely as any chat show host. He turns to face the middle of the room. 'Everyone, quiet! I think Sarah here has an announcement.'

'Bloody hell, Del, why, oh why did I invite you?' She looks around the room for support but sees only questioning faces staring back at her. 'OK, OK, look, I'm bloody pregnant... although why that should interest Hampshire Police, who should be–'

The remainder of her sentence is drowned out by cheers, applause and cries from Old Jones of 'about bloody time.' A bottle of champagne appears, covered in dust, from behind the bar and Jackie pops the cork with a loud bang, saying 'this one is on the house'.

The afternoon becomes early evening and Jude and Danielle are in deep conversation. Eventually they both nod and then Jude sidles up to his editor. 'Jimmy, I've got something to tell you–'

'Lad, no you don't, I know what you're going to say.' Jimmy may be a seasoned drinker, but even he can't prevent his gentle swaying as he speaks. 'I've seen it coming and I'm just pleased you stayed as long as you have to see the trial through. You were always going to get offers and you'd be a mug not to take one of them. So don't tell me, tell everyone.' The editor picks up a spoon and loudly taps the side of his pint glass, causing Old Jones to worry the glass is going to smash and he'll have to clear up the mess. 'Listen up, everyone, young Jude here, and maybe Danielle, have an announcement. The second surprise, well, the third, if you count Debbs' sentence from the court, today. Jude.'

Jude walks to the middle of the lounge bar, is about to start talking, realises his mistake and grab's Danielle's arm and gently pulls her into the centre of the room to join him. Only slightly self-consciously, he holds her hand and starts. 'I don't want to piss on Sarah's bonfire, but as this is a day for revealing our secrets, here's my, well, ours. I've been offered a job on the Evening Standard–'

'Doing what,' Old Jones heckles, 'will you need to borrow one of my brooms?'

Jude smiles, 'I hope not, I'll be reporting, news and some investigations.'

Sarah is smiling. 'Bugger, I'm just about getting used to having you around. And you, Danielle, what are you going to do, sell advertising? There must be lots of great opportunities in London?'

'Don't take this the wrong way, Sarah,' Danielle pauses for effect, 'but if you and Jude can make a living as journalists, well, it can't be too hard, can it. I've got myself accepted onto a National Council for the Training of Journalist course in London and, I hope, can just about afford to pay for it.'

The whole rooms laughs and Jimmy stands to make a toast. 'Jude, it's never been boring with you around and I'll miss you. But I'm sure I'll have an easier life when you're gone. Now, with you going and Sarah will, I suppose, be taking maternity leave, it looks like I'll be training up two new wet-behind-the-ears reporters soon.' He raises his glass. 'All the best to Jude and Danielle!'

The End.

Printed in Great Britain
by Amazon

78331642R00154